A  Humpty Dumpty Field

Andy Bracken

A Morning Brake Book

Copyright © 2018 Andy Bracken

All rights reserved.

ISBN: 1985238268
ISBN-13: 978-1985238268

First Edition.

ANDY BRACKEN

For C & R. With love.
x

ACROSS THE HUMPTY DUMPTY FIELD

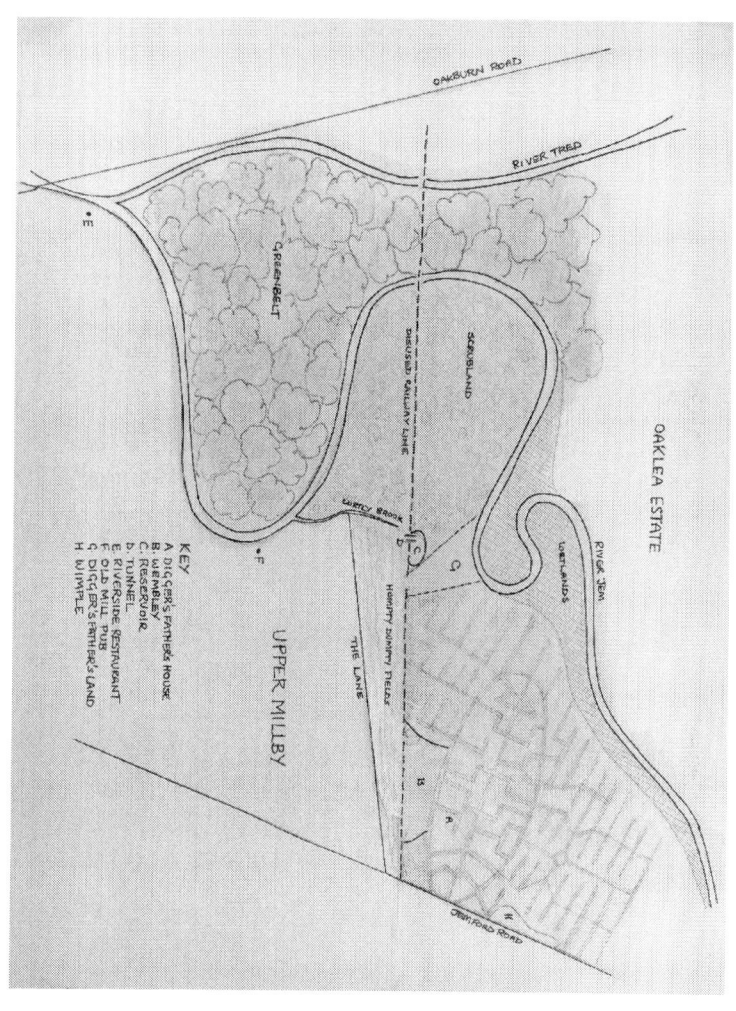

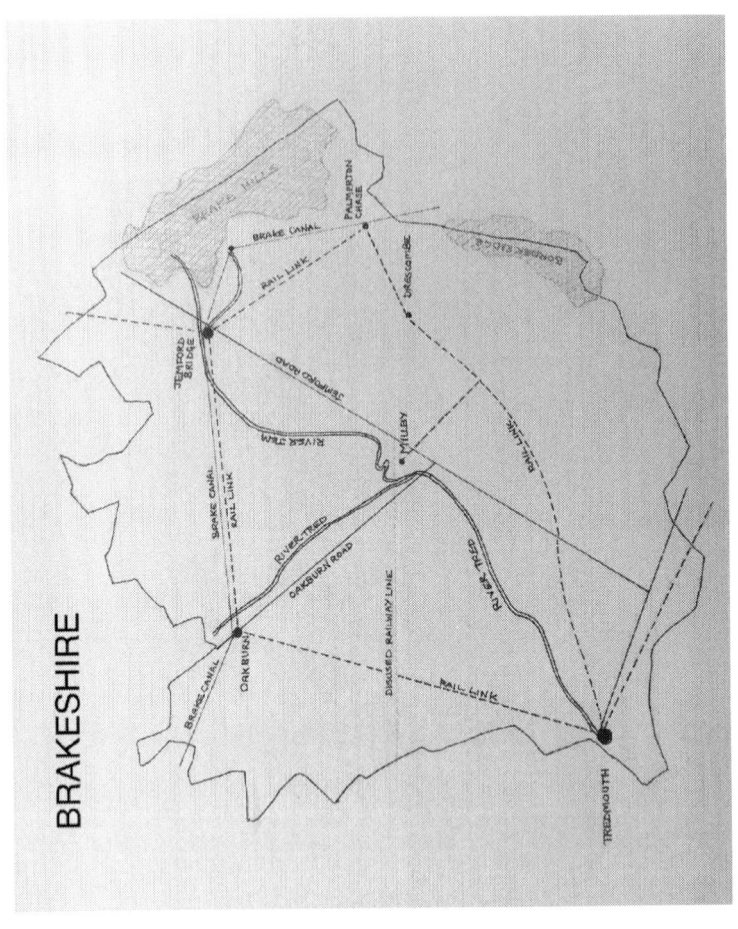

'If equal affection cannot be,
Let the more loving one be me.'
W H Auden

Introduction.

Picture a lower-case y, with one branch descending from the approximate northeast and another from the northwest, until they merge and become one line bearing south-southwestward. And now raise your eyes a little from that point of convergence, and spy the angled attenuated line leading off one of those jubilantly aloft arms. That is the Lane.

It was never named beyond that most basic title. At least, not officially; not by cartographers and the like. That scratchy line stretched from a dirt track on one edge, and went all the way to seemingly nothing. I say seemingly, but, as with everything, it came to exist for a reason.

The lay of the land and the obstacles, or exploitable characteristics nature throws up, determine what mankind does in the locale. Geography, as shaped by biology, is a science, and the engineering and cultivation of the terrain is always governed by it.

Thus, the Lane is actually a spur, and the path it followed was dictated by two things. Firstly, it was a level unobstructed line of land, or, vitally, the path of least resistance. Secondly, it led to a fresh waterway known as Curtly Brook, so-called because of its lack of length. Its accessible banks and slow current, as it emerged from beneath ground, were essential for the cattle and sheep that would be herded down this way from the rural pastures and hilly-fields to the northeast, as they were driven to the market towns in the southern region of the area.

Upper Millby, in whose bounds all of this is situated, was, and still is, the median point between those two environments.

Millby was crop country in those days, the land in the centre of the county lending itself to that particular trade, aided by the fact that the arable terrain is coursed by rivers and streams as they run from the high ground in the west and north of the region, before entering the middle-country as the rivers Jem and, ultimately, Tred.

All of this takes place in the county of Brakeshire, the administrative crux of which is in the southwest corner; the city of Tredmouth.

Aside from being the sole place with city status in the county, it is also a misnomer. To find the sea into which rivers pour and such contextual mouths are formed, you must travel a further five score miles, through Hardy's Wessex, before you come to a pleasant but enforced halt at Tinbury Head. However, there is a mouth of sorts, as the river Tred merges with a mightier waterway before flowing down to sea level.

Millby to Tredmouth is, as near as makes no difference, thirty miles, or the better part of three days hard travel on foot and hoof. Hence the need for water prior to that final leg being undertaken.

Ergo the formation of the Lane.

Millby took its name from the close-by mill that had operated here for hundreds of years. The Lane can be found a mile or so northwest of the now dilapidated mill. A lichen-bitten wheel and the Old Mill pub are the only indicators as to the site's former function. Above ground, at least.

There was no mill when the livestock were led to water. Millby didn't exist; neither Upper nor Lower. How could it? There was no need for people to reside here in any numbers back then, and it is, after all, people who name things. It's done to assist communication via a quick concise reference. 'Up by the mill' became Upper Millby in relatively short order.

The Lane, then, was established by animal feet, rendering it a muddy quagmire of putrid excrement in wet weather, and an arid desert of excrement dust in the heat of summer.

Year on year, millimetre by millimetre, it was carved into the earth by friction and displacement. Now, in our time, it stands nearly six feet below the level of the rest of the terrain, with steep banks cut out. Gnarled thorny hedges and interlocking stone walls add more to that depth perception. A man of average height can walk along the Lane, and not be seen by a person of equal stature standing just two yards from the lip at the natural ground level.

Trees break the hedgerow along the way, their roots visible, clinging desperately to the nigh-sheer walls of dirt that form the banks, those roots and other green growth binding it and holding it all together. Without them, there would be no structure, and the whole would fall in on itself. One heavy downpour, and all of it - earth, silt, stone and gravel - would slide down and fill in the trough. There are no drains here. A gentle slope assists the water in dispersing westward to the curt little brook, where sprats swim in abundant shoals, those silver darts of translucence too swift and sleek for my hand and eye. That said, a simple net on a stick will snag them, as long as the mesh is of a tight weave.

How do I know all of this? Because my father taught me, and his father taught him. It is the lore of the land.

Is it all true? Perhaps not all of it. But in the main, it's based on fact, some elements of which may have become skewed and embellished during the long passage of telling and retelling. Equally, though, some of the history must have been lost along the way. We can never know the all of it. But the land doesn't lie; not really. It all exists for a reason, and it continues to be in flux, as the impact of every change, great or small, plays out its knock-on effect.

And, I ask myself, how is that any different to me?

This is the route I took when I left here thirty years ago. So it seems suitable to retrace my path now that I'm forced to return.

Forced? No, I have choices, and I chose to come. But I wouldn't have come under any other circumstances.

It took something seismic to bring me back.

It took my Dad dying.

1.

With one hand on a branch, I slide sideways down the steep bank, the outer edge of my left foot accumulating a ridge of dirt before snagging calculatedly on a horizontal root to control my descent. Letting go of the branch, I jump the last three feet and slap down resoundingly on the hard asphalt of the Lane, the displaced dust from my boots spray-painting around my footprints.

I stand motionless, my arms remaining in the position they naturally found on landing; bent at the elbow to sixty degrees, hands instinctively splayed ready for an unintended impact that doesn't arrive.

It feels like I'm crossing a threshold, as though a resisting force exists as a means of discouragement. Or, perhaps, a warning. So much so, that I have to mentally will myself to break my pose and relax my limbs, enabling me to walk across the quiet roadway.

Pulling myself up the other side, again utilising a branch and adroit foot placement, I clamber on to the low stone wall and swing my legs up and over. I sit for a minute, the stone cold under my rump, and I light a cigarette. I'm down to five a day, though I brought enough for nearly thirty a day, given that I plan on staying here for one week. I had a feeling that I might need them.

The grass is always so green here. I'd forgotten. In my mind, the grass was always greener on the other side.

Slipping down, I amble out onto that lushness. I'm in no hurry. There's nothing I can do for Dad now. Everything else can wait. Moreover, everybody else can wait.

Beth Orton's 'Tangent' comes to mind, the lyric suiting the moment, and matching my pace this day. I carry it, along with thousands of other songs, but not on a device. I have it in my head, having purchased the album, 'Trailer Park', in the nineties. As a result, I listened to it properly and absorbed it. That's my version of a download.

I bought it because of 'She Cries Your Name'. It brought someone to mind; someone I once knew.

Mounting the first small incline, I pause on top of it, my head turning to one side and then the other, the long rolling smooth ridges and troughs smaller than I remember them to be.

And I re-cross the Humpty Dumpty Field.

I'm going 'home'.

2.

It was the limit to our world.

Parents would instill it in their children: 'Don't go across the Humpty Dumpty Field.'

You could go on it, right up to its stone-walled and hedged limit on the south side, but that was it. The Lane was the boundary, and woe betide anyone caught going a step farther.

It was a part of our language, that phrase. It became euphemistic. To 'cross the Humpty Dumpty Field' was to explore the other sex. To be 'across the Humpty Dumpty Field with the fairies' was to suggest someone was barking mad. It was a parental threat - 'I'll send you across the Humpty Dumpty Field with a flea in your ear if you don't bloody well behave yourself.'

But, despite that and because of it, it became a fascination. It became where all young people aspired to be. It came to represent sex and freedom and adulthood and independence and adventure. It was, to our minds, the rest of the world lying just over there.

A Humpty Dumpty field is a plot of land with humped ridges running across it. They roll gently up and down, so that a bike may be ridden across them with clement ease, though over-riding will make you feel a little queasy, much like a succession of hump-back bridges. From a distance the ground appears flat, as one mound merges in to the green of the next, and only when you get close do you notice the phenomenon.

Ah, but phenomenon may be the wrong noun to use, as there is good logical reason for it. Dad knew that it was, and I quote, 'the best surviving example of medieval strip agriculture in the area,' but as kids we'd speculate wildly on what on earth - or not of this earth - could have caused it.

Me? I believed it to be formed of once active waves, frozen in place during an ice-age, mineralising over millennia and now covered in tons of dirt. If we could only dig deep enough, we'd find evidence of marine life preserved down there. After all, those sprats got in the brook somehow.

My brother, Paul, two years my senior, knew it to be a landing strip for space craft from other galaxies, the design done to signal to them like an ancient barcode, the mounds themselves matching up with the landing gear, and here to act as ramps, thereby raising it up, allowing air in, and stopping it from overheating. Paul always understood such mechanical things.

Mucky Micky thought all of that was a pile of utter bullshit. He knew, without doubt, that it was an ancient burial ground, dating back to pre-Saxon times, and that virgins were sacrificed here to pacify the gods. And, furthermore, they were naked and beautiful. And mostly female. The mounds show where they were buried after their throats were cut, the blood drained into the ruts before being daubed all over the bodies of the revellers, who would then indulge in an orgy of humongous proportions...

Micky was my best friend. In truth, he was my only childhood friend. Brothers don't count.

Pausing on a ridge, I look left and right again, before resetting my eyes to the north. Through a thin line of trees, I can see the small strip of land that denotes the start of the Oaklea housing estate. In my day, that singly-treed and relatively flat wedge of grass was our football pitch.

Moreover, it is the lea with an oak in situ for which the estate is named.

On the south side of the development the houses are a mix of efficient private detached homes, and equally practical but more land-efficient semis, each with a small back garden and an even smaller front one.

They were built for, and sold to, those young married couples who were born into the generation known as the baby-boomers. The problem for local authorities came about because so many of them married and begat children of their own in the late-sixties and early-seventies. There was a baby-boomer bottle-neck.

Besides, the Millby region was suddenly booming, both with babies, and more generally. Perhaps not booming, but thanks to its location at the hub of the Brakeshire wheel, it was certainly attracting an influx of labour as it established itself at the heart of the distribution network. It was, so I once read, logistically pretty perfect.

In twelve years, between 1968 and 1980, the population of the Millby area grew from 3,500 to 17,000+. Or five-fold.

Oaklea housing estate was one of the first attempts to accommodate the influx, and the only one built to the north of Millby. Back when Paul, Micky and I were calling this area ours, there were no more than 200 homes, offering roofs over some 800 heads. There was never a shortage of kids to play football with.

And that's what strikes me as I look around; where are all the children?

It's a Sunday, eleven in the morning, on a bright and breezy October day. Where do the children play?

As soon as that thought completes in my mind, my brain hops to Dad's funeral, and I wonder which song by Cat

Stevens might be used. He was a big fan of the early Island LPs when I was a child. To the point that 'Tea For The Tillerman' is the first album I ever recall hearing.

Tillerman.

Till.

Dig.

Digger.

That was my name. It still is. It's one of the few things I took away from here and kept. Everybody calls me Digger.

Nowadays they assume that it's because of my job. What do I do? I choose music for media. My official title is Media Music Consultant. It is what it sounds like, though it goes largely uncredited. I read scripts and screenplays that are earmarked to be made into televisual or radio programmes, and build a playlist to be included as part of the soundtrack.

So, yes, I dig through the archives and music libraries, and find something suitable. My own music collection, and somewhat obsessive crate-digging for second-hand vinyl, helped cement my vocation and nickname. I have a knack for digging something up.

But I was Digger long before any of that.

Dad named me one summer afternoon, back when six-week school summer holidays lasted for months, the sun shone every day, Summer Special comics cost less than twenty pence, and the twenty pence coin hadn't been invented...

I stop myself from thinking nostalgically. It's what I was afraid of. Going back in life is seldom a good move. And it's why I stayed away from here as much as possible during the intervening time.

Oh, I'd come and visit, perhaps three times a year, planned to coincide with some event on a calendar;

birthday or Christmas or... No, just those two. And not even always. Toss in a couple of Father's Days, and that'll be the sum of it.

Work was my excuse, both for lack of visit frequency and for shortness of duration. It's invariably a safe cop-out, and hard to argue with. I'd drive up, park up, enter the house, sometimes stay a night so that I could have a drink with Dad, and then slip away. If it hadn't been for Dad, I would never have visited. And even when Dad was alive and kicking, it was always so much easier for Paul, being twenty minutes or so away in Drescombe. Okay, half an hour with traffic, as he's always quick to point out. Or an hour round trip. Or a gallon and a half of petrol. Plus wear and tear on the car. And with him being married and having kids, and me not...

Anyway, so it goes when dealing with Paul.

I've not been back to this humpy field since I strode purposefully across it on that miserable May day of departure in 1987. I was eighteen. I was of independent age. But I could have described it in minute detail during my thirty year absence, so ingrained is it in my being.

I know where the softest grass and most comfortable mounds are located, and where the screen of trees is most dense and private. Or I can show you every navigable path in and out, whether that be via the tunnel leading to the reservoir on my left, or through the copse and along the slight ridge on my right.

It's all the same as it was, but smaller. Childhood memories tend to be like that; they shrink the self and magnify the extraneous. Look at a child-drawn family portrait, and note the proportions; see the size of daddy's hands.

What do I feel, being back here? I'm not overjoyed, of that I'm sure. There is a trepidation, but no revulsion. This soil and place are in me, after all, imbibed and infused and imbued over the most formative years of my life.

I was less than one when we moved here in 1970. This was all I knew until I walked away, arrogantly thinking myself fully-formed. I was not. But, I will concede, my time here set me up to cope with all that life could throw at me. I got away and somewhat prospered in spite and because of it.

Paul's always quick to point that out, how he remained behind, and I got all the opportunities. He did venture as far as Drescombe, and those twelve miles are a fair measure of his ambition. But he only moved there when he was thirty-five or so, and only then because his wife was from there, and she convinced him that the schools were better, and the air cleaner, and the... I forget what else. Anyway, she was adamant that it was a much better place to raise children.

And that's the thing, as I walk on this field: I can't think of a better place to have grown up than right here in Oaklea, just to the north of Upper Millby.

My childhood here was never really the problem. It was as I matured into young adulthood that things started going awry and getting complicated.

And neither can I think of a better time to have grown up than during those years where freedom could be revelled in, as we benefitted from the wars fought and won, and the social revolution of the sixties, as those revolutionaries became our parents and teachers.

"Where do the children play?" I say out loud, as I turn south and begin making my way back to Upper Millby where I parked my car.

3.

To this day, as I pull up outside the house I grew up in, I've never understood how or why, seeing that it sits on the corner of the street, it came to be numbered number three. As children, we'd call it Number Three On The Corner.

It should be number one. Opposite is number two, and next door is number five. Number two is correct, but number five should be numbered three. And number thirteen at the far end should be eleven. Unlucky for some. And it was unlucky for them, because every time a new postman took over the round, thirteen would get eleven's mail, and have to walk next door with it. We'd simply sit and wait for number five to bring us ours.

I have no idea what happened to number thirteen's actual mail.

It is, clearly, a short stretch of road on which I grew up; a tight community of twelve small detached houses. The gaps between them were calculated to accommodate matching gates, running off which was a shared fence sufficiently high enough to contain dogs and children, whilst offering a modicum of privacy in which the mothers of 'my generation' could sunbathe in their period-wallpaper inspired bikinis. Or not. Toplessness was commonplace in those days when ozone was a word challenged vociferously should anyone dare to place it on a Scrabble board.

Being on the corner, we had more land than any other house in the street, courtesy of a narrow strip of unfenced green that ran the length of the property to the left. The reality of it was that it meant more to mow. But it was somewhere to sit and watch the world pass by, or even a great place in which to play badminton on the few days a year when the wind was sufficiently calm.

A sharp rap from a walking stick on the side window of the car startles me to a degree that my heart rate spikes, my adrenal glands having reacted before my brain can process the information.

"I say, I thought it was you, Digger! Best to check, though, with the house being unoccupied," the muffled words inform me, emitted by a tight lipless mouth, the wrinkles cascading from which all head downwards, giving the distinct impression of sourness. Like he's sucking a lemon, and has been for years.

Forcing a smile and a jerk of my chin, I open the door. "All right, Mr Glenn?"

"I said to myself, I said, that's probably Digger, but I should go and have a look-see just to be safe. Well, so, your father's dead, then. Shame, I say. A real shame. We had our differences over the years, as you know, but I'd known the man for nigh on fifty years, and that's saying something. There's something to be said for that, by my reckoning."

"That's, erm, good of you to say," is the best I can muster.

"Yes, well, you can't park there, Digger. We have an agreement as neighbours, that the corner of the road should be kept vacant so that anyone turning has a clear and unimpeded view of the street on entry, and so that people crossing the road can see if anyone is approaching."

"Sorry, I..."

"No criticism intended, Digger, I say, none intended. You weren't to know, after all, but you can see that it forces vehicles to take a wide berth as they turn, and, as I said at the meeting, I said, what with that adverse camber it could result in a catastrophe. That got their attention, I can tell you - nobody wants to see blood on the streets, Digger!"

"Yeah, I was just going to drop my bag in, before I park on the driveway round the corner," I manage to say.

"Oh, right, right. Well, why didn't you say? Good job I'm here, then. I shall stand guard while you perform that duty, and warn any turning cars, or vans - because they are the worst, those delivery drivers with their deadlines and targets - or, indeed, motorised cycles, for who the adverse camber is probably most hazardous, especially in wet weather. You leave that to me, Digger, and get your stuff inside. I say, look sharp now!"

I glance up at the clear blue sky this Sunday morning, a few thin white clouds skating across it, before noting the dry road surface and total absence of anything moving, whether that be vehicular or more organic.

Still, it doesn't stop grey-suited, tweed-capped old Mr Glenn walking to the rear of my car and holding his brown walking stick horizontally at chest height by way of highlighting the fact that my silver glinting large shiny metal car lurks several yards beyond the apex of the turn.

It's only when I reach the porch door that I remember there's nobody inside to answer my knock, and I don't have the key. I need to collect it from number five. For now, though, I deposit my case outside the rickety old porch that Dad built one summer rather than take us on holiday, and head back to the car.

"All safe, then?" I call out to Mr Glenn, having completed my twelve yard round trip and not heard a car, van or motorised cycle in my wake.

"Lucky I was watching out the front window!" he says, and means it.

There was no luck at play. He's been watching out of that front window for forty-five years that I know of, him and his wife taking the duty in shifts. Until she died some eighteen months or so back.

Dad told me about her death, and hinted at me coming up for the funeral, but I used work as an excuse to get out of it. I didn't even send a card. I should have, perhaps.

"Thanks," I call to him out of the wound-down window I didn't have to wind down, a button performing the function. A buttoned-down window doesn't sound right, and only serves to make me think of the white shirt and black suit in my case.

Old Glenn magnanimously nods his acceptance of my disingenuous expression of gratitude. Feeling compelled to say something else, I add, "I was sorry to hear about Mrs Glenn."

A flicker of emotion passes over his rheumy old eyes, as a rare glimpse of softness and vulnerability momentarily relaxes his tight mouth. But he quickly gathers himself, looking down briefly at his stick as it taps against his foot. A nod and a snatched breath fortify him as his head comes back up just high enough so that he can look down his aquiline nose at me. "I said to your father, I said, those flowers were beautiful. And when I asked him how he knew that they were her favourites, he told me that you must have told him." A decisive nod of, I think, slight regard and borderline respect summarily dismisses me.

Dad must have put my name on the card.

A three-point turn is executed competently outside Micky's old abode. Only when I reach the junction and come to what I was anticipating would be a brief pause before turning right, do I look in that direction and see Dad's car is parked on the single-vehicle driveway. I don't know what to do, so I sit for a while, the indicator click-tracking my life away. I could park on the grass, but the car is low-slung, and will probably scrape on the kerb. The rockery on the corner destroys my notion to park on the front lawn.

Eventually, I reverse up, and park outside number five, racking my brain in a futile bid to remember the occupants' names. They moved in a few years ago, and aren't part of my history. That said, they were always good to Dad.

Bob and Diane, I learn from the piece of paper taped to the door with my name on. '*Digger - in case you arrive while we're at Church, key is at number nine. Hope you had a good journey, and so sorry for your loss. God bless, Bob and Diane and family xox.*'

It had to be number nine, "number nine, number nine," I chant in homage to a crap Beatles song. Even I've never felt the urge to use that one in a soundtrack.

A heavy sigh propels my about-turn, as I fight the urge to walk across the front lawn of number seven. My reluctance isn't born from any sense of respect or regard for property, but solely from a desire not to again encounter the occupant - Mr Glenn. Besides which, the rose thorns tend to snag your clothing.

Number nine is called home by Pat and Pat, as in Patrick and Patricia.

He-Pat and She-Pat were how we always referred to them. He-Pat answers the door. Have I spoken with him in thirty years? I feel as though I have, but perhaps that's simply based on Dad mentioning him. On reflection, I may have raised a hand of acknowledgement once or twice as I turned the car round to leave, but can recall no conversation.

He looks solemn, but I'd anticipated that. People feel obliged to assemble their features into a face suitable with which to confront the bereaved. It's infectious, like yawning, but I flash him a closed-mouth smile nonetheless, before reverting to lugubrious.

His soft green eyes find mine for the briefest moment, before he blinks me away. He has the inoffensive, non-judgmental look that his profession requires. He's probably retired now, but you never fully lose the past. For years Dad thought he was a Councillor, and would chunter on to him about the state of the roads or his rates being so high. He was in fact a Counsellor, the nature of which discouraged him from ever correcting Dad's misunderstanding.

"Sorry for your loss," he says, and hands me the key.

"Thanks," I tell him, and add, "are you and Pat well?"

"Fine," he succinctly replies. People don't want to tell you they're really great at such times, I suppose, and rub your nose in it. It probably wouldn't be wise to be too complaining either, given that anything they might gripe about almost certainly wouldn't be as bad as death.

"And Elle?" I follow up when it becomes apparent he isn't about to add anything.

"Fine. Will you let us know about the funeral, please?"

"Sure," I reply.

I can smell food cooking, as he nods and closes the door on me. He's recognisable. His hair is greyer and thinner, but, then, so is mine. Similarly, I would have recognised Mr Glenn had I encountered him out of context. They are both merely older versions of their former selves.

Does that mean that Elle is as I remember her? Does she still retain the form that I've attempted to hang on to in my mind for thirty years? Does her chin still form a soft point when viewed face on, and can she still ignite me with a smile that barely disrupts any facial feature except her eyes?

Is she in there, through that door? Could she be just on the other side, within touching distance were there no barrier between us? Did I breathe air that she has exhaled for that brief time the door was ajar, and the warmth from within sought to escape?

Do we all have our Elles; the one that we lost; the one who ended it with us, rather than us with them? The one who broke our heart to such an extent that it never truly healed. Or, if it did, it seems to have knitted itself back together in a way that isn't quite right, as though a small fragment went missing, perhaps. Or the chambers that constitute it are somehow in the wrong positions or wrongly wired; slightly out of whack.

Elle was the reason I left. I should thank her, really. My life would be very different had I remained.

And is Elle also the reason I stayed away so resolutely? Yes. I couldn't bear to see what I'd lost. Thirty years, and it still gnaws at me.

And I know that I've idealised her over that time. She was prettier, no doubt, in my mind than she ever was in reality. Wasn't she? Isn't she?

She was cool and wise, because I was young and knew only the people I'd grown up knowing, and they all knew what I knew. She was exotic purely by virtue of being the one who came from elsewhere. That was what we called people from other places - Elsewheres.

Now I am that Elsewhere person. I left her behind, in that sense.

She had the most magnificent body, because the other bodies I'd seen up to that point were less mature, less developed, or too mature and too far in advance of me. Her voice haunted me because it didn't use local inflections, and her clothes and music were what she'd absorbed and brought with her. Now...

Now I am the one from the outside, the one with the clothes and music. I'm the one immersed in culture. She will be the one with the housing-estate, new-town, small-town sensibilities and surroundings.

Yes, I should thank her for getting me out of here.

I should genuinely tell her that dumping me was the best thing that ever happened to me. Because it was. It made me. And it made me determined not to fail; to never have to come back and swallow my pride, and pick up where I left off. Or, rather, where she left me off when she threw me aside.

That's what I'll do if I ever see her. I'll thank her sincerely for making me what I am. And what I am is okay. What I am is content. I like my job, and how many people can honestly say that? I like my house, my lack of debt, and the fact that there is nothing I really hanker for. I have what I want, and I want all that I have.

Oh, but Elle! There's still - despite all my protestations to the contrary - there's still this little fissure somewhere in the very core of me that feels like it could rip open and tear me apart at any second, if I just succumbed to it.

And for that, I can never fully forgive her. Let alone thank her.

I did nothing wrong.

There were no signs.

There was no gradual disintegration - we didn't begin to crumble before the whole lot came tumbling down. It just suddenly crashed without warning.

One day we were going to spend the rest of our lives together. And the next, we weren't.

And I held on. For years... For all the years, I've held on and waited.

After all, it was she who ended it, so she who had to reach out. I couldn't. It would have empowered her further, and opened me up to a fresh rejection. I couldn't have suffered that twice. Once was bad enough. I honestly don't think I could have survived a repeat performance.

She never did contact me. She never once stretched that olive branch in my direction. There was nothing for me to grasp. And that told me all that I needed to know. Sometimes it's silence that paints a thousand words.

It wouldn't have been difficult for her. She could have contacted me through Dad or Paul at any time. He-Pat and She-Pat continued to live three doors up. It would have been the simplest thing in the world.

I carry my case into the hallway and set it down.

My jacket slides from my arms, and I hang it on the bannister at the bottom of the stairs.

Rummaging, I retrieve my cigarettes and lighter, and enter the kitchen at the front of my childhood home.

The kettle's cold. It's like Dad. Were he still alive, the kettle would never get to become fully cold during waking hours. His next cup of tea would be in preparation before it could ever get there.

Flipping the lid, I see it has water in it - just the residual leftover from his final brew.

I don't want to throw it away and replace it with fresh.

So I add to it from the tap, and vow to myself that I will always add and never empty. That way an ever-decreasing but ever-present amount of his likely last action will remain for the time that I am here.

And as it begins to burble to a boil, so I stand with my hands gripping the sink edge and resist the urge to cry in my isolated grief, as I consider all of my losses.

4.

"All right?" I say to my brother as the door swings open to reveal his darkly-grey-stubbled face. "You shouldn't park there, apparently," I add, pointing at his van, but he ignores me.

"All right?" he replies, coining the local vernacular.

It's all rhetorical. Nobody expects an answer; we know we're not. For reasons I can't explain, I'm relieved to discover he's alone. No wife. No kids.

Not quite alone. He has Dad's dog with him. The mongrel's called Bean. Not for the number of varieties that constitute its lack of pedigree, but because, as a puppy, it would invariably have just 'been' on the carpet.

Dad always had a dog. Not the same one. Before Bean was Heinz. Again, not for the obvious reason. The truth of it was that, prior to Heinz, he had a mutt called Eddie. And Heinz was... You guessed it - 'Just Like Eddie'.

And prior to Eddie, came Ringo. There you have it; a life mapped out by dogs. Fifty years and more recalled by which dog was present, and its approximate age. 'Let me think now. Heinz hadn't quite grown into his paws, so it was 2001 or 2002.'

Bean makes his way methodically from one room to another, sniffing the carpet as he goes. He's looking for Dad. I hope that's all he's looking for.

"Have you been smoking in here?" Paul asks.

"I just had one with a cup of tea when I got here."

"Christ, Digger! We've got to sell this house. You can't smoke in here."

"Dad smoked in here for nearly fifty years," I point out.

"Yes, and that did him the power of good in the end, didn't it? I mean it - this place needs tidying up and airing. No smoking."

I shrug and fondle the lighter in my pocket as I open the kitchen window.

"Do you want a cup of tea? Coffee?" I ask, as much to change the subject as anything else.

"I can't stay. I'm just dropping the dog off."

"Dropping it off where?"

"Dropping it off here."

"Why?"

"Because we can't have it at ours, not with the kids' allergies."

"But I've never had a dog of my own. I don't understand how they work," I protest.

"Feed it twice a day from the tub in there. Make sure it has water, and let it out in the garden every few hours. It isn't difficult. You might even want to take it for a walk every day," he concludes, handing me the lead.

"Fantastic," is my considered reply.

"And make yourself useful while you're here. Start getting rid of some of the crap. We'll need to get this place on the market as soon as possible."

"Can't we bury Dad first?"

"He's being cremated..."

"I thought he wanted to be buried?" I interrupt.

"Cremation's cheaper."

"Hang on. He wanted to be buried, Paul, you know that. He'd tell us about being eaten by worms, and recycled back into the earth. He'd joke about us making sure he was dead first, though!"

"It was just one of his stories, Digger. It doesn't matter. He won't care now, will he?"

"It's wrong."

"It's arranged."

"Already? He only died on Friday night."

"Jen arranged it. She's done this kind of thing before, when her grandparents died, so she knows the form."

"What's it got to do with Jen?"

"She's my wife, for starters. And she's the mother of Dad's grandchildren. And she's been bloody brilliant. What were we supposed to do, wait for you to get here?"

"Yes!"

"Really? And you think that a burial and all the arrangements can be made in the week you can grace us with your presence?"

Fuck you.

I let it go. I fondle my cigarettes and lighter, and let it go.

"Are you working?" I ask, again to change the subject, as I nod towards the van visible through the window.

"No, but Jen came round yesterday and sorted out some stuff for the charity shop or something. It's in those boxes in the hall. I figured I'd make a start and get them out of the way. As I said, the house will need to go on the market as soon as possible."

"We don't even know Dad's Will yet."

"Well, I kind of do, because I actually spent time with him and spoke with him about it," Paul mutters, another barb lodging in my person. "Anyway, what possible scenario is there where the house won't be sold?"

I can't think of one.

"Right," he responds to my lack of response, "so it'll need selling, then. And I certainly can't afford to pay the bills and maintain the place, so it'll need selling pretty bloody sharply."

Again, I shrug my understanding.

"So," Paul continues, "start sorting out what needs to go to the tip, what can go to charity, and anything you want to keep. And there are a couple of boxes of your stuff in your old bedroom. Stuff from when you were a kid. Those need sorting out or slinging. And the house could do with a clean. If you find yourself twiddling your thumbs, try painting the place and tidying up the garden. Don't forget the dog. And no smoking in the house. Okay?"

"Sounds great."

"I've got to run. Give me a hand with these boxes," he orders, and I follow him to the hallway.

I light a cigarette as we stand at the rear of the van, the boxes wedged along the clear central aisle. The van interior smells of oil.

"Look, I'm sorry if I'm a bit ratty," Paul conciliates. "I'm just stressed, that's all. Someone has to sort things out, Digger, and you simply aren't around. I've got Jen and the kids to think of. And if I seem a bit... A bit cold-hearted, I suppose, then it's only because of that." He pauses and smiles sadly at me before tipping his eyes ground-ward. "Let's just get through this week as best we can."

"He-Pat asked me about the funeral. Have you got a day and time?"

"We won't know until tomorrow. The weekend didn't help. We've also got to get the death certificate tomorrow, and go to the Millby Registry Offices. As I said, Jen knows her way around all that, and she's happy to help. Her mum's minding the kids after school this week, so we'll get that side of it all taken care of. The best thing you can do is to get this house sorted out."

"Okay," I concede, "I'll do all I can."

Paul awkwardly takes the hand I offer him, and shakes firmly without making eye contact. He hides behind grief on this occasion, but it might be by watching his children or checking the weather on another. There's no slyness in that averted gaze. It's simply a lack of self-confidence manifesting itself; a shyness. I once read that a sizable percentage of men have a problem with a handshake, and there's a myriad of different reasons for it.

"I'll ring you tomorrow," Paul calls out as he walks to the driver's door.

"Speak to you then."

With a foot resting on a large stone that is part of the rockery, I smoke on, watching as Paul waves a hand and ascends the sloped tarmac that half forms the corner on which number three erroneously stands.

When did Dad build this rockery?

Ringo was grown up, no longer needing to be tethered, so it was the summer of 1978. It wasn't the scorcher of 76, nor the jubilee of 77. He added the porch in one of those years.

As with many such schemes, he conceived of the notion after hearing something about it on the radio. Being a heavy goods vehicle driver for virtually all of his working life, the radio was his constant companion.

That was why we seldom had summer holidays. The last thing Dad wanted to do during his two weeks off was sit in a vehicle in traffic. It wasn't much of a hardship to go without. Being off school, and having the countryside to play in compensated.

We had no idea what a rockery was prior to Dad informing us that it was a rock garden. 'So we'll need rocks!' was the logical next snippet to be revealed. And that was where we came in.

Furnished with a wheelbarrow, Paul, Micky and myself were despatched to seek them out, the promise of twenty pence a load being sufficient to ensure the enthusiastic participation of our nine- and ten-year-old selves.

Dad estimated five barrow loads, and a whole quid was a fortune in those days. Admittedly, it was difficult to divide by three, but seeing how Micky gave up after the third trip, declaring it slave-labour, he only ever saw a Paul-negotiated twenty pence of the booty, Paul and I pocketing the remaining eighty between us.

I say pocketing, but in my case I bought a Matchbox car before the day was over. Paul probably still has his.

We knew where the best rocks were to be located in sufficient quantity: We'd get them from the Old Railway On The Moon.

I don't know who named it. It could have been Paul, or it could have been a name passed on to us. But I do have a vague memory of walking along the elevated former railway, and someone stating that the anaemic powder accumulating on our footwear looked like moon dust. Had we ever seen moon dust? It looked like what we expected moon dust would be like.

The railway was active until the nineteen-fifties, running roughly east-west through the heart of Brakeshire, linking the north-south lines running between Tredmouth and the rest of the country. It ran straight and true through the middle of the county, where Millby is situated, heading for the easy path north of Border Ridge in the east. Only here at Oaklea did they have to elevate it, and build bridges and a steep-banked spinal moraine under which the waterways could flow.

How much did it cost, and was it viable for the eighty years it was in operation? I have no idea, but would assume not, as the roads replaced it, and it was determined that rail goods would be better running south to Tredmouth and back out from there.

Did it cost lives, building that railway?

We were convinced that it did, just as we were certain that lives had been lost during its time in service.

And just as I am certain that a life was lost there one day when it no longer carried anything except the scampering fleet feet of boys inevitably venturing to the places they weren't really supposed to go.

But we had permission that day, and we loaded the barrow from the blasted remains of a bridge that once spanned a dry valley that was, perhaps, once a river. We selected our rocks from the low land, where pickings were easy and plentiful, and where a barrow could gain ready access.

Was that the day? Was it on that pristine summer day in 1978 that Dad called out, 'here they come, the Diggers Of Brakeshire!' or was that some similarly different day when I was re-christened Digger as a consequence?

It was before then. It was when he built the driveway on the side of the house, and I assisted him in clearing the land and levelling it out.

Prior to that re-christening, my name was Douglas. Doug - the past tense of dig. And I was pleased that Digger stuck, and I could cast off the old name that I never much cared for. The new one sounded more vital and current. There was a coolness to it.

I always liked digging. I still do. I enjoy shovelling snow to this day. There's something satisfying in sinking a spade into the earth, and removing a piece of it. Others like to build and add, but I like to clear and subtract, before planting and burying and covering everything back up again.

It pleases me to know that I was nicknamed for those agricultural revolutionaries, those Diggers of this county and Warwickshire, along with the Levellers and other such bands across the country, who rose up in the early sixteen-hundreds to dig up the hedges and level the walls, and fill in the ditches put in place to control the land and assign ownership and stewardship and subservience.

Bending down, I stub out and bury my cigarette butt in the earth between two slate-hued boulders, forty years of rain and wind having washed and blown the light moon powder from them.

Laying a hand on one flat rock, I remember the race track Paul and I made here for our Matchbox cars one summer, and I smile as I recall Mr Glenn complaining about the rockery being a tripping hazard as it sat so close to the pavement.

As I rise, I see movement in the kitchen, and for the briefest moment forget that Dad is dead.

It's only the net curtain moving in a breeze that has arrived suddenly from the northwest. I breathe it in, and smell the earth readying itself for rain that I know will be imminent. There's no sign of it on the Wedgewood pottery sky, but I trust the earth more than I do the heavens.

It's coming.

A storm's brewing.

5.

"Bean," I call coaxingly, having discovered the dog lying with his nose at the foot of my Dad's bedroom door.

He smells him in there; his residual smell at least; the strongest remaining scent of him in the house. Can he perceive that the scent is diminishing?

"Come on, come outside before the rain starts."

He follows me to the back door, his tail lazily swaying in time with his gait.

What will happen to him when all of this is over? He's about six now, or middle aged. Eddie and Heinz both made it to twelve or thirteen. Will he be dropped off at some shelter and put up for adoption? Will anybody want him, or is there only demand for puppies? Perhaps a neighbour will offer to take him. I'll ask around. That would be better, to keep him in the area he's familiar with. Or would that be cruel, his loss having to be confronted every day, and would he better off with a fresh start elsewhere?

It worked for me.

He circles the garden as I observe, cocking his leg up a bush, but his heart's not in it. We both glance up at the muddy sky as the first drops of rain splat fatly down on the paving slabs.

It's his cue to head back, but he stands in front of me, as though he's asking my permission to enter his own home. He knows things have changed, and that more changes are in the offing.

"Come on, boy," I say, and tap my thigh by way of invitation. His umber eyes spark for the briefest moment, a finger-click of time and no more, and a solitary wag of his tail shows his appreciation. I get the impression that he doesn't want to be alone.

It feels later, the gloom adding to that sense, but it's only two in the afternoon. Will this be a brief storm? I could do with getting out of the house for a while. Perhaps I'll take the dog for a walk if it stops.

I don't want to be here. I want to be in my own place with my own things. I could do some work, I suppose, but I have no inclination. The time will drag if I do nothing. So, I may as well act on Paul's suggestion, and start sorting through things. I certainly feel an urge to keep busy.

Heading up the stairs with a cup of tea in hand, I discover Bean again lying outside my Dad's bedroom door. It can't do any harm, so I open it and let him in, whereat he scurries rapidly about the room, his nose painting a picture for him. Resting his chin on his paws on the edge of the mattress, he gives out the smallest of sad whimpers at the realisation that the room is empty, the bed unoccupied.

The sheets are straight and the pillows propped. Someone made the bed. Was it Dad?

He died on Friday night, but they found his body on Saturday morning. Christ, that was only yesterday.

Bob and Diane next door suspected something was wrong when they didn't see the dog being let out, and when Dad failed to emerge for his newspaper.

I'd gone out to get breakfast at a greasy-spoon when Paul had called, and, only intending to be an hour or so, I hadn't taken my phone. I knew it wasn't going to be good news when I saw seven missed calls on my return.

He hadn't been ill, Dad. Or, if he had, he'd kept it a secret from us. Which would have been typical.

A heart attack is the unofficial cause of death, but we should know more tomorrow. The specifics, I suppose - the gory details.

Bean settles down in the hallway, where he can best keep a sorrowful watch on me, but also see the front door through the balusters as he forlornly awaits the return of his master.

Did he go to Dad at the end? And did he comfort him in his final throes, however long they lasted? And when it was over, did he remain with him, either at his feet, or on his lap as he attempted to infuse the body with his warmth that meant life? Through that contact, did he notice the lack of a heartbeat and the absence of a rising and falling chest?

Did he know?

He couldn't have. If he knew, he'd know that he isn't coming back, and wouldn't feel a compulsion to watch the door.

Paul's way of coping is to keep busy. Bean's is to mope and grieve. We all have our own way.

Dad kept our rooms made up for us. For thirty years, he kept 'my room' ready. Mum and Dad had the larger room at the rear of the house, and Paul and I decided on 'my room' and 'your room' purely, I think, by size and age - older meant bigger. But there isn't much between them. They're both boxy small, but with mostly window across the front wall offering a sense of light and space. Mine is painted as it always was, with the almost-white-but-hint-of-blue paint I never thought to question. It was, after all, just a background on which to hang things - posters mostly, and a couple of framed pictures above the headboard of my single bed.

The gloom of the afternoon prompts me to flick the light switch on entry. I'm greeted by two cardboard boxes with 'DIGGER' indelibly inked on them. The bed looks clean and is made. The posters are gone from the walls - Siouxsie and her Banshees evidently put up a fight, judging by the touch-up marks on the painted surface.

It's strange that I never noticed them before, but I was always in a hurry - a flying visit. Besides, I'd always be back, so I could see it properly the next time. But this will be my final stay in this house, so I absorb it more as a consequence.

All of those years elapsed, and Dad didn't repaint the whole room, preferring to touch-up with some mixed approximation of the original hue, or, perhaps, an old tin or jar of leftovers that hadn't weathered like the walls, and remained brighter and cleaner because of that lack of exposure.

By peeling away the strip of barely tacky tape along the seam of the box, I break open my childhood and teenage years. Nothing comes spilling out other than a musty smell of paper and cardboard. And my eyes alight on a green baize sheet that I know without unfolding is my Subbuteo football pitch.

Lifting it clear, two boxes of players tumble free from its folds, a few falling out and attempting to make a getaway. One has a broken base that will probably hinder his escape. And I smile at the terrible paint job I applied in a bid to customise my team. The box informs me that they were once Liverpool.

Micky had all of it - the floodlights and grandstand; the spectators and corner flags and scoreboard. If he didn't, it felt like he did. He was given so much - he had so much. Yet it never satisfied him. He always wanted more. He always wanted what he didn't have. Some people are like that.

I set the green bundle to one side for the bin. Or for the charity box. Do children play with such things now, or is it all digitised and high-definition and impersonal? Subbuteo was the football we played inside when it was too wet to play football outside. That was all it was. A poor substitute from back in the days before substitutes. The box contains only ten outfield players and a goalkeeper.

A stack of seven inch singles dominates the rest of the space. I flick through them - Undertones, Generation X, Siouxsie And The Banshees, The Cure, Adam And The Ants, Visage... Buggles - what was I thinking? 'Toast' by The Streetband, an empty sleeve of 'Lucky Number' by Lene Lovich, 'Cruel To Be Kind' by Nick Lowe, 'Up The Junction', 'Down In The Tube Station', 'Temple Of Love', 'See You', Talk Talk, 'Ever Fallen In Love (With Someone You Shouldn't've), 'New Year's Day', 'Ghost Town', 'True Faith', 'Bigmouth Strikes Again', 'That Was Then But This Is Now'. 'Shine On' by The House Of Love - the last record she ever bought me before I left in May 1987.

Time and place. The soundtrack of my life. Some of it good, some of it bad.

Padding out the bottom of the box are a selection of Warlord comics and annuals, some Tiger and Scorchers mixed in. My name is written inside the annual cover, along the top margin. My name in my hand. I recognise it, despite writing very differently now. Not so different, perhaps, but more practiced; more perfunctory as a consequence.

Writing now is always hurried and scratched. Notes, not letters. Lists, not dreams. Reminders, not aspirations. Prompts, not plans.

A half completed Panini football sticker album forms the foundation on which everything was stacked, a bundle of swaps bound by an elastic band wedged down the side. Season 1981-82. That was probably the last year I bothered with such things. Priorities changed as teenage years commenced.

The records are all I wish to keep, so I load the rest back in the box and open the other carton.

Cassette tapes rattle in their cases as I shift the box and sit down on the carpet next to it. I know the sound, despite not having handled cassettes in two decades.

Before I get to them, my secondary school report book arrests my attention. Flicking through it, it's better than I remember. Mostly B's, a couple of A's offset by a couple of C's. Bearing in mind this is from back in the days when children could actually fail, I consider it pretty good.

'Could do better' seems to be the predominant line of feedback, along with a minus for effort. It's true that I never tried too hard. I didn't see the point. I still don't. Yes, it's nice to have an understanding of things, but how has any of it affected my life?

Ironically, a C- for music points the way to my career path.

Until I get to late 1984, when everything changes. The comments are kinder, more understanding of my lack of effort. The marks are reflective of that - A's and B's across the board. There are no minus signs.

Did I put in any more effort? No. The truth is, I put in less.

But I was a victim by then. There were very clear and understandable reasons for my performance. It could all be explained.

Even if I couldn't explain it.

I can feel a darkness descending on me. It comes into me like a wisp of smoke at the edge of a closed hatch. Before I know it, the blackness will be pouring through the four sides and hinges. And I know that there is no way out of the room except through that hatch. But to escape means flinging it open and letting everything in. Or everything out.

Dropping the report book, I walk to the window and lift the bar at its base and open it up.

Greedily, I suck in the damp clean air, the storm passing, almost gone.

Averted for now.

The smoke I inhaled, the blackness, leaves me, and my mind and nerves settle. My tea is lukewarm, but I drink it, clearing the acridity from my throat, flushing it down to my core where it can be processed and ultimately flushed away.

Something touches my leg, startling me, my fist clenching. It's Bean.

"Hello, boy. Fancy a walk?" He knows the word, and his ears flick rigidly upright. "We could both use some air, I think."

As I turn, having re-secured the window, I see a piece of paper that slipped free of the report book. It's dated November 1984.

And I see the outline of her face looking up at me.

C+ for art. It's very telling. The one subject I tried hard in, I was no bloody good at. I never could draw. No amount of practice would improve me. I was simply no good. Paul got the arty gene, though he never took advantage of it. He wasted that nature-given gift.

I couldn't fill in the details. All I could accurately depict was a broad outline - an impression. As soon as I attempted to add the eyes, mouth, nose, hair, etcetera, it would look less and less like her. But I could sketch out the outline and fill in the details in my head.

I can still draw her outline. I know that, because I still do.

Thirty years on, and I sit from time to time, and draw the outline of Elle's face, because it's my way of holding on to her.

I've drawn her in sand on a beach, and on scraps of paper on a train. I've seen her in pubs and restaurants and walking along the street. She's looked out at me from notebooks in meetings, and on the front of manuscripts I've been tasked with soundtracking. Bits of her, most of her, but never all of her have appeared to me on screens in cinemas and on television at home. I've frozen the image, and traced her facial outline with my finger, just to see how close it is. Once or twice I've had to look up an actress online or in the credits, just to make sure it wasn't her.

For thirty years I've been in love with a somewhat empty frame - a featureless perfection. I kept no photos, and my memory has done what memories do. But I know the shape of her face, and that's been enough to keep the merest flicker of an inextinguishable flame burning somewhere in me.

It's a hollow and transparent flame - the kind that can catch you out and destroy. It's like an ember or tip of a cigarette being held to the centre of a piece of paper, and as it burns through, there's no telling if the sheet will ignite or simply brown crisp and be ruined, leaving a residual outline of potential destruction and nothing more.

The ignition is determined by fluke; by a sudden rush of oxygen, perhaps, or a perfect match of paper and ember, the ember containing enough energy and the paper thirsty enough to take it on. Or even a complete stillness, so that no movement of the air can extinguish the dalliance before it can properly bond. Either way, every way, it is dependent on outside influence whether the flame is to prosper.

Elle, pronounced L, signed L, 'Love L x.'

L and Elle derived from Eleanor.

Named for Eleanor Rigby. The song, not the woman. An old-fashioned name, I suppose, but not in 1967 when she was born, as it was in the public conscience courtesy of the Beatles.

But she could just as easily have been named Rita or Lucy.

Her writing adorns the cassette spines on show in the box, but I can't face that now. So I fold and slip her characterless outline in to my wallet, and head downstairs with Bean at my heels.

6.

Damp grey monochrome's the streets and houses, as we traverse the gentle declivity towards the greener rim of the estate. The dog seems happy going this way, as I allow him, to some degree, to dictate the route and pace.

Before it can be unsighted by the corner house of the adjacent road, I take advantage of the dog sniffing the metal pole of the street sign to turn and look back at number nine. It's too early for the lights to be on, and I see no signs of life.

In my head I hear a snippet of a song, and at first I can't get purchase on it enough to fill in the rest. Only the refrain 'I never saw you again' is accessible. It's a b-side. The Cure. 'The look before I go is a look for you.' It was in the box and, as a result, subliminally suggested.

I carry the song with me as we continue down the slope. 'A Few Hours After This' I remember.

Of the six houses on our side of the street, it seems against the grain that, up until Friday, half of them should have been occupied by the same people for nearly fifty years. I don't know the average length of residency in the country, but I'm guessing it's unusual. Dad at number three, Mr Glenn at number seven, Pat and Pat at number nine are the originals.

Micky's parents moved away from number thirteen in 1985, and there have been a few people come and go since then, none of whom I can tell you much about.

Number eleven was home to Perry in my time. That said, he wasn't an original, but whoever predated his arrival has slipped from my memory. Perry appeared on the scene in 1977, or thereabouts. Micky fondly referred to him as a 'hippy wanker' as part of his eight-year-old punk persona, so far as he could understand it.

Still, it didn't stop him obsessively spying on Perry's succession of hippy girlfriends as they paraded around the house and garden in nothing, or next to nothing.

Perry upped and left a few years after I departed, having transmuted into a smart-suited and booted late-thirty-something Yuppie wanker. It seems that Perry was destined to always be a wanker.

That leaves number five, or next door as we more commonly referred to it.

Bob and Diane live there now, with their churchy superiority and developmentally stunted offspring. They're late-fifties, both in terms of age and morals, with kids they should have had when Bob could still kick a ball with them, and Diane didn't have to rely on prayer and fertility treatment to conceive.

That said, when did my Dad ever kick a ball with us?

Ah, they're nice people who would never knowingly do you down, and they were kind to Dad.

But my sense is that everything is forbidden. Their son and daughter, twins in their mid-teens, are angelic little delicate bundles of wrapped-up-ness. I doubt they have sharp objects in the house; that even the crucifixes are filed down or fitted with those corner protectors you get for cupboards. Scissors are always, always carried up and down stairs with the hand enclosing the pointy bits.

They are the polar opposite to the family who lived there before them.

Debbie, Donnie and Davie, the alliteratively named trio, called it home, along with their mum and dad, Dee and Colin. Surmise from that who wore the trousers. Or all-in-one trouser suits.

The boys were born there at number five, but Debbie came as Micky and I did, without memory of elsewhere. We shared a classroom as a consequence. At least, until we were twelve and different educational options were available.

There were enough children in Oaklea to warrant the formation of a first and middle school, at which we were founder members in 1974, Paul transferring from Upper Millby Infants and joining us.

Dee and Colin were Mum and Dad's best friends. Which was handy given that they lived next door. Whether they would have been friends, best or otherwise, had there been any effort involved is debatable, but people in the seventies were good at making the best of what they had to hand. It was probably a hangover from the post-war years and rationing.

Dee was one of those people who had to have a bigger or better version of whatever you had. My Mum inherited a gold watch from her grandmother. It wasn't anything special, but it was gold and old and she loved it, mostly for sentimental value. Within two days of seeing it, Dee had a diamond-dialled, eighteen carat Rolex on her wrist, which she proudly exhibited by wearing short sleeves in the middle of winter.

Similarly, when Dad got a new car, within a week, next door had the same car. Except it wasn't. It was the next model up, with the red paint job that screamed 'notice me, notice me!'

But all of that passed me by as a child. It was only the overheard comments between Mum and Dad that flagged it up as being anything out of the ordinary.

Just as long as Debbie was keen to play nurse to us wounded soldiers, it was absolutely fine by Micky and I. She had her uses.

Does everybody encounter those people in their childhood - the ones who seem to 'know things'? Micky and Debbie were cut from the same cloth when it came to biblical knowing. And to this day, I can't tell you where their knowledge came from. They simply seemed to know.

And because they knew, and because we lived in the same street and they were my friends, so that information was passed on to me. My sexual education was administered and imparted, not by awkward parental chats or biology based clumsy school lessons, but by exposure to Debbie and Micky. Exposure being the operative word.

Those were the players in the early acts of my life, those good folk who shared the same side of a quiet little cul de sac on a new housing estate called Oaklea, north of Upper Millby.

Even residing on the other side of the road, in an even-numbered house, relegated the occupants to mere support actor role. How strange that a strip of asphalt should make such a difference? But that was how it was.

Bean and I cross the road at the bottom of Oaklea, a road that once looped all the way around the estate and formed its circumference, but now cuts through it on its northern and eastern curves, large detached abodes built from imported red brick with matching charcoal ceramic roof tiles and cream-coloured paved driveways having bitten away the countryside on two fronts.

In my mind I hear the roar of the crowd as I step onto what was once our little Wembley. It's scrubland, really, but as level as any open piece of land in the area, so it served us well enough. Playing football on the Humpty

Dumpty Field was a non-starter. So many hours of my life were spent on this patch of grass; my sweat and blood must, to some unmeasurable extent, still be here in the soil.

Is that what Bean scents as he busily follows his nose zigzaggedly over the ground? He must have terrier in him, with his upright pointy ears and proportionately short legs, and the terra firma that informed that part of his breed retains an instinctive pull on him. The sky holds little interest, and I doubt that water would either. The earth is his natural habitat, just as it is mine.

And as I think back on them, all of Dad's dogs had that terrier base to them. We're an earthy lot, I suppose, Dad driving over land for a living, as opposed to flying through the air or sailing the seas. It's born, I believe, of coming from the landlocked county of Brakeshire, and the earthy heart of it at that. Water passes through it, and the sky is large given the lack of any high ground worthy of the title, but soil and sod predominate. Crops and grain were the stock-in-trade. Until more recently, when the movement over the earth of goods came to base itself here. Paul plays his part, servicing and maintaining those engines that lug, and the machines that sow and reap and load and unload. Oil tattoos the bitten skin around his fingers, and stains the nicks in his knuckles.

Dad smelt of diesel. Paul smells of oil. What do I smell of?

Tobacco, I decide, and light one up.

Without considering the route, Bean and I emerge on the edge of the Humpty Dumpty Field, and take the barely discernible impression of a footpath along its top edge bearing westward. We work our way along the thin line of browning trees, their crisping cast-offs saved from disintegration by the malleability injected by the recent downpour.

Leafy fragments adhere to the shining wet toes of my boots, a couple hanging from the low-slung belly of the dog as he sinks his nose in piles of foliage and sniffs for a verminous prey he may or may not be capable of dealing with should he encounter it.

Does he still have the killing instinct, or is he too far removed from it now?

I click my tongue, and he looks round and up at me, his face seeming to smile, as his tongue overhangs the side of his wet muzzle. I'm glad I did this. Bean needed it.

Checking the weather and light, we decide to push on and loop round to the north. We pass through the arched brick tunnel that the old railway trains once trundled over, that nostril-like arch ensuring it could bear the load. The almost black damp brick glistens as though I'm inside a slug, as my footsteps chase me and pummel me from both sides and above. Until, as I pass the midpoint and have to keep right to avoid the sitting water, those sharp shots of my steps seem to be coming from in front of me, as though they're happening before I can make them as they seek the light and air and a way out.

Emerging on the north side of the defunct railway, a weed-strewn gravel path bordered by a tall rusting black metal fence encasing, but not containing, even taller weeds skirts the reservoir. I don't know, and have never known, why the reservoir exists. My best guess is that it served some purpose for the railway when it was active, but that's purely speculation.

I recall cub scouts gingerly maneuvering canoes on it a couple of times a year, and every few years it would be drained and all of the shopping trolleys and bits of discarded car removed. Sadly, there were never any be-woggled cub scouts in its murky shallows. But that aside, it played no memorable role in our lives, other than as something that required circumnavigating. After all, even Micky would rather go home for a drink than refresh himself from the water in the reservoir.

The river Jem is crossed by the old railway a mile or so to the west, but the fading light puts it out of our reach on this occasion. We follow the congealed gravel path and take a short detour to emerge at the blasted gorge where Dad's rockery rocks were mined one sunny day too long ago.

Shrubs, undergrowth and stunted brittle trees cover the sharp-sloping banks of the railway. Something about it tells of its manmade-ness. It's slightly alien in the context of its surroundings, and perhaps too precise and straight. Nature tends to be a little more charming and curvaceously attractive in her doings. The charm, I believe, lies in the imperfections.

But the rail is like a long set of molar teeth rising from the gums of the earth, a single extraction leaving the gaping gorge. They planned to build a road through it, thereby opening up the land to the west of Oaklea to housing.

As a result, an abandoned old line of grey stones runs for scores of unbroken miles before suddenly, without warning, ending for an un-jumpable gap that is, in actuality, wider than it appears. Nobody I witnessed could ever manage to stand on one lip and throw a stone onto the other. Any attempt would die in the air, and hurtle down to crash-land in the gorse below, thwacking a rapid succession of leaves and branches before thumping the earth in frustration.

I have time to go there, I decide, as I pick out the best route up the bank by eyeing the density of the shrubbery.

And once ascended, the railway is less lunar than I remember it as the residual damp darkens the stones to slate and holds the pale dust at bay.

Bay: As in horse; a dark reddy-brown that I know to be Elle's natural colour. But she was bleached blond and shorn punkily when I first saw her.

I pause to bend and give Bean a pat and rub on his densely coarse neck. My boots aren't hiking spec, and I'm not sure I'd have had the traction had he not somewhat pulled me up through the lead. He's a strong little dog, with a barrel of a chest and short muscular legs, his squatness making him an excellent climber, I think, and probably an excellent digger, as well.

Digger. And then Elle and Dad. My thoughts involuntarily go in that order, despite me knowing that my priorities should be different. It should be Dad first and foremost. And probably Paul coming in second. But I'm controlled by the thing that leaves the biggest hole inside me.

It's all related to itself, as all roads lead to here; Millby at the hub of my world. Round and round it goes, relentlessly churning and grinding like the scarred millstone that is all that remains above ground; all that can be seen of the past.

The sun appears, and sits an inch above the moon rock as I look at it along the track stretching away behind me.

I walk away from it, my shadow elongated and narrow, and jerkily moving ahead of me as though it trembles with fear.

And I am a little anxious being here. But I felt a need to come; a compulsion, almost.

They fenced it off. If only they'd done that before. A solid metal barrier about four feet high seals off the drop, a red triangle warning of danger, a crude depiction of falling rocks, and a yellow and black sign ordering people to stay away from the edge.

Advancing to that barrier, and no further, I rest a hand on it as I gaze out over the chasm beneath me. Again, it isn't as large a drop as I recall, perhaps only forty feet; not much higher than the average house. In my mind it was twice that at least.

I can see the individual leaves on the trees below, and in the gaps I can discern the long yellow grass growing amidst the rocks that season the landscape as though salt and pepper were applied from a giant grinder.

I didn't bring my phone. I didn't want intrusion. And I don't wear a watch. But I know by the position of the sun that it must be about six o'clock, and that it'll be dark in twenty minutes or so. It would be wise to be on paved ground by then.

"Are you hungry, boy?" I ask Bean, "are you ready for your dinner?"

The final word is recognised, and his eyes meet mine, fiercely orange as they catch the sun as it kisses the ground.

He looks happy, and that makes me happy.

Just before turning to leave, I peer over the precipice again, and try to remember exactly where it was that Micky fell and perished.

7.

A knock at the door brings a warning bark from Bean. It's the first time he's barked since Paul dropped him off.

It isn't a knock so much as a rattle, as bare knuckles make contact with the wooden frame of the off-kilter door on the porch.

Elle is my first thought, forcing me to check my attire, and run a hand through my hair.

It's dark, and there's no outside light, so I flick the hall light on as I pass through, Bean leading the way, curious to know if it's Dad returning. We each cling to our forlorn hopes.

A man confronts me, his face somewhat hidden under the rim of a waterproof safari style hat. There isn't much big game around here.

My immediate concern is that I should recognise him, so I greet him with a smile and a nod, but no words.

"I heard about your father. My condolences," he says, quietly but audibly, a scratchiness in his voice that makes me think of Clint Eastwood. The hat adds to the impression.

"Thank you," I reply.

Who are you?

"You don't recognise me, do you?" he adds, raising his chin a little so that the light from within accents his features.

But before he can do that, I know who he is, his vocal inflections more apparent when he asked a question. Oh, and he had a lot of questions for me on a few occasions. His northern accent comes to the fore; grimly Yorkshire. My jaw tightens, a little angry tremor prodding at the joint on the right of my face. But I catch myself, and relinquish it via a smile.

"Detective Immleigh," I confirm, "it's been a while."

"Detective Sergeant," he feels the need to point out, before adding, "retired."

I'm relieved to hear the last bit. But I should have known that. He was a keen early-thirties when I was fifteen, so he must be mid-sixties now. One promotion in all that time, but I'm not surprised. He'd not long before transferred from uniform, and I was his first case as lead investigating officer.

"And how's that going?" I ask him, resting my hand on the doorframe at shoulder height, my arm blocking the way and sending a message of 'you're not coming in.'

"It suits me well enough. Lots of time to fish and lots of time to think, you know?"

"Not really. How long have you been retired?"

"Three years."

"And you've been fishing and thinking for all of that time?"

"Not all of it. But you think back on your life - the ones you nailed, and the ones that got away."

"Fish?"

He actually laughs very slightly, from the back of his throat and through his nostrils. "Those as well."

"Well, as I said, thanks for your condolences," I say by way of getting rid of him. I offer him my hand.

He takes it. No warm pump of renewed acquaintance comes, but he holds my hand firmly enough. Perhaps a little too firmly. The dog low-growls from behind me - *good boy.*

A glint of light tells me that Immleigh's eyes are watching me from beneath the rim of his hat. I can make out the grey beard on his chin and lip, those tight lips that adhere to his teeth to such a degree that one can't open without dragging the other with them. I remember his crooked mouth, rising on one side more than the other so that a permanent smirk seems to blight him, just as a mild stroke might.

"I know you did it," he soughs.

"What did I do?"

"You killed that kid up the road for starters."

"I did. But I didn't mean to."

"So you said. Or, rather, you didn't say. And then there's the missing girl that I think you know more about than you ever let on."

"Try not to think too much," is my advice, as he releases my hand. I feel an urge to wash it.

"I can't help myself," he responds, "and given your history, it's always played on my mind that you left at the same time as she disappeared."

"Coincidence. I told you that."

"You did. Yet you were seen with her on two occasions that day."

"She asked me a question about the trains. I've told you that a few times."

"So you maintain. Been keeping your nose clean, have you, down there in London? Been keeping that temper of yours under control?"

He already knows that I've had no trouble. He'll have checked on a regular basis, and run my name through the database. A nod, therefore, seems to suffice.

"When's the funeral?" he asks.

"We won't know until tomorrow."

"And then what? Back to your important life in the big city?"

"Something like that," I reply, and smile at the thought of it.

"You can't hide here like you can there."

"I have nothing to hide from."

"Well, I'll see you around, then."

"Only if you intend being around."

"Oh, I'll be around," he calmly informs me.

Immleigh turns on his heel and strides away without looking back.

Just leave me alone. All I've ever wanted is to be left alone.

8.

I inhale the cassettes, but they smell of old cardboard and plastic, her scent long since departed from them.

But if I had access to a crime lab, a modern crime lab far in advance of what was available in the eighties when the tapes were compiled, it will surely show her fingerprints, and her skin fragments and hair will be retrievable and analysable; her presence would be confirmed.

Elle would make them for me. It was part of my education; the most vital part, in that, to a large degree, it led to the career I now enjoy.

She'd sit up at night, putting them together from her own records, or records she borrowed from the library, and they were done solely for me. That was before we were together, but it played its part in us getting together.

She suffered from insomnia for years. She was, quite literally, afraid to go to sleep.

Perhaps that isn't true. As she told me once, she was more afraid of waking up if she did sleep. It was irrational, she'd readily admit, and laugh critically at herself.

But, I reason, if you'd been woken up in the pitch black of night at the age of eleven and taken away by a uniformed stranger, sat in a starkly lit white room, and told that your parents had both been killed in a road accident, you might begin to understand it. To further learn that the man you called Dad for all of your talking life wasn't actually your father, but, rather, that he had married your mother and taken on her burden, and that, when that burden became too great, he purposefully drove the family car into a bridge support at ninety miles an hour, killing his wife and himself, and orphaning a little girl, you might understand it a bit more. She went to live with her maternal grandmother for four years, but awoke one morning to discover her dead in her bed.

When Eleanor went to sleep one night, her life was perfectly happy. If only she could have carried on sleeping for ever.

But she couldn't sleep forever. And from it all, Elle pronounced L was moulded.

L. That barest of names adorns all of the tapes. 'To Digger, from L.'

And later - 'To Digger, love Lx.'

And even later - 'To my Darling Digger. All my love forever, Lxxxxxxxxxxxxxxxxx.'

Well, that was a lie.

She came to live with Pat and Pat when she was fifteen, almost sixteen. It was the summer of 1983. She-Pat was her mother's cousin, and closest relative on her maternal side. Her father's side, birth or adoptive, didn't want anything to do with her.

He-Pat being a Counsellor probably helped with the placement. Besides, Pat and Pat didn't have children of their own, so it filled gaps all ways round.

I was a year younger than Elle - one school year, but close to a year and a half separated us in actual time. And when you're that age, and add in that girls invariably mature earlier than boys, there was what seemed like an unbridgeable gap between us initially. Now, though, later in life, the age difference would be nothing.

Still, it didn't stop me being utterly captivated by the mere sight of her from the moment I first set eyes on her. From the very beginning, I drew the outline of her face and vainly attempted to add in her features. I did it then, just as I continue to do it now - so that I might never forget her.

Because I must have known, deep down, that I would lose her - that she was too good for me; too sophisticated; too classy.

Her statuesqueness was arresting. Unlike Debbie, who sought to attract by revealing, Elle seemed to hold allure by revealing nothing.

Oh, and how Debbie hated Elle. Not that she didn't befriend her at first, but you could see the envy. In one fell-swoop, simply by coming to live here, Debbie was relegated from favourite to also-ran. She tried to compete, getting Dee to take her to a salon in Tredmouth to get her hair styled and coloured, and her dad brought her clothes back from business trips to London, but she couldn't carry them like Elle could. And anyway, Elle created her own clothes, adapted from charity shop finds, clothes that were essentially fifty years out of date, but held that deco period cut and pattern that tied in to the post-punk and emerging scene of the new decade. She invented it, as far as I was concerned, and Debbie tried to buy it - one a leader; one a follower.

And I had no desire to follow a follower.

All of that said, though, Elle was so far out of my reach, and Debbie was next door, where she'd always been, and she was attractive. And available. She was attractively available.

Ah, I'm being too... Debbie was...

I don't know the extent of the majority, but I believe that more than half of men, and women for that matter, would find Debbie more attractive than Elle. Debbie was more classically pretty, with her English-rose features and complexion, her light-brown - blonde when the light caught it - hair, and her porcelain skin with a natural blush of rouge where her bones were closest to the surface on her dimpled full round cheeks. She had the requisite smattering of random freckles on her nose, and a naturally full mouth that lent her a perpetually happy disposition. Further, she had large open blue eyes that I still recall gazing up at me earnestly every time I think of her kneeling in front of me.

Her body was early-developed and extremely well formed. She was bestowed with breasts that stayed where they were no matter what position she took up, adorned with nipples that were always erect, and only became more pronounced when suckled or tweaked. And they were incredibly sensitive to any and every stimulation. Prior to Micky and I being sexually mature enough to attempt to satisfy her in other ways, we could somewhat satiate her by breast-play alone. Somewhat.

Debbie adored sex, and she adored her own sexuality.

Her hourglass figure was completed by her perfectly proportionate hips, and at an age when she should have been braiding the hair of her little pony, she was instead obsessively maintaining her 36-22-34 figure. I'd often be ordered to hold the tape measure.

Yet, and as with a lot of people I've known, she always focused on her self-perceived flaw. She hated her legs. There was nothing wrong with them, as far as I could see. But she insisted that they were too short and a little heavy on the thighs, and thin at the ankle. And it obsessed her beyond all other fixations, that overly-self-critical imperfection. As I say, I never saw anything wrong with her legs. But that didn't matter - she did.

And the legs she would have liked to own were on Elle.

Elle was less shapely by comparison, and more lean with an angularity next to Debbie. She had a harder look, no softness of feature here, until you got to, as I did, see through the barrier she faced the world with. Penetrate that, and the softness and vulnerability would come flooding out. Her angularity would become willowy as it softened and flowed more naturally. And I never knew such warmth of person as I unearthed in Elle. I have never known such tenderness.

Yet, to all appearances, the warmth and comfort that most men desire, if not all, was more overtly present in Debbie.

And that, I believe, is why most men would opt for her over Elle. Elle was too aloof and cool, too impenetrable and strong. But it was a facade - in both instances, it was all a facade.

Dirty Debbie was the name Micky bestowed on her, but never to her face. And whereas Micky's moniker came from his unquestionable obsession with sex, it also existed because he was a grubby sod. If there was a single dog crap anywhere in the vicinity, he was certain to stand, sit or lie in it.

Debbie, by contrast, was immaculate. Dee saw to that. Before Elle entered the scene and altered Debbie's wardrobe, Dee would dress her in her own image - less Mini Me, and more Mini Dee.

And Dee was keen to hang on to her youth. 'Mutton dressed as lamb' was the phrase Dad always used to describe her. Pop-socks and little flared gaudily-coloured ra-ra skirts had supplanted the Charlie's Angels one-piece trouser suits that had carried her through much of the seventies. Toni Basil appeared in John Travolta's stead.

As far as Debbie was concerned, none of it mattered much, as she'd shed the lot at the merest of suggestions.

Anyway, thankfully Madonna came along in 1983, and that was a look that Debbie, and Dee to a lesser extent, could carry off very well.

Elle, though... Always Elle. We'd see her coming and going, and that was about it. We didn't interact. We were fourteen, and a long way from fifteen, and Elle was nearly sixteen, so the gulf was huge.

I remember the first time she smiled at me. It was barely a smile, and more a flicker of mirthful recognition as she swept by in the passenger seat of Wanker Perry's MG Midget. I was busy cleaning Dad's car on the driveway half way up the hill, him having decided I was more deserving of a bob for the job the cubs were happy to perform for the same. 'Keep it in the family' was his line of negotiation. Anyway, he gave me fifty pence, which was enough to top up the cigarette fund to the price of a ten pack.

Micky had his church plate money safely stashed. He'd become quite expert at feigning a drop in the tray, and palming the money away. He'd spent hours practicing with an old upturned frisbee and some washers from a jar in his dad's shed. Anyway, not only could he now mimic the apparent dropping of a coin, but had recently managed to develop his technique to an extent that allowed him to snaffle a larger denomination coin in the process. Ten pence became fifty pence. 'It was a miracle,' he claimed - 'praise the lord!'

We'd need Debbie to write a note for the shop, forged expertly to uncannily resemble Micky's dad's handwriting and signature. She really did have a gift. But it would cost us two of the ten ciggies, and we'd have to take her 'across the Humpty Dumpty Field' as payment. Still, beggars couldn't afford to be choosers.

So, I was cleaning the car, and a toot on a horn startled me. I dropped the water bucket, and turned just in time to see Elle trundle by, Wanker Perry with an arm proprietorially draped around the back of the passenger seat, the roof lowered on his throbbing bright blue Midget. It was a shade that Paul brilliantly dubbed 'Perrywanker Blue'.

And as I stood there, a suddy sponge depositing white foam down the front of my Pepe button-fly jeans, that was the first time I was aware that she was aware that I existed. A smile threatened to part her lips and show me her teeth before she looked away, Wanker Perry laughing his head off as he winked at me.

Winker Perry.

A couple of years later, I reminded Elle of that day. She remembered it, and said that her smile was genuine, and that she'd admired my backside in my new jeans I'd picked up on a day trip to Jemford Bridge to visit my auntie and cousins. It was my cousin who gave me the black suede winkle-picker boots he'd outgrown. They were barely used, and I was probably wearing them with my Pepe button-fly's that day.

The truth is, though, that she was smiling at the 'boy' on the corner washing the family car in his best clothes, and desperately trying to look cool as foam dripped down the front of his new clothes.

It was I who adopted the L to depict her name. Did I do it to rebrand her; to make her in some way uniquely mine? Or was it simply a code I employed, so that I could write about her in my notebook, and disguise the object of my desire should the notebook ever be brought to light? Similarly, was that why I never drew her features on to the blank outline of her face?

I sound like a stalker.

Ah, but my obsession with Elle was amateurishly lightweight when compared to Micky's.

Whilst I was a little ashamed of my feelings, and harboured no real hope of anything ever happening between us, he was convinced that she held secret desires for him. He would sometimes blur the lines between fiction and reality. He'd struggle to differentiate between the thoughts in his head and real events.

It killed him in the end, that not knowing when to stop; not seeing the point at which a laugh and a lark became something more dangerous.

Debbie didn't help matters. She'd gone from being a bit distant and intimidated by Elle, to fawning all over her, as she'd regale us with tales of their, frankly, dubious sounding interactions.

Elle was, apparently, "certainly bisexual, and most probably a full-on lesbian," Debbie informed us, as she twirled one of the black ribbons she'd had woven into her soft-permed hair, as she lay back in the long yellow grass down at the foot of the bank of the old railway, where the leaf-laden branches of the Gnarly Ash tree offered both shade and privacy.

Apparently, nobody had ever touched Debbie like Elle had, and, she supposed, "it took a woman to really know where and how to touch another woman."

And as Micky clumsily humped away on top of her, so she'd set those saucer-sorcerer blue eyes on me, and watch me unblinkingly all the while, her tongue poking out a quarter inch between her parted lips, her eyebrows raised high, her lids painted blue. And as Micky relieved himself on the grass, she'd whisper so that he couldn't hear, "you can have a go if you like."

9.

At the very bottom of the carton are three shoe boxes with the lids taped down. Lifting one free, I pick at the ends of the tape strips and open it up on my bedroom carpet.

Inside are Elle's letters to me.

Did I seal them away, or did Dad do that, and keep them for me? And if he did, to what end?

I didn't do it. I'm sure of that. They were all stashed in my fishing box the day that I left here. I should have burnt them before leaving.

They're in the envelopes they came in, their top edges split. It was a thing we had, the sending of letters. It was nonsensical, as we lived three doors apart, but, at the outset, it was the best way that we could communicate. It was the best way that I could communicate, to be more accurate.

And once that was established, we carried it on. I think we could both more ably put across what we felt in letter form rather than verbally.

Does she still have my letters to her? And, if so, are they similarly stored away, having lain dormant and unread for three decades? Or does she take them out from time to time, perhaps prompted to do so by some event or thought? A song, perhaps, heard on the radio and taking her back to a time when we were together?

Does she see me in the countenances of actors on television, just as I see her? And has she attempted to project the aging on to me, and failed to conjure up anything that makes sense, always having to revert to a mental image of how I was? Is she as locked into the past, like a frozen still of film that no amount of fast-forwarding, rewinding or attempts to eject will fully remove?

It isn't healthy. I know that. I should have let go a long time ago.

Avoidance was my tactic, but it hasn't really worked. I stayed away so that I wouldn't have to see her, yet I looked for her everywhere. I rarely asked Dad or Paul about her, yet I longed for them to mention her name. And even when I did inquire, it was in the broadest sense.

Her handwriting is so distinctive with its heavy slant. I imagine her writing lying down, the pen in her right hand, the bulk of which glides along below the line of text so that all of the stems and tails are scored at forty-five degrees to vertical. Perhaps it's the reason that there are no true straight lines in the font, as every line has a curve to it, however slight. Had I not known, I would have said that it was penned by the hand of a woman.

August 11th 1985 "... My Digger! I don't possess the words to tell you how you make me feel. I don't think the words have been invented, which is why I struggle. And that tells me that nobody has ever loved anyone in the way that I Love you. You tell me that I'm beautiful, and I've never believed myself to be that. But when you tell me, I begin to believe it. At least, that I am beautiful in your eyes, and that is the only place that matters to me. Thank you for making me feel so special and Loved. I hope that you know you are Loved so very much by me. Lx."

Another. *January 2nd 1986 "...I miss you, and I only just saw you. I still smell you on me. And I still feel you on and in me. I didn't know that it was possible - this thing that we have. I honestly believed that love was fictional, some label invented by someone, and no different to any other noun and verb - no different to dog or cat, and walk and* nap. Love was what people said, what they called someone, how they hoodwinked them - love was a lie, as far as I was concerned, and I was on my guard against it. But now Love is everything. My Love for you consumes me entirely. I'm fascinated by you. Just the way you light a cigarette enthralls me, and I bet you don't even know that you do it. You always flick the lighter with your right hand, and then release it so it can drop into your left, and in one fluid motion you put it in your pocket. It's like art, Digger, like water and air! Oh, my Love, everything you do - just the way you move turns me on! I Love you so completely. Lx."

And another. I can't stop reading. *May 22nd 1985 "...I'm so sorry, my darling Digger. I was wrong today, and I admit it freely! It must have hurt you, and I'd never knowingly do that. But you were wrong, as well - I am NOT ashamed of you! It's just that what we have is nothing to do with anyone else. It's nobody's business but ours. Nobody! I love you! There, I wrote it down. I said it. I Love you with a capital L. I LOVE YOU! I am in LOVE with YOU! And I don't even know what that means, beyond knowing that I am. I feel something that I can't explain, and that both terrifies and delights me. Do you believe me? Love Lx."*

The next, randomly selected. There are scores of them; two a week for at least two years. Two hundred letters.

October 20th 1986 "...they should be heading off to the conference in mid-afternoon, and staying there for the night. Come to me as soon as the coast is clear. Come under the cover of darkness! Oh, come to me, my Love! We can spend the whole night together, wrapped around one another. It will be our time - my first time falling asleep and waking up with someone! Will I snore? Do I snore? Would you tell me if I did? Perhaps we shouldn't sleep, just in case. I wonder what we could do all night instead? Any ideas? My tummy rolls over on itself when I think of it. But be careful. Don't get caught. Come to the back door, but only when you know it's safe! We mustn't ruin our chance, okay? Come to me! I ache for you. I throb and pulse and beat and breathe, all for you! We will bath together, you and I. We will immerse ourselves in one another, and I will show you all of my Love. Lx"

I have to cease.

How? How can a person write all of that, and lots more besides, and not actually mean it? Is it, as she wrote, all fiction? Love is fiction. Literary bullshit fiction. It's all words for the sake of words. But it seemed so genuine. I was hoodwinked by it all. I was naive and young. I craved something, and she provided it. That was all it was. I instigated it all - she was simply reciprocating. I told her that I loved her, and she told me back, because that's what people do. It's a trigger response, with no substance. It is nothing but words.

I should throw them all away. No, I should destroy them. This is the moment I should let go, and move on. Finally, and at last.

But I know that I shan't throw them away, or burn or shred them. I will retain them, and I will look at them all at some point. And I'll do that because I'm weak; too weak to let go of her. It's easier to hold on, just as I've always held on, than to open my fist and relinquish her. If I did that, I might feel an urge to grasp something else in her place.

Relinquish her from what to what? Christ, she is bloody relinquished - she relinquished herself thirty years ago, at the same time as she relinquished me!

It's me that needs to renounce myself.

What time is it? My legs are numb and locked beneath me, so long have I squatted here in the same position.

Bean lies in the hallway, watching me through the open bedroom door, where he's also able to monitor Dad's bedroom and the front door from his strategic placement.

Dad is dead, he reminds me. Yet all of my mind is filled with Elle. It's selfish. It's wrong.

What did Dad ever say about Elle after I left? What was his take on it all, and why did he keep these letters?

He once said that she was 'a good one', and that it was a shame things didn't work out between us. She was a 'lovely girl, once she stopped wearing those daft clothes and tidied her hair up a bit. She turned into a very fine looking young woman, once she realised she was actually a young woman!'

That was about it.

Paul would tell me snippets on the phone. I'd run through a list of people to ask about, and slip Elle in the midst of them, usually bolted on to Pat and Pat as an afterthought - 'oh, and what about Elle - is she doing okay?'

Through that I learned that she went away soon after I left. To college, I think; teacher training.

God, I never had teachers who looked like Elle. I might have enjoyed school more had that been the case.

But I know very little. Did she ever marry? Have children? I don't think that she did. Where does she live? Is she still a teacher? Paul said something about moving back with Pat and Pat a few years ago when she transferred schools.

Is she still there, living with them? Was that just a temporary arrangement?

Does she ever give me a thought?

She'll be fifty now. I was with her for two of those fifty years. One in twenty-five - four percent. It isn't much. I saw a woman called Michelle for longer than that, but I ended it.

She wasn't Elle.

Dad lived with Bean for six years, the poor little pooch. A hundred percent. He must be in turmoil, but he can't communicate it. He shows it, though; he shows it better than I do.

"Come on, fella," I say to him, and he rises and follows me down, tripping expertly off each stair, his body at an angle that I wouldn't care to attempt.

He still hasn't touched his dinner. I can talk; I haven't eaten dinner myself.

Are we pining, he and I?

We slip into the dark back garden, a dull yellow bulb outside the door casting just enough of a glow to help avoid the snails - the scant light enough to be tossed around by the pampas grasses in the borders as they hula in the breeze.

Lighting a cigarette, I turn to my right and count the rooftops against the thinly-veiled but moonlit sky - number five, seven, nine.

~~~~~

The Glenns were my concern that evening I went to her. They were always watching, and always ready to interfere. So I went up the hill and around the rear of the houses, before dropping down the alley on the other side of the fence by number thirteen. That way Dad and Paul would see I was heading to the schoolfriend's house I was purportedly staying at that night.

It hadn't been removed, the swing that Micky and I had placed there a few years before so that we could slip in and out without detection. So, with my arm fed through my bag handles, I used the streetlight to ascend the seven-foot high fence on one side, and the frame of the swing to silently slide down on the other.

Sinking to my haunches, I listened for any sign of the dog belonging to the new occupants. All clear. The flicker of the television lit up the small patio area, so I gave it a wide berth and used a hand on a post to side-vault the fence into Perry's garden.

His home was in darkness, his MG not parked on the street. Still, I exercised caution, lest old Mrs Glenn be gawking out of an upstairs window. I slipped along the brick until I was at the fence bordering Elle's house. Rather than run the risk of destroying one of the bushes planted in the border along the fence, thereby leaving telltale evidence, I opted for the gate, the side of Elle's house offering me cover.

I waited while a car came along the street, its lights pouring through the gaps between the houses as it three-point turned at the end of the road, and then came to rest outside the house I was so recently pressed against. Wanker Perry was home.

At the moment his headlights were extinguished, I slipped through the gate into Elle's back garden and froze.

My heart pounded in my chest - part fear at being discovered and deprived, and part excitement at what lay ahead if I wasn't discovered.

'The bastard, the bastard!' I was thinking, as the buckles on his cowboy boots rattled their way towards me. He must have bloody seen me. I could hear his flares rubbing against each other as I held my breath so that no mist would be exhaled.

The latch lifted, and there came a push against my back as the gate was opened. I went with it, stepping in time as it swung ajar because there was nowhere else to go. My nose was jammed into a fence post, my form shielded by the gate itself, as I released my breath as steadily and silently as I could and blew the condensed fog of it away into number eleven.

My bag was pressed into my shins, but I remained there stock-still.

Daring to turn my head to the left, I saw Perry out of the corner of my eye, lit up somewhat by the light from within. That was all he did for a while - stand there staring. It dragged on, the time, though it probably wasn't nearly as long as it felt.

I dreaded the thought of him tapping the back door, and Elle thinking it was me. But he didn't. He did nothing, and made no sound. Suddenly he was striding back towards me, sandwiched behind the gate, the delicate chink of his buckles and the rub of his trousers informing me of all I dared not expose my face to.

The gate left my spine and swung silently back into position, the latch lifted and gently returned to the clasp. I was glad that my black trench coat from Army Surplus covered my clothing, my grey cap shrouded my fair head of hair. He hadn't noticed me.

Perrywanker strode to Elle's front door and I heard the ding-less dong of the chime as he pressed the button.

"Oh, hi," I heard Elle say.

"Hi. Just thought I'd look in on you, with Pat and Pat being away. Is everything okay?"

"Fine, thanks."

"Well, if you need anything, I'm back home, so just give me a shout."

"Thanks, but I'm sure I'll be fine." Her tone was dismissive, her answers closed.

"I know, but Pat asked me to keep an eye on things. So, if you need anything…" He left it hanging. He always did that.

"I'll let you know," Elle said, closing the statement for him.

"Right. Well, I'll leave you to it, then."

"Thanks."

"Oh, hey, I was going to open a bottle of wine and chill out tonight. You're welcome to…" he suggested.

"Share it? No. I have college work to do."

"Oh, right. Anything I can help with?"

"That would defeat the objective."

"Ha! Yes, I suppose it would. Good point. Well, I'll be, erm…"

"Going?"

"Yes. Next door. So you know where I'll be?" he said suggestively.

"Next door."

"Okayyyyy! Well, catch you later, potat-er!"

What a seventies DJ wanker.

It was hard not to laugh and ruin everything.

The door closed, and Perry jingle-jangled his flappy way back home.

I made my move after I was sure he was in his house, but before he could hit the lights at the rear and expose me.

A barely audible tap brought Elle to the back door, the outside light purposefully left unlit. She looked for my face through the window before opening it, her relief at seeing it was me eliciting a beautiful smile. Her smile meant so much more because it wasn't a part of her public face. It was reserved for me, because she felt safe.

And she looked so homely and comfortable in her worn old jeans with the frayed bottoms, and the baggy-yet-clingy red jumper that overhung her hands a little and accentuated her willowy form.

She looked like somewhere I could live for the rest of my life.

And as I stepped over the threshold, and into her arms, my mouth on hers, I had an incredibly strong urge to cry.

I didn't, because I hardly ever do. But I felt it burn my larynx and diamond my vision. Why? Why at that happiest of times did I feel that way?

Those chiselled cheeks and warm smokey grey eyes held such an allure to me; a lure, even, that I was powerless to resist, willingly devouring it and wanting to be snagged and captured by it despite its ability to rip into me and cause me such pain, as it would ultimately remove me from my natural habitat and leave me gasping for air.

Oh, I went willingly every time because I was bidden and because there was nowhere I'd rather be. I went where others longed to go, but were not bidden.

I never did tell her about Perry watching at the back window. I don't know why.

Instead, we drew all the curtains and cocooned ourselves for a night and the best part of a day.

We'd had sex many times before that night, but it was often snatched and with us both on our guard. Yes, that made it fun, that risk, but clothing had to remain so that decency could quickly be reestablished. For the same reason, it mostly had to be hurried and rushed and, therefore, less fulfilling.

But that night we ate a meal like adults, and we shared a candle-lit bath that we kept topping up until our skin went wrinkly, before we fell in to bed together.

That was it - the only full night I ever spent with her.

And it was, by a considerable distance, the best night of my life.

~~~~~

I have such a compulsion to retrace my route from that night, and to find myself in her back garden.

Oh, god, and I understand Perry! I am Wanker Perry. For I would do the same, and sneak in and look furtively through the window at her, because that would be enough when compared to nothing.

10.

I slept fitfully. Tea and more tea is all I can handle as Dad's water content diminishes.

"Hello?" I say into my mobile phone. It barely ever rings.

"Morning! It's me! Paul said you were at your father's."

"Hi, Mum. Yes, I'm here now."

"Ugh, it's terrible isn't it? I still can't believe it!"

"I know, it's..."

"He was only a couple of years older than me, your father was."

"Yes, I know that, Mum."

"It really has taken me aback. I was married to him for twenty years, don't forget, and a couple of years courting before that."

"It's a shock, Mum. It is a shock. For all of us."

"Ugh, I don't know how you can stay in the house."

"Well, he's not here, is he?"

"No, no, I know that. But it was where he, you know... Passed." She whispers the last word.

"I don't think he had the plague."

"Ha! You are funny! His heart, wasn't it? That's what Paul told me. A hard heart like his! Oooof! What chance have I got with my soft heart? But I do have a kind heart, I think, because it's softer."

Fucking hell.

"So, what's the weather like there, Digger?"

"Erm, overcast at the moment," I reply, looking out of the window, "but it might brighten up..."

"It's beautiful here where I am. It's one of those beautiful days with a clear blue sky, although it's cold, but it is beautiful."

"You're lucky living by the coast."

"I suppose I am, aren't I? Do you really think I am?"

"Oh, yeah."

"Well, you should come and visit me more, then. After all, you won't have to visit your father so much now, will you?"

"Not so much, no."

"I just spoke with Paul. He was on his way to see the doctor to get the death certificate. And he'll know more about the funeral later today. Jen's doing a lot of it, which is great."

"Yes, it's great," I confirm.

"And what are you doing with yourself? Paul said you were sorting out the house."

"Yes, I made a start."

"I've already started on mine. All this stuff, Digger, we accumulate all this stuff! I'm getting rid of it, and having a good sort out. I made over a hundred pounds at the car boot sale, did I tell you about that?"

"Yes, you..."

"People don't want to pay anything for anything nowadays, that's the trouble. And you and Paul don't want any of it. I suppose it's old fashioned, really, stuff I got when my mum and dad died. It still upsets me, you know? Even after all these years."

"I know, Mum."

Don't start bloody crying.

"I'm having a good clear out, I am. There won't be much for you to do when I pass! And I've paid for my funeral, did I tell you that?"

"You did."

"It probably sounds a bit morbid, but I wanted to do it. You and Paul won't have to worry about me when I go. Not like your father. I'm all taken care of."

"Well, that's good."

"You will miss me, though, won't you? There's nothing like losing your mother. I know. It's different, I think, because you come from inside your mother. I carried you around inside me for nine months, don't forget. Yes, it's different, losing your mother."

"I try not to think about it, Mum. You'll be around for years yet."

"Phhhh, well I don't know about that. Look at your father - here one day, and gone the next. Do you think I should come to the funeral? Paul thinks I should."

"Yes, of course. If you want to."

"Well, I want to be there for you boys, really. And Jim might come with me - you remember my friend Jim? I told you about him? We're only friends, nothing more. He wants more, I think, but I've sat him down and told him that we're just friends, and that's all there is. He can like it or lump it! But he's good to me. He does jobs around the house for me, and he's very generous. Jim's offered to drive me up there and back, but I'll give him some money for petrol. He's very good at funerals, Jim. He has the face for it."

"I'd better run, Mum. I think Paul's trying to get hold of me."

"Oh, okay then. Well, I'm here if you need me, don't forget. You know where I am. You can call me anytime."

"Thanks, Mum. Speak soon. Bye."

Seizing my smokes and lighter, I head to the back door and let the dog out, simultaneously taking the call from Paul.

"All right?" I mumble, as I flick a flame from the disposable lighter, the disposability of which reminds me that I plan on giving up. The Zippo Dad got me feels a bit permanent, as though it will outlast me.

"All right? Are you smoking in the house?"

"No. I'm in the garden with Bean."

"Hmmm. What have you been doing?"

"Ah, not much. I walked the dog yesterday evening, and made a start on the house. The bin's pretty full. What do you want me to do with stuff that needs slinging? And what day do the bin men come?"

"Tuesday, I think. But check with the neighbours. You'll see them put the wheelie bins out the night before. They won't take anything not in the bin. Look, stash stuff in the hall, and I'll swing by in the week and run it up to the tip."

"Fair enough," I say, because I suppose it is.

"I've just left the undertaker. We can get in on Friday. They had a cancellation."

I try to think of the circumstances leading to a cancellation, but draw a blank. "Okay."

"I figured you'd be happy. You said you had to get back next week for work."

"That's fine. It'll save me having to make two trips."

"But we'll need to jump on this to get everything arranged. Jen's printing up the invites, and we'll need to get them out today and tomorrow. She's doing them at home to save money. I'll drop a bundle off to you later, if you can spin round and deliver them."

"Why doesn't she just post them?"

"No time. Besides, it's cheaper. Look, we'll be hard pushed to make today's pick up, which means they'll not go out till Tuesday. You know what the post's like. They probably won't get there till Thursday at the earliest, and that's not enough time for a Friday funeral, is it?"

"I suppose not, no."

"There are only about twenty. And most are in Oaklea or Millby. We'll do any over Drescombe way, and the others will have to be posted. But Jen will ring them, as well, just so they know their invites are coming. Look, Jen's keeping a log of her expenses, and we'll need to take that from Dad's money. But there's no rush. We can just about cover it."

"Thanks, Paul. And thank Jen from me, as well."

"Right. Anything else? Any questions?"

"Just one," I say.

"Go on."

"Where's Dad's television gone?"

"We took it back to ours on Saturday."

"Why?"

"Because the house was going to be empty, and Jen saw something on the news about thieves targeting houses from the obituaries."

"Right. But you knew I was coming."

"Digger, it's hardly at the top of the list of priorities."

It clearly was on Saturday. Was it still warm? Was Dad?

"No, I suppose not. It's just a bit boring in the evenings."

"Then get on with doing stuff. There's a lot to get done, Digger. You haven't got time to watch television, anyway. Look, I'll be over later. I've managed to borrow a trailer from work."

"A trailer?"

"For Dad's car! It'll have to go before we sell the house. I'll swing by later and pick it up, and I'll drop off the invitations."

"Where's it going? The car, I mean."

"Jen's having it. She needs something more reliable for running the kids round. It'll hardly be worth anything second-hand. And we can't all afford a brand new car every couple of years."

Every five years, you tosser.

"It's only fair, Digger. My car has nearly two-hundred thousand on it, running back and forth to see Dad every week. You don't want it, do you?"

"No."

"Right. So what are you going to do, ring a man out the paper to come and take it away? He'll charge you for that."

"No, no. It's fine."

Everything's bloody fine.

"I'll see you later."

"I might be out with the dog," I point out.

"I've got a key."

"Right."

He hangs up. Actually, I don't suppose he did. He probably just pressed a button.

Elle, you did me the biggest favour by breaking my heart, and simultaneously breaking my desire to live here because I couldn't bear to be close to you and not be with you.

11.

For three hours I empty cupboards, drawers and wardrobes. I do it so that Paul will see how much I've done. Dad's radio alarm clock churns out music tinnily.

If I have to go out later and deliver the invitations, I'll swing by the Do-It-Your-Fucking-Self megastore down at Lower Millby and pick up boxes and a marker pen. 'Tip', 'Charity' and 'Sell' seem to be the three options. I kidded myself that I might add some keepsakes to my boxes upstairs, but I can see that all the good stuff has been picked vulturine clean. They even took Dad's wedding ring, which he kept in the little pot-cupboard by his chair for over thirty years. The price of gold must be high.

Even as a child, Paul was cautious when it came to money. There is certainly something inherent that makes him that way, but I believe it was augmented by timing. He left school in 1983 when unemployment was rife and prospects were low. He spent a few months on the dole before landing a job at the place he still works at to this day. He's risen from yard assistant to mechanical supervisor, the company having put him through his apprenticeship.

Is he happy? I hope he is. He was a good brother growing up, and we were close for all of our formative years. But we went off on tangential paths at some point that I struggle to pinpoint or explain.

Was it when he left school? It may have been. There was an immaturity about him prior to then that bridged the age gap and brought us closer together, but responsibility forced him to begrudgingly grow up, and the repeated rejection he met with when applying for jobs shattered his self-confidence.

I use the word immaturity, but it's unfair. There was a softness in Paul that served to alienate him from the crowd. He was arty and thoughtful - far more so than I was as a child - and he was the creative one, both in physical deed and in thought. He would create and invent; he could draw and paint; he could conceive and imagine far more readily than the rest of us.

And he was a dreamer. If he could think it, it could be done!

But at some point he gave up on thinking and dreaming, and he lost all aspiration. Get him in a lighter moment, perhaps with a few drinks in him, and he'll admit it all, and explain it as 'having all creativity stripped out of me to be replaced by a robot that does. I'm a doer, and that's all I am now.'

So he does stuff, and he does it to provide for his family.

He met Jen through work. I never knew her, and I still don't really know her now. She's an Elsewhere from all of twelve miles away in Drescombe. That said, I always liked her. She's good for Paul, I think. Dad always said that about her. She's safe and supportive. Between them, a boat shall never rock and caution is kept away from even the gentlest of breezes.

No rainy day shall ever catch them out.

Paul never made a bad choice; he simply didn't make a choice. He stuck every time, rather than twist. And all of that is fine.

Right up to the point where he hits middle-age and begins to reflect. Through that comes a resentment that I resent. Because the truth is, if I had been given any say in the matter, I think that I would have remained here with

Elle and missed all of the opportunities that came my way as a result of leaving.

Leaving worsened the already fractured relationship between Paul and I, as, I believe, absence made Dad's heart grow fonder.

Is that always the curse of the first-born? He arrives in a world where he is the undiluted centre of attention. Then I came along, and he's downgraded to, at best, fifty percent as attentions are divided. But it's even worse than that, as I am younger and less independent, so command more than my half share. That must be hard to deal with, even at a subconscious level.

But he's a good man, my brother, despite all of that. And he's smarter than he ever gives himself credit for, because he doesn't give himself any credit. All of his praise has to come from outside of himself for it to hold any value to him, and external praise is hard to come by.

Through that, Paul never sees what he has, only what he doesn't have. He has a good marriage and two beautiful girls. Okay, so Jen was never going to set the world on fire, but who wants to live in a burning world?

Would I honestly trade with him? Would I take domesticity and comfort with Elle in place of the life I have? Ah, I tell myself not, but I think I probably would.

The promised brighter weather doesn't arrive, but, in spite of the sky threatening otherwise, the earth tells of no imminent rain, so I set off with the dog at two in the afternoon. Again, I trust the earth more than I do the sky.

And again, I turn when the dog stalls to check for interest on his earlier deposit and make another withdrawal, and I glance along at number nine.

What is my song for this day? If I were reading this scene in a script, what would I pair off with it? It requires music, as there is no conversation, and no other sound to fill the void in this moment. My thoughts are all I have to contend with, which is a relief, but I dare say that my solemnity is apparent in my demeanour.

Perhaps an instrumental piece would work - something to match my footsteps as they slap down on the leaves plastered to the pavement.

I opt for John Renbourn's non-lyrical version of 'My Johnny Was A Shoemaker'. The flavour of it suits the terrain here.

Bean chooses the route, and I'm happy to be steered. With me acting as navigator I always head down the same path; Elle.

Would Albinoni's 'Adagio In G Minor' be a good choice for the funeral? Dad loved it, and it has a funereal feel to it. Will I even get a say? Paul and Jen seem to be playing the whole bereavement handbook out, and in record time. But, then, what's the sense in resisting and waiting? It suits me.

As I packed my case on Sunday morning, I told myself that I would get in, get through it, and get out - and that's what I intend to do. I only packed seven pairs of socks. Was that only yesterday? It feels like longer.

Is this the last time I'll ever come to Oaklea? There's nothing here for me now. Dad was the last reason for visiting. Mum's down near Tinbury Head, and Paul and his family are away in Drescombe. I'll go and I'll visit, perhaps twice a year; birthdays and Christmases. And I know that they'll never come and visit me, but that's not the point. Paul has Jen and the kids. How old are they, Charlotte and Hannah? They must be fourteen and eleven. Something like that.

I should know their ages. I should care more. Why don't I? I mean, I do care, they're my family. 'Mollycoddled' Dad called them, before adding, 'but they all are these days.'

Not that he saw his granddaughters very often. Paul would swing by, usually when he was in the area anyway, but Jen didn't like the kids to visit because of the smoking. And then there was the dog, and the kids' allergies.

Dad laughed at it all. That was Dad. If he didn't have it, or have experience of it, he didn't believe in it. He wasn't very empathic.

Mum left because of that, I think. She needed emotional support. She wanted to be made to feel like a princess, and Dad wasn't the princely type.

In fact, when Prince died, he said, 'never rated the bloke anyway.' But around the same time, when he heard that Ada, the final surviving chimp from the PG Tips adverts had died, he went, 'oh, what a shame! Poor thing. How old was she? Do you know what she died of?'

That was Dad. I think he liked animals more than he liked people.

It's probably truer to say that he felt more comfortable showing emotion with animals than he did with people. And that was why Mum left.

It was no big deal. They weren't getting on, so they split up. I was sixteen, and loved-up with Elle. Paul was nearly eighteen, and getting on with his life, so it was one of those things that happened without much fanfare or effect.

To be perfectly truthful, it made things simpler. Dad worked a lot, driving his truck, and Mum lived up towards Jemford Bridge. As a result, I enjoyed a lot of freedom.

All that said, though, Dad kept quiet about his imminent inheritance of the land from his father. He didn't want

Mum getting half of that. And, tellingly, he didn't trust Paul with the information either. But he told me.

It has to come out in his Will, that land. And I am aware of a foreboding. It tells me that as much as I plan on making an effort to stay in touch with my family, it may not be possible.

Bean and I walk westward along the far edge of the Humpty Dumpty Field, as we loftily follow the Lane to where the land levels out, and the rain-swollen Curtly Brook chuckles merrily in front of us.

~~~~~

Initially the sprats scuppered any plans to develop the land above the Lane.

Had the sprats not been discovered, and the brook and surrounding land consequently placed under protection, Oaklea would have been a very different place. In fact, it wouldn't have been Oaklea. It would have simply been an extension of Upper Millby as the lea and oak that gave birth to its name would have disappeared.

We would have had no Humpty Dumpty Field on which to ride bikes and cavort, the earth from those humps scooped up to fill in the reservoir, the banks of the old railway levelled and used to further destroy the character of the land, before forming the foundations on which more houses would have been built.

Dad was always adamant that it would have happened. But the sprats changed everything. And later, the humpbacked field changed it further still.

And my family was somewhat responsible for all of it surviving.

I feel pride as I look on it; this natural playground. We didn't need parks with swings and climbing frames, because we had them all right here. A simple tyre strung from a sturdy tree limb would achieve that. Neither did we need spongy asphalt on which to safely fall, because we had soft green grass. And we certainly didn't need organised sports and supervised activities on plastic pitches.

Ah, but then I think of all that happened here, and I wonder if we did need that. Would we have been better off without the freedom and liberty? Should we have been exercised on much shorter leashes?

Would Micky still have been Mucky? Would Debbie still have been Dirty? Would I still have killed my friend?

Or was it all inevitable? Outside unsupervised, or inside supervised - would it have made any difference?

It made no difference to Debbie and I. The first time I had sex with her was in her bedroom, where we'd been banished because my Mum was downstairs with Dee enjoying, or enduring, a tupperware party. It didn't take place in the woods, on the bank of the railway, or on the humpy field. It took place with our legal guardians no more than twelve feet away as the crow flies.

And after I'd done it with Debbie once, I did it with Debbie as much as I could that Spring of 1984. Because that's how it goes. She was my instructor, and she taught me most of what I knew at the time.

But I never loved her. I loved Elle, even then. And I don't think Debbie ever loved me. She'd say that she did, but she had too much love for herself. There wasn't room for her to love anyone else.

Love? I use the word so readily; almost flippantly. But looking back as a middle-aged man, I still believe that I did love Elle.

Ah, but that's where I trip over myself. I also believed that she loved me, but I now know that she didn't.

Stop thinking about her!

Bean follows the brook away from the river, against the current, northward in the direction of the old railway.

I surmise that he heads there because it was where Dad would have taken him. And Dad would have gone that way to keep an eye on his little piece of England.

My grandfather, Dad's dad, bought the half dozen acres of land from the railway company. And he got them for 'a snip' according to Dad.

It was in the nineteen-fifties, when the railway was disbanded, the metal salvaged, and anything else of value removed. He was part of the operation, a canny self-employed businessman with nothing so restrictive as a definite trade. Rather, he would turn his hand to where the money was in that moment. And in the mid-fifties in Millby, it was in the cessation of the East-West Rail Link.

And as he salvaged the metal for weighing in, so he looked down from the lofted track, and saw the extent of the terrain that the railway owned. A hundred years prior, they'd purchased a broad swath of land, far more than they needed, through the heart of the county.

The other thing that he saw from there, was the need to replace the thing that he was destroying. And so, I imagine, he looked at the relative nothingness all around, and foresaw the future; the inevitable growth of the Millby area.

So he took a punt, and snapped up his acreage. But it wasn't a random plot that he invested in. He knew the land. He understood the earth hereabout. He was from here, as was his father, and his, and his. This terrain was in him, just as it's in me.

Access from the west was too cumbersome and expensive given the two rivers that would need to be crossed, the railway bridges not suitable. The wetlands around the river Jem had to be preserved in the north, so the only way in was from the south or east. The eastern access was the simplest. So that was where he purchased his property.

But when it came to it, my Grandfather refused to sell the land. Whether he refused for fiscal reasons, or because he didn't want the area urbanised is debatable. Dad said that it was financial. I think it was conservational. Perhaps it was a bit of both.

So the focus shifted to the Lane; that ancient lane to seemingly nowhere. But it led to, and ceased, at Curtly Brook. On paper, it would have been a minor inconvenience to widen it, bridge it, and open it up to allow the heavy machinery in and out, and ultimately form the access road for those residing there.

A survey was performed, and the project was close to being green lit. Until the transparent little sprats were spotted. Tests were performed, and those sprats were identified as a rare species, the brook itself, as curt as it was, flagged up as an area of great natural interest and importance, as it was the babbling spawning ground of the entire endangered genus.

The final nail in the development coffin was Dad getting the county to recognise the historical significance of the Humpty Dumpty Field as 'the best surviving example of medieval strip agriculture in the area.'

Dad had a theory that number three became such because the builder, having had enough of being scuppered at every attempt to build on the south and west quarters of the region, walked away without building the final house on the street. A different builder then came in and added the road abutting it.

The Will shall reveal all. I may well find myself owning those few acres of land in the coming days. But perhaps not. It wouldn't surprise me to discover that Dad has left it to Paul, or donated it to the county as a conservation area. No, I don't think he will do any of that. He will instead pass the mantle to me.

What's it worth? Dad thought maybe a million, but who really knows? It's worth what someone is prepared to pay for it. And it still wouldn't open up the entire area. The Humpty Dumpty Field and little brook would always be protected and off-limits. But the western side, and the land before the point where the rivers Jem and Tred merge would suddenly be accessible and exploitable.

And as I look down and around from the high ground on the railway at the lack of any person, young or old, and the fading routes that foot hasn't trod and maintained throughout the summer and autumn months, I wonder what the point of keeping it this way is? Why keep it as nature intended, when the nature of people is to ignore it or be afraid of it? 'It isn't safe for children to play down there,' Jen and Paul have said within earshot of me. 'You never know who might be lurking down there.' 'It isn't like it was when we were kids.' 'You see it all the time on the news.'

Ah, but I can't let the land go. History is in that land. Secrets are contained beneath its crust.

So, for the same reasons Dad rejected even recent overtures, as the money being offered went higher and higher, I will have to do the same.

The difference is, everyone will know about it. It won't be a secret between he and I. So I'd better come up with some bloody good excuses as to why it shouldn't be sold and the money shared between those with a valid claim.

12.

Bean eats a few of my chips. It must ignite his appetite, as he slopes off as soon as he's established that there is no more coming from my plate, and I hear him crunch his lamb and brown rice dry food that, in truth, smelt and looked more nutritious and appetising than my dinner. It gladdens me to see him eat.

Paul came by when I popped out to the chip shop, leaving a bundle of white card invitations in matching envelopes, both with a minimal black border that tells of the contents.

A dry oblong is all that remained of Dad's car. I covered it with my own vehicle when I returned and saw the driveway empty.

Thumbing through the unsealed envelopes, I recognise about half of the names, if not the addresses. People move on, I suppose, even if not that far.

There isn't an envelope for Elle. Pat and Pat's makes no mention of her. I double-check in case her surname has been matrimonially altered, but the use of full first names for both genders satisfies my curiosity. I'm unsure whether I'm relieved or disappointed by her absence.

It's too dark now, I won't be able to read the road signs and house numbers, so I decide to defer their distribution until tomorrow.

A rattling rap on the porch door startles us both, Bean barking an alert on the off-chance I didn't hear it. Immleigh is my first thought.

It's a relief, therefore, to be faced by Bob from next door.

"Hello, Digger, I hope I'm not disturbing?"

"Not at all," I say, shaking his hand. Not firm, but genuine enough as his earnestly peering brown eyes attempt to wash his faith into me.

"Diane and I were wondering if you fancied popping round? No sense in sitting here on your own, after all, when we're only next door. Come and have a drink. You'd be very welcome."

"That's very kind of you both, thank you."

I can't think of a reason not to go. I could say that I have work to do, or that I really should get on with sorting out the house or making arrangements, but the truth is, I crave a bit of company. Even the puritanical variety.

"Well, no time like the present!" Bob beams.

So I give Bean a rub and tell him I shan't be long. In twenty-four hours I've picked up the habits that come with dog-ownership. Even down to the fact that I know I can use him and his need to relieve himself as my excuse for extricating myself when I'm ready to leave.

The television screen is off, but a classical CD or streaming service plays inoffensively through the speakers. They aren't quite the dark-aged family Dad had led me to believe. The sitting room I'm ushered through to is comfortable and warm. I felt a need to lever my shoes off on entry, and I'm glad I did when I see the cream carpet, plush underfoot.

Diane rises to greet me, a heavy lady but with the skin of a child on her face. Her small green eyes glitter when she smiles at me, and I happily accept her embrace, her arms clasping my shoulders and pulling me down to her.

My chippy breath rebounds off her neck as she says, "we're so sorry for your loss, Digger. Your dad was a good man, a good neighbour and a good friend to us. God rest his soul."

"Thank you," I reply as she pulls away from me, finding my hands with hers as she does. It prompts me to say more. "And thanks for keeping an eye on him. I believe it was you who realised something was wrong on Saturday?"

"Well, yes. I didn't see the dog in the garden, you see. And I said to Bob about it, so he went round the front and saw that the paper was lying in the porch. Well, we rang 999 straight away, didn't we Bob?"

"We did. But there was nothing to be done, Digger. I've racked my brain, but I don't think there's anything we could have done differently. I'd only seen him the previous morning, on the Friday, because he was out with the dog as I headed off to work. But with it being a Saturday, and not a work day, I was up a bit later and I thought I might have missed him. But when I saw that paper, I knew, didn't I, love?"

"You did, love, you did."

Diane looks up at me, my hands still partially enfolded in hers, and I think she's expecting me to cry. I settle for a tightening of my mouth and a slight nod of understanding.

It prompts a little squeeze from her, and the comment, "he's in a better place."

He's in a morgue. How is that better than at home with his dog, watching Helen Mirren?

"Now, let's get the man a drink, Diane. That's what we need, a drop of sherry!"

"Ah, I'll skip the sherry, thanks, Bob. A hangover from trifle as a kid."

"Oh, right, understood," he says in a way that implies he doesn't. "What about a beer, then? There are some cans left over from the summer barbecue."

A can of warm lager is decanted headily into a sparkling glass that is placed on a ceramic coaster on the dark wood table by the side of the chair I was instructed to use by Diane.

I'm trained to use coasters. As Dad used to say, 'there's many a slap twixt a cup and a lap.'

And it's nice. They are nice people. They care in a world where people no longer generally do, yet they're perceived as oddballs as a result. I'm as guilty as anyone of judging them harshly, despite not even knowing them.

Their children - twins aged sixteen: Mark, just started at Millby College where he's doing his A-Levels; and Kerry-Anne, so good they named her twice; recently entered the sixth form at Millby Girls School - are polite and thoughtfully intelligent.

Yet, I can't help feeling that there's a naivety and an innocence about them that won't serve them well in the world. Am I right, or does a Micky and a Debbie lurk behind that curtain of innocence? Is there a Digger in there, masked from view?

They sit attentively as the gentle conversation ebbs through the room, Diane saying a little silent prayer before first sampling her sherry. I answer questions as I'm asked them, about my job and what will happen to Bean and Dad's house.

I present Bob with the funeral invitation I thought to bring with me, and they each silently read it in turn before Bob sets it in pride of place next to the glass-domed brass clock on the white mantle above the gas fire, a clock that is either stopped, or time is passing very, very slowly.

By way of checking, I keep my eye on that clock, but Diane presumes I'm staring at the black-bordered white card and whispers to me about understanding, and it must be a difficult time for me. She tenderly pats the back of my hand to make it all better.

It is a difficult time. She's right in everything that she says, and most of the reasons why. I understand, as I sit here occasionally sipping my beer, that I've had very little of this - this family thing.

Dad worked. Mum mothered, until she left. I have no kids, and have had no real relationship. Michelle was a friend as much as anything, who I happened to go out with for two and a bit years and have sex with infrequently. Elle was it for me, I think, and I only got to sample this togetherness in a home environment for one night and day with her.

Looking again, I see all of Bob, his sincerity and open face and eyes, his bald pate with a rim of monkish grey-black hair skirting his ears, and his ever-smiling amiability. Dad used to say that nice was a poor word to use as a descriptive, but it is the only word that fits here.

Diane, with her unblemished skin and grey curly short hair, that I think was once borderline ginger but lost all character when she was in her twenties, her eyebrows telling of a more colourful past. She isn't even as rotund as she seems, her largeness of head confusing her proportions, and her choice of clothes, a sack of a frock in dark blue with puffy long sleeves that truncate her arms, disturb her true form further. She is the perfect match for her husband when measured in terms of niceness.

The twins aren't identical, but they are very clearly twins. So, if I have this right, Diane's ovary didn't split, is that how it works? Or did the fertility create more than one egg, or did Bob get the treatment, and two of his bionic little sprats arrived in a dead heat? My mind can't recall how it happens, and it isn't the lager addling my brain.

Mark sits upright, his hands resting on his thighs, fingers splayed. I note his index finger tapping. Is he counting the time until he's excused? It's a steady beat, perhaps matching his heart. I see no evidence of shaving, yet he's sixteen, but perhaps that's down to his fair wispy hair. And his voice hasn't fully broken, a youthfulness retained that he's conscious of as he speaks lowly but clearly. Has he ever been with a girl?

And what about his sister? Similar, but different. I try to imagine her with the long braid missing, and her hair not so swept back and matronly tight to her head. She'd be blonder then, with the light able to run through it, she'd be softer and less strict looking. She has her feet tucked under her, sitting to one side, her cheek resting on an open palm as her elbow sinks into the arm of the chair opposite me. Her hands and face are the only skin she exposes, along with a little sliver of white flesh where her long grey skirt doesn't quite meet her white fluffy slippers. She's pretty…

They aren't his, I suddenly realise. They have trace elements of Diane in them, but they aren't their father's children. The cleft chin and eye shape of both is absent in mother and father. The colouring is all wrong, his brown eyes absent despite the dominance of that gene. A sperm donor, I wonder? I hope it's nothing more illicit. I can't believe that it would be.

"The clock needs winding," Diane says, and heads shoot round to confirm her announcement.

And as those heads pivot, only mine and Kerry-Anne's decline the invitation to check. Mine because I already knew, and hers because she was aware that I was watching her.

She smiles at me coyly, sexily, lustily. Yes, dirtily. And as she swings her legs from beneath her, so she allows them to part for an instant before her bunny-rabbit feet connect with the creamy unblemished carpet. It's just long enough for me to catch a glimpse of the gusset of her white panties, and done in a way that it could very easily have been excused as accidental. But it wasn't.

"I'll do it, Daddy," she trills innocently, skipping towards the fireplace.

And as I rise and thank them for their hospitality, citing the dog as my reason for dashing off, and Kerry-Anne retrieves the key from behind the clock and begins to wind it up, so I wonder if the key to a happy family is to not be related to one another. Because nothing else has really changed.

~~~~~

April 14th 1985 *"...I didn't see any of this coming because I wasn't looking for it. I knew that I liked you, and that I was attracted to you, and I kind of knew that you felt the same about me. But yesterday...! I'm afraid, my Digger, terrified that you'll hurt me. You know me now, and you know that I'm not what I appear. I'm not strong. Not really. I'm fragile, and this - us! - it terrifies me, because I know that you'll hurt me. You won't mean to, I suppose, but you will. Everybody does in the end. You know about my life, and you'll understand that I need time. Please, just give me that. Let us carry on as we are for a while, and don't push me too much, my darling. I admit that my feelings for you run deeper than I've ever told you. They run deeper than I've ever allowed myself to admit. With love. Lx."*

June 1st 1985 *"...I'm so sorry, my Love, I don't know what was wrong with me today. I think it's because I worry about losing you - losing us. Losing me, I suppose, because I never discovered myself until recently, and that* was because of you. You showed me to me, and I liked what I was all of a sudden. But DD is so much more womanly than me, despite her being younger. She has her perfect tits and arse, and big blue gazing eyes. And I know that you had a thing with her. You told me, after all. Sometimes I wish you hadn't. She wants you, Digger. I see it when she looks at you. And when she looks at me, I see that she wants to take you away from me. But none of that is your fault, and it was wrong of me to take it out on you. Forgive me? Ultimately, the thing I desire most in the world is your happiness. And if you decide that happiness lies elsewhere, you should go with my blessing. Only ever be with me because there's nowhere else you'd rather be, my Love. Promise me that? I want you more than anything, but only ever if you come willingly. All of my Love is yours for as long as you want it. Lx."

June 28th 1986 "...Darling Love, I got my period today, and I thought I would be relieved and happy. But I'm not. I felt a sadness when I did. I know that we must be more careful, but it's so difficult. I crave you. I relish the feeling of your heat inside me - of your life force. Yet, I don't want a child. Not yet. I want you all to my selfish self for a while before we start a family. Oh, heaven help me! I never wanted children until I met you. I was adamant that I would never marry and never have children. What have you done to me? Whatever it is, thank you! I have never been so happy, and yet so sad at times as well. Such as today. Such extremes of emotion wash over me like tidal waves, and as a result, I've never felt so alive! I Love you and our life. Lx."

13.

It was late-morning when I began my deliveries, and now early-afternoon as I work my way back towards the house. It was a good time to pick, as most people are at work or otherwise occupied, it being a Tuesday. The decent weather has coaxed people out of doors, the sun warm now that it's had time to dry out the pavement and bleach it back to light grey.

In North Millby the door of a scruffy end of terrace opens before I can reach it.

A man in his forties, though it's difficult to say more specifically, fills the opening. He's heavy-set but out of shape, and with the flush in his face that tells of an imbalance in how hard his system has to work to keep his body fuelled. And all he did, as far as I know, was walk to the door.

"All right Digger! You haven't changed, have you?"

I have. But evidently not as much as you, because I have no idea who you are.

"All right," I say back, and smile. The name on the envelope means nothing to me.

"You don't know who I am, do you?"

"To be honest with you, no I don't. Sorry."

"Don."

I must still look blank, as he adds, "Don Smith. I used to live next door to you."

"Bloody hell. Sorry, mate, out of context, and all that."

"Ah, it's been a while. I still recognised you, though."

"You did. How are your mum and dad, and Davie and Debbie?"

"The same, you know. Nothing really changes around here. Hey, listen; I was sorry to hear about your dad."

"Thanks."

"Is that the funeral invite?"

"Yes," I confirm, handing him the envelope. The name Don and Sara Perkins-Smith suddenly making a little more sense.

"When is it?" he asks, rather than open it in front of me.

"Friday at eleven at the crematorium in Millby. Then back to the Old Mill for a drink."

"I'll buy you a pint, Digger," he offers.

I smile at him.

He adds, "this is where you're supposed to say that it's a free bar."

"Paul organised it."

"Ah. Understood. I'll bring some cash. They have some nice real ales on at the Mill."

"I'd better get on," I say, offering him my hand. He shakes it firmly, the sweat evident on his palm. "It's good seeing you, Donnie."

Be baulks a little at his childhood name.

To put it right, I follow on with, "and I'll take that pint, Don, as long as you let me buy you one back."

A grin pushes his cheeks out, restoring his youthfulness a little, resulting in me thinking that I might have recognised him after all.

Ten minutes later, and I'm at a large detached house in the northeast segment of Oaklea estate, one of the recent new additions.

Back when I was a lad, it was all fields!

It's a very pleasant situation, here on the edge of the housing, a thin finger of gentle slopes being the backdrop. The Wimple was the name given centuries ago to the wrinkle in the land, a name that's endured. What happened to cause it? All about is relatively flat pastureland, yet here, inexplicably, is this out of character spine. We'd speculate as children that a dragon slept there, and viewed from a distance, or from above, it does resemble such, with the lower gentle slopes of the tail and head rising a hundred feet or so to the wider midriff of the beast. And the black exposed rocks at its head show the final fiery breath it exhaled before the cold-induced sleep overcame it, and the grass grew richly and hid it from view.

But it wasn't dead. No, it simply idled there, benumbed and waiting for the fire to come that would recharge and reanimate it. And then woe betide all in Oaklea, Millby, Brakeshire and the world!

"Don said you might be heading up my way," Debbie calls to me as I pace from my car to the front door. The driveway is constructed of cream pavers that abut the red brick of the house, a line of mortar splicing the two.

I recognise Debbie from her voice alone. It still has a sing-song fakery to it, that I know disappears as soon as displeasure or dissatisfaction enter the fray.

My head looks to the door, but there's no sign of her there.

"Cooee! Up here, Digger!" she adds, my face drawn upwards.

I wave the envelope at her towel covered head and proceed to the door.

"Come round the back. I've just got out the shower," I'm instructed.

I pause, more than half of me wanting to drop the letter and run for my life. But a small piece of me is curious. I think I know which small piece of me it is.

A tall arched solid wooden gate, with a six foot high wood panel fence that smells of creosote, seals off the half acre of land running back to where the land begins to rise up the dragon's rump.

It swings freely open as I enter, and I turn to secure it behind me.

She stands at a sliding door that opens on to a patio, one white towel knotted on her head, and another tucked under itself by her armpit, and ending somewhere closer to her naval than her knees. All the skin I can see has an orange tinge to it.

"Hello, Debbie."

"My Digger!"

I was never yours.

"Sorry about your dad," she says seriously. The smile drops away, until a quick lick of her lips resets it.

"Thanks," I reply, because I don't know what else I'm supposed to say in response.

"Oh, bless. It's so sad. Come here and give me a proper greeting," she orders, her arms opening up to me.

I do as commanded, the towel damp against my stomach, her size dictating that her head only reaches my chest, the knotted top of the towel beneath my chin. She smells clean and fresh. She always did. I note that she took time to add some make-up rather than clothes after her shower.

"I'll fix us a drink. Bet you could use one," she sings, and spins away, finding my hand with hers, and gently pulling me inside the house. I notice the tattoo on her scapula. I can only see half of it, but it looks like a mermaid. The tail would complete the picture, I suppose.

"I'm driving," I protest.

"One won't hurt you."

It won't be your first of the day.

She's kept her shape. Yes, her face is older and her skin sun-leathered, but she remains an orange version of herself. The towel skirts down from her most protrudent feature, her breasts, and skims nothing else before it ends at the top of her thighs.

After pouring two glasses of white wine from a bottle that was opened but full, she tugs the towel from her head, and shakes her hair free like a dog might on a wet day. The trusses are syrupy and neck length, the dampness binding and darkening them. When dry, I imagine that they'll be not much fairer than her natural colour. Her natural colour before we all went grey, at least.

She's aged well, I have to admit. I admire her for the effort she must have put in to achieving it; all the more so given that I know she's had three children. Or was it four?

I take the wine I'm proffered.

"You look well," I say, and kind of wish I hadn't as soon as it's too late to take back.

She glows a little more confidently orange before me, and tips her head over as she chews the inside of her cheek and contemplates me.

"So do you. And you kept your hair."

"As did you."

As I sip the wine, I gaze around the kitchen. It's immaculate, with white everywhere - white marble countertops and white cupboards, white tile on the walls and floors, and white paint on the ceiling. Even the lights have pure white recessed surrounds, and all of the appliances are white. I bet the lights, when illuminated, give off a stark white light. The white towel disappears amidst it all, leaving the impression of two orange legs, orange shoulders and arms, and an orange face floating in front of me like goldfish swimming in milk.

She retains the appearance of pureness, of a virgin, despite her being anything but. And this is the princess's virgin palace where impurity doesn't exist.

I place the white envelope on the countertop closest at hand, and only the black border and the words 'Debbie Smith And Family' remain as a result.

There's no husband mentioned, and she uses her maiden name. Unless she happened to marry another Smith. It could happen.

And I wonder if that's why I'm here, and why I left Debbie till almost last on my delivery round. Only the rest of Dad's road remain in my car.

One of those houses is Pat and Pat. And possibly Elle. Yet I came here first, before going there. Why was that? Yes, it made sense geographically, and yes, I wanted to wait until a little later before calling at number nine; I wanted to wait until school had finished, and teachers might be at their homes.

But here I am, two hours before that might be possible, drinking wine with a woman clothed in nothing but a towel.

"You're quiet," she says, breaking my train of thought and averting my eyes from the envelope. My being quiet has always been a cause of concern for people who know me... Knew me, I correct myself.

"Sorry. It's not easy."

"What isn't?"

"My Dad. Everything."

"Being back, you mean?"

"That. And other things."

"When is it?" she asks, her blue eyes on the envelope.

"Friday at eleven at Millby crematorium. Drinks in the Old Mill afterwards," I trot out.

"I'll have to wear black. I hate black."

"You like white," I point out.

And orange.

"How did you know?" I'm not sure if she's being ironic. I'm not even sure if she knows what irony is, despite her looking rusty.

"A lucky guess."

"Shall we sit outside? Make the most of the weather?" she proposes.

For some reason, getting out in the open appeals to me.

I head that way, patting the invitation as I leave.

"I'll just slip on something less damp," she calls after me, "make yourself comfy, shan't be a minute."

Taking a seat, I feel my heart rate lessen as the clean fresh air, abundance of green landscape, and the wine settle me down.

A noise brings my eyes back on the spacious home. It was, I realise, the sound of a towel being tossed aside and thwacking down on the tile.

And with no apparent self-awareness, Debbie nakedly bends down to zip up a pair of white leather boots with tassels at the tops that she stepped into. She takes her time in hoisting a flimsy white armless dress over her orange hairless body. It hangs to an inch above the heeled boots that raise her up a couple of inches. She never did like her legs and height. Another tattoo, depicting a dragonfly, decorates her pubis on one side.

She's still Debbie, unmistakably, yet she's also half Dee it shocks me to think. Am I half me and half my Dad? Is that why I'm so identifiable, because I've morphed into my father as I've aged? Is it that which people recognise, and not me at all, as they fill in the blanks and merge us together? I've seen myself every day, so the changes in me have appeared gradually. I am not the same. Yes, I kept my hair, but it's thinner and greyer, despite the touch-ups I have done at the salon.

Michelle used to do them for me, applying a noxious concoction as I'd sit perched on the edge of the bathtub, my legs going to sleep under me. And we'd usually copulate after I'd showered.

I use the word deliberately. We didn't have sex, because it wasn't that sexy. And we certainly never made love. We used a condom and copulated, to scratch an itch and sate an urge. It suited both of us that way. It was never anything more. It was simply convenient.

Anyway, so it became established that once every couple of months or so, I'd decide that my hair needed colouring. So I'd call Michelle and she'd come round with the dye. I'd get a bottle of wine in, and she'd apply. We'd drink while it took, she'd continue while I showered, and then we'd copulate. I'd then continue with the wine while she showered, and when the bottle was empty, she'd go home.

And I did it because, in the very slightest of ways, she resembled Elle. Get into the detail, and she was nothing like her, but her outline wasn't a million miles away. Even her name, Michelle, contained her name.

Whereas Debbie is the polar opposite of Elle. And perhaps that's why I'm here.

"You were miles away across the Humpty Dumpty Field," she coos, snatching me back. I'd forgotten about that euphemistic application; a dreamer.

"Just admiring the view," is my retort, and again I didn't intend it in the way that she takes it; selfishly.

"I always loved you," she says suddenly. "I always have."

I stare at her. She's serious. I nod my understanding.

"I still do, and I think I always will," she says, and closes the circle of time.

Am I her Elle?

I think of W H Auden...

'If equal affection cannot be,
Let the more loving one be me.'

No, no, no. He was wrong, so very wrong.

I dump before I can be dumped. I grasp and execute the thing that comes with being the one who cares less, and I ditch before I fall; before I can be hurt again.

"Say something," she pleads. She knows that she's in that most vulnerable of places.

"I don't know what to say," I respond, because I'm not callous enough to say what I'm thinking.

But Michelle was a friend. That worked because of the lack of love. But that lack of love has to be equal. If one begins to feel love, and that imbalance enters the field of play, it's doomed.

By telling me that she loves me, Debbie is killing it. Whatever 'it' is. Because I love Elle. Still, and always. I simply can't help it.

"It's all fake, you know," Debbie sings at me, draining her wine in a greedy gulp.

"What is?" I call after her as she clips her way across the patio to get the bottle.

"Everything!"

I shake my head blankly as she reemerges.

"This," she says, using the bottle to indicate everything in view. "The house is mortgaged up to the hilt, and will have to be sold or repossessed. The car is leased, and I can't afford the payments. Half the furniture is on the never-never, and anything that isn't came from mum and dad. Even this expensive wine is taken from a cheap carton that

I refill the bottle from when it runs out. Even these are fake," she adds, and tugs down the front of her dress to show me her perfect domes of flesh. "And you know the worst bit?"

"No," I answer, because I can't imagine.

"My nipples are senseless now, thanks to three kids sucking them dry and shredding the nerves. Well, that and the fucking implants that my husband wanted me to have when things went a bit droopy."

"I'm sorry."

"He still left me. He still bitched off with a younger model," she snarls.

"I didn't know."

"No, how could you? You never bothered to stay in touch; you never once came back to see me."

The singing voice has gone, replaced by a bitterness that emanates from the pit of her stomach.

"I never came back to see anyone but Dad," I protest.

"Not even her?"

"Who?" I ask, but I know exactly who she means.

"Fucking Eleanor," she spits out, and I think it hurts her to say the name even more than it hurts me to hear it.

"No, not even her," I answer honestly, and she softens a little at learning I didn't play favourites with my absence.

"Have you seen her since you've been back?"

"No." She likes that answer.

"But you came to see me?"

"I came to deliver an invitation to a funeral."

"I'm lonely, Digger. I'm so bloody alone."

"Where are your children?"

"Away. Gone. They're in their twenties now, with lives of their own. They come and see me when they want something."

"Are they local?"

"One is. The other two are in Tredmouth."

"It's not that far."

"Far enough so I'm out of mind. I'm a bloody grandmother!"

"Congratulations." She shoots me a look to see if I'm taking the piss.

"I don't want to be old, Digger. I don't feel old. Do I look like a grandmother?"

"Not really."

"What about you? You never married, I heard."

"No, I never did."

"That was wise. Any kids?"

"No."

"Why not?" she asks.

"I never met anyone I wanted to have children with."

"I used to dream that I'd have your babies."

"We were kids, Debbie."

"No, not just then. I dreamt it until I actually had my first. And then I dreamt that you'd come and take me away from it all."

"You shouldn't say that," I tell her sadly, staring down into the top of the wine I'm nursing.

"Why not? It's true," she snaps, pouring herself another.

"It's not right. They're your kids, Debbie."

"And if I could do it all again, I'd do it all so differently." She's softer when she says that; more whimsical.

"Such as?" I probe, wanting to keep her level, and sensing that what might have been is a safer road than what was.

"I'd have been yours. Not Micky's or anyone else's. Just yours Digger. We'd have been great, you and me. We still could be."

I shake my head.

"Why do you do that, and why so sad?" she continues, "I'm alone; you're alone. We're old friends. It isn't like you've not been there before, is it? It makes sense! Oh god! Just screw me, Digger!"

"Why me?"

"It was always you."

"But I'm not what I was. I'm nothing special, Debbie. I wasn't then, and I'm not now."

"You are to me."

"I don't deserve it."

She levels her eyes on me, those blue eyes that were once so open and deceptively honest-looking. Now they're narrower and cynical; more true to her nature. But they're still attractive for that added guardedness.

"You were always that bit different. Micky was more attractive, with his messy blonde hair and freckles, and his cheekiness. But I could see that you were always going to age better. Shit, I know Micky died, so didn't get to age, but you know what I mean?"

"Not really."

"And there was a maturity about you. A steadiness. That's the most attractive trait in a man, Digger, that strength and steadiness. It was why I wanted to have your baby, I think. There was some subliminal thing I'd feel, where I just knew that you were right for me. We both fucked up, Digger. And life hasn't worked out perfectly for either of us. But, at the end of the day, here we are, both alone. And we are left with each other. What a waste of thirty years. And all because of her."

"Elle?"

"Yes! That bitch came along, and she changed you. She changed us all. She was like an alien species that escapes and infiltrates the world - like a grey squirrel. And she killed off and drove away all of the natural ones; the ones that belonged here. Do you see? Or think of it like this - she was Dutch Elm disease, and as soon as she got here, we were all doomed."

"She didn't do anything, Debbie."

"She did! Micky wouldn't have died, would he? And you wouldn't have changed as a result. You wouldn't have had all that trouble. Your mum might not have left. We'd have been together! I know it, Digger. I know it in my heart."

"My Mum would have left anyway. Elle had nothing to do with that. You can never know what would have happened."

"I know what did happen! She drove you away, didn't she? All because of a letter."

"How do you know about the letter?"

"Everybody knew. She played you along, and then dumped you, and you went away broken-hearted."

"How do you know about the letter?" I persist.

"Paul showed me."

"Why did Paul show you my letter?"

"Oh, jeez. He didn't, okay? I was with him, in his bedroom, and when he went somewhere, I went into your room and found a letter."

"You read my letter?"

"Yes. It was lying there."

"No it wasn't. I always kept them hidden in my fishing box at the back of my wardrobe."

"Okay, okay, so I snooped around a bit..."

"And you were with Paul?"

"Yes, Digger, I saw Paul a few times," she says dismissively, "grow up. I was only seeing him to get closer to you. It was over thirty years ago."

"Which letter did you read? The last one?"

"No. It was all lovey-dovey bullshit."

"Then how do you know that I went away because of a letter?"

"I guessed. There were so many letters, it had to be that. The bitch dumped you in a letter. Not even face to face. I'm right, aren't I?" she laughs.

"I should go," I assert, leaving the dregs of my wine in the glass and placing it decisively on the table.

"Don't go! I'm sorry, okay? I'm sorry that I snooped. But I loved you, Digger. I still love you."

'I don't think you're capable, Debbie. Not really."

"Oh, and she is, is she?"

"I thought she was."

Debbie puts on a plaintive voice, and makes quote marks in the air, "...I love you more than life itself, my darling Digger, nobody's ever loved anyone in the way that I love you, blah, blah, blah." She sneers at me, and adds, "and how did that work out for you? The lying bitch!"

I rise to leave.

"It was all crap, Digger, that's all I'm saying. Don't go, please don't go. Stay. Let's make love. For old time's sake. No! For new time's sake! We were always meant to be together."

"Goodbye, Debbie."

"I can't do this on my own!" she calls after me, her voice creaking and ready to falter. I've heard it all before.

I walk towards the gate. Dad always said that you should leave a place the same way you entered. It's bad luck not to. "Can't do what?" I ask, checking my stride, her sobs getting to me in spite of myself.

"I need a man in my life. I need you in my life! There, I admit it!" she says to my back.

"And I need nothing in mine," I say turning, "at some point, life has to be about what you want, not what you need."

"I know what men want," she sniffles. Leaning back, her booted heels rise to the table and lock on its rim, and her legs fall open so that I have a blurry view of the dragonfly and her most intimate parts through the mottled glass table top. "I've always known what men want," she repeats as tears trickle down her orange cheeks.

"Is that why they keep leaving you?" I ask.

"Well you left her, so I must know a thing or two!" she screams, as she swipes at her tears, her legs still propped up on the table. The tears cause her more shame than her position.

As I sink down into the driver's seat of my car, my hands resting on top of the steering wheel, I look out and see Immleigh parked in the turning circle watching me from beneath the rim of his dark blue safari hat.

I have a sense that everything is steadily being ground to a narrow tapered point; that a head will be reached on which not everything can continue to sit side by side as it has.

14.

"I hope I'm not interrupting your dinner, Mr Glenn?" The smell of boiling vegetables and the fact he's wearing a pinafore prompt the comment.

"No, no, Digger, not quite. Seven minutes until readiness is reached. I heard the door, and I said, I said, that might well be young Digger coming with the funeral details. Am I correct in my guesstimation?"

"You are," I say, and hand him the envelope.

These few envelopes are slightly fatter than the rest. I slipped a piece of paper in each, handwritten on which is: 'Bean the dog - free to a good home! Six years old (I think), house trained, no issues. I believe that my father would like him to stay in the only street he's ever known and called home. Comes with all you'll need - bed, bowls, toys, etc. Call Digger on...'

"Well, it's a grim business, I'll say that, but it needs seeing to, lad. And there's no sense in stringing it out. It comes to us all. Now, will you stay and share a plate of supper with me?"

"Oh, I can't. But thanks for the offer. I've got to get these envelopes delivered. The funeral's on Friday."

"Friday, you say? Oh, no, no, no. That'll take some sorting. I was thinking it would be next week."

"They had a cancellation."

"I'm supposed to be at a very important meeting on Friday. A cancellation did you say?"

"Yes."

"What on earth would cause a funeral to be cancelled?"

"That's what I thought."

"Foul play, probably, I say. Oh yes. If they suspect foul play, they have to keep the body for the investigation. Strange that there's been nothing in the paper about anything untoward. They must be keeping it quiet for now. We should be extra vigilant, I say. There could be a murderer on the streets. No offence meant, Digger, no offence intended."

"Erm, none taken."

"Now, did they confirm what he died of, your father?"

"A heart attack."

"Oops! Three minutes until serving up," he says, a bell ringing in the kitchen.

""Well, I'll hopefully see you on Friday."

"Why wouldn't you? I'll be there. Your father and I may have had our differences over the years, but I'd known the man for nigh on half a century, and there's something to be said for that, I say."

With that he closes the door on me.

Will she open the door at number nine? No, it's She-Pat.

"Hello Digger. How are you?"

"Ah, as well as can be expected, Pat, thanks."

"I'm so sorry for your loss, I really am." She's such a kind lady. I don't think I've ever seen her angry or unhappy.

"Thanks. I just wanted to give you this," I tell her, handing over the envelope.

"Friday at eleven, I heard."

"Yes, at the crematorium in Millby. Did Paul tell you, or Bob and Diane?"

"Oh, no, I heard from Eleanor."

"Oh, right. I wonder how she heard?" I say, trying not to show any emotion.

"She didn't say."

"Well, she's not on your invite, but please let her know she'll be very welcome."

"I think she's hoping to get back for it."

"Good. I mean, it'll be good to see her," I add hastily.

Hoping to get back for it. Hoping? Get back from where?

"Well, I'll see you on Friday." Pat smiles her pleasant smile, and the door swings to. She has Elle's tallness and eye colour, but that is as far as the genes were shared when it comes to physical appearance. Her general form is sinewy, and a little skeletal as a result. The familial commonality is more apparent when applied to their caring natures and sensitivity. She was always very kind to me.

There's no answer at number eleven, so I slip the envelope through the letterbox, Wanker Perry long gone along with his MG Midget.

An inexplicable nervousness accompanies me to the front door of number thirteen. The last time I made this walk was a few weeks before Micky died. I never went back after that. What would have been the point? He was dead, and his parents certainly didn't want to see me.

Yet, despite them being gone from here for over thirty years, a lingering presence hangs over the place. It's more likely that it hangs over me.

Three young children come bouncing to the door.

"Who are you?" one of them asks, which kindles the others into asking who I am in chorus.

"My name's Digger," I tell them.

"That's a silly name."

"I suppose it is."

"What do you want?" they chime.

"Is your mum or dad there?"

A man approaches and playfully wrestles his way through the bouncing throng.

"I know you," he says.

"And I know you. Tony Swann! All right, Swanny?" He was a year above me at school. Elle's year.

"All right, Dig? What can I do for you?" he asks, giving me a handshake that turns my fingers white.

"I just wanted to drop this off," I say, handing him the envelope.

He glances down at it, and beams at me, "congratu-bloody-lations, mate. About time."

"Er, there seems to be..."

"It is her, right? Who you're marrying, I mean?"

"Who?"

"Elle?"

"What? No. That was years ago, Swanny."

"Ah, but true love never dies... Shit. This is for a funeral."

"My Dad. He died at the weekend."

"Kids - in!" he orders fiercely, and waits until they've disappeared before continuing. "Oh, buggering hell, Digger, I'm so sorry. I don't know what I was thinking. I've been away for a week working, and I just got back this afternoon. I didn't know."

"It's alright. Don't worry."

"I'm a prat. A first rate prat."

"Are they your kids?" I ask him to shift things along a bit.

"Grandkids. We get lumbered with them, me and the wife, every evening after school, and most of the weekend. I don't know why young people bother having children nowadays. Actually, I do. Because us mug grandparents do all the bloody work for them."

"What made you think I was with Elle?"

"You were in my head, as strange as that sounds. It was the weekend before last, and me and the wife bumped into Elle down at the Riverside restaurant. She was there with Pat and Pat. They'd taken her for her birthday - her fiftieth. Anyway, we had a few drinks and got chatting. About the old times. You know how you do when you've had a few."

I nod that I do, even though I don't. I'm afraid to interrupt the flow.

"Anyway, I asked her why she never married. I told her that she wasn't too bad looking when she was younger. That earned me an elbow in the ribs from the wife, that did. So the wife jumped in with, 'she probably never met the right man' or words to that effect. And Elle looked kind of sad then. Suddenly, I'm at the bar with Pat, and the three women are off to the toilets together. I think Elle was a bit upset."

"So what happened?"

"Well, I only know what the missus told me. But she had a good chat with Elle, and your name came up as the one she would have married. That was why you were in my head. And when I saw you with an envelope in your hand, I thought, 'aye-aye, something's happened here!' I hold my hands up, Dig, I never was the sharpest pencil in the box when it comes to that kind of thing."

I laugh and shake my head.

She would have married me. She made a mistake, and she knows it.

"It'd be great to see you there on Friday, Swanny, if you can."

"I'll be there. You can count on me."

"I'd better be going."

"Yes, and I'd better get these children fed, I suppose, as their parents seem bloody incapable of it."

It's been quite a day, I decide, and head back to Bean.

~~~~~

May 9th 1987 "...My Darling Digger, I'm dreading going away from you. I'm writing this at three in the morning because I can't sleep as usual. I say 'as usual', but I've been sleeping better this past year, and that's down to you being in my life. And no, not just because you tire me out! I feel safe with you. I sleep because that way the time will pass more rapidly and I can be with you again. And the safety comes from knowing that you'll be there waiting for me. I Love you. Come with me! Find a way, and we'll run away for the week. We can share a bed every night and wake together every morning. I love watching you sleep. Have I told you that? That night we had together, I watched you for ages as you slept. I watched your eyelids move as you dreamt, and I wondered what you were dreaming about. Were you dreaming of me? I know you were, because you opened your eyes and smiled at me in a way that told me you expected me to be there. And, I have to break the news, you did snore gently, but I didn't mind. After all, what is the alternative? A silence that means you aren't there. So snore away by my side, my Darling Love, and I shall never complain! Lx."

September 1st 1985 "...P&P know about us, I'm sure of it. They know that we're having sex, I mean. They told me to be careful. But they can't possibly know how special that sex is, and how perfect our Love is. They can't. Nobody can, because if they did, I would see it on them. I can recognise it, Digger, because I'm living it. It feels unreal, don't you think? Yet, when I see you it becomes real again. And that's why it's so hard - as each time we have to be apart I doubt it exists. I ebb and flow through my life like a tide, declining and regrowing every day and night - yes! I decline when I am not with you. I am dormant and without energy, waiting. And when I am with you I become alive again as I regrow. I think I'm losing my mind! Is that what is meant when people say that they are madly in love? I am madly in Love with you, my Love, Lx"

July 18th 1985 "...I'm lying awake in bed and crying! I must have nodded off, unusually for me, and I dreamt that you had met someone else! I know, I know - it's pathetic. And I know that it isn't real, but the thought of me without you is unbearable. I felt physically sick. I must have been sobbing loudly, because H-P came to the door and asked if I was okay? It felt so real, Digger. You know me. I never cry. I don't do drama and overreaction. Yet, here I am, having turned into something not unlike DD - lying in my bed sobbing into my pillow over a boy! Okay, a man. A young man! And I am a young woman, I now understand, and something has changed within me since I met you. I've opened up, I think, and as a result I've softened. I am open to love because of you. But that fissure, Digger - that crack in my protective shell! - it scares the life out of me. I will be okay, won't I? You'll make sure that I'm okay? You won't hurt me, will you, my Love? Only you know how fragile I really am - only you know the true me..."

Which ones did Debbie read? When was it? Early on or later? She must have taken them out of the envelopes and replaced them neatly. I never knew.

It feels like a violation. An invasion of privacy. It occurred to me that Dad might have read them when he boxed them up and stored them, but I don't think that he would have done. Or Paul may have stumbled across them after I left, but that was after the fact. Debbie did it when they were current, when they were... I was about to say true. But, of course, they were never true. Not really.

Debbie was right about that. She was right that it was all lies, and she was probably correct in saying that life did change when Elle appeared on the scene, and that it didn't really work out well for any of us.

15.

I laughed at the vulgarity, and ran with the pack because that resulted in me being socially accepted.

In reality, though, I was as sensitive, if not more so, than Paul. I was simply better at hiding it.

As I matured, I became more confident, and my quietness was a result of that growing belief in my own character. It was why Micky and I had drifted apart as we turned fifteen in the spring of 1984, and had been for several months leading up to it. I dare say that we both shared the same desires and dreams, but our means of achieving them and dealing with our emotions was vastly different.

Similarly, Debbie increasingly bored me. I had sex with her because, in the end, I wanted to. I wanted sex, pure and simple, and I knew that she would permit me to. That was all it ever was.

More importantly, I chose to. It was my choice, and not something Micky dictated or Debbie desired. I ensured that I was getting only what I wanted from it.

Bean led me back here to the old railway.

It's early - about eight o'clock on a beautiful Wednesday morning. Bean slept across the threshold of my bedroom door last night, rather than Dad's. It's the first time that he's done that. He's coming to terms with the loss, I think, and accepting it as he allows himself to move on to his new master. I should discourage him from getting too close, as it will hurt him all the more when I depart. It would be doubly cruel to lose everything twice in little more than a week.

Mist fills the troughs on the Humpty Dumpty Field like smoke between plump splayed green fingers, and, as usual, there's only us present to witness it. It diminishes before my eyes, and will be gone entirely by the time I finish my smoke. It occurs to me to take a photograph, but I left my phone behind. I'm tending to leave it more and more as any concern about being contactable and playing my part in the world seems less important the longer that I'm here. And no photo could ever do justice to the scene as seen through my eyes in this moment. How will a photo capture the freshness of the air? How will it preserve the sound of the birds coasting hither and thither as they playfully break their fast?

As children, we'd come here after dark, despite being forbidden, and wait in the bushes on the north bank of the line. We'd see the pale apparition of the signalman emerge from the box in his dusty blue uniform. He'd stand in the middle of the rails that had appeared like silver plane-trail mist.

The old signalman would look our way, something having caught his attention, and he'd sniff the air before sinking down and laying a ghostly hand on the equally ghostly rail.

'Don't let him see you!' came the whispered instruction from the older boys.

So we'd sink our faces down into the dirt and grit and lie as still as was possible.

The sense of fear was real, and I remember the hairs on my neck standing upright, the goosebumps covering my arms despite the warmth of a late-summer evening.

And as the very ground would begin to tremble beneath us, so little gaps would appear around the stones; the moon dust being shaken away. The smallest stones would fall and trickle down under us and around us as though the whole of it, the very earth itself, was about to disintegrate.

Our imaginations filled in all of the detail.

The train was coming.

But the bridge was out, blasted away twenty years ago, and just a sheer drop remained!

The signalman began waving his arms and mouthing words that never reached our ears above the din of the speeding train.

He'd remove his hat and wave it above his head frantically, his eyes moonlit and horrified, the whites punctured by two black dead-looking pupils that left no room for irises.

'Don't let him see you,' came the call, and I'd feel Micky shaking beside me, keeping close for comfort and support, our lithe svelteness wound in and held, ready to run, like a paper glider when the elastic band is at its optimum - one more quarter turn and it'll snap.

The signalman stood panic stricken in the direct path of the train, the sweat beads on his brow picked out like stars by the moon, and anguish twisting his features and stretching his mouth to a point where I felt it must split.

Until he broke, sank to his knees, covered his head and waited for the impact.

And a cheer came up, as two dozen boys, most of them older than us, ceased beating the ground with whatever they could find, and the tape recording of a steam train copied from a sound-effects album was clicked to silence, as the breathy roar from the mouths of those assembled ended abruptly.

Laughter rang out to replace it, and shot through the bushes and trees until it reached the ground and filled the trenches on the humpy field below. A wall of mirth slammed upwards and bounced back to us off the very moon itself.

Such larks!

And we ran for home - objective achieved - as someone called out, 'the daft bastard, he falls for it every fucking time!' And we laughed some more.

Except me.

I ran silently; sadly.

And I carried in my mind the image of the homeless man in his once smart blue suit, now ingrained and talced with dust, and I wondered what his story was and how he came to be there?

That night in my warm bed, I didn't sleep for hours, because every time I closed my eyes I saw him, kneeling on the gravel with his mouth wide, and at the very last, as the sound ceased and there was a second of silence before the laughter began, I saw his face and I noticed the tears running from his eyes and off his cheeks and into the dust that covers everything here.

Years later, when I recounted the experience to Elle, she wrapped herself around me and kissed the tears from my eyes and mingled them with her saliva before taking them into herself so that I might not have to taste them ever again. And she told me that I was different, and that was why she Loved me.

Elle walked from this direction one hot evening in August of 1984. I saw her over Micky's shoulder, but opted not to make him aware of her presence.

I was humming a song, 'Waves' by Blancmange because I'd got the single from the cheap box on the counter at Millby Hardware for 20p, and I liked the tune. It made me sad. Micky thought that it was 'miserable shite like that twat Morrissey.' I didn't tell him that it made me sad because it reminded me of Elle every time I heard it, even though I wasn't sure why it should.

I'd stopped sharing my secrets with Micky by then, which probably told the state of our friendship better than anything else.

Half of me hoped that Elle would turn back that day, but an equal amount of me wanted her to advance and for us to encounter one another. I suppose I knew that Micky being there might be a problem.

He was obsessed with Elle, and whereas I kept my desires hidden as best I could, he was completely open about what he'd do to her given a sniff of a chance.

Micky's head shot round when he noticed that my eyes were pointed down the line. Elle was perhaps twenty or thirty yards away and still oblivious to our presence.

We chose our location carefully because of the cover it afforded, and so that we could see along the track one way, and not be surprised on the other. Micky's parents had an intolerance for smoking, so he needed to be vigilant or they'd cut off his pocket money.

"She knows we're here," Micky hissed in my ear.

"No she doesn't," I corrected him.

"She knows. And she's coming here because she wants something," he insisted, stubbing the smoke out in the gravel.

I stand where we lay that day, and Bean sniffs the recess with the solid foundation where once a signal hut stood before someone burnt it down in 1979.

She was less than five of her strides away from us when Micky sprang up.

As he did, I noticed her flinch, and felt a pang of guilt and protectiveness, but I did nothing.

His head was pivoting between Elle and myself, because Micky was a coward really. He needed me next to him, just as he had that night with the signalman, and just as he did when he was 'doing it' with Debbie.

I sat and stewed, and Elle tried to push past. Why didn't she turn round? But that was the thing with the old railway, more so when the sun was high and bright and the grey stones shimmered diamantine like - you couldn't see the drop until you were upon it; it was as though the path continued unbroken.

So Elle walked on rather than back, inadvertently trapping herself. All of which Micky misread as her secretly wanting to be there with him.

Still I did nothing but observe.

Micky began pawing her, walking by her side and grabbing her behind. He was so used to Debbie and being able to do whatever he wanted, everything being giggled at as he was told that he was a 'mucky sod.'

Elle tried to spin away, swiping at his hand, and I could see Micky getting more and more agitated, his face flushing in frustration. He still believed that he was right, and that she was there for him.

"Leave her, Micky," I said, but he ignored me like even the best trained dog will ignore the strictest command if prey or sex is scented in the air.

She tried to rise above it, but I could see that her lips were tight and dry as she persisted in her attempts to fend Micky off.

It dawned on her that she'd reached the end of the line. There was nowhere to go.

"I'd like to go back now," she said, sounding calmer than she was.

"What's the password?" Micky teased, blocking her way.

"Is it 'get-out-of-my-way'?" Elle snapped at him.

"Nope. If you don't know it, it'll cost you a kiss."

Elle ignored him.

I sat watching, rubbing a bit of gravel between my thumb and finger.

She glanced over at me, and I faintly smiled apologetically.

Later, she told me that it emboldened her, that smile. She knew that I wasn't going to jump in on Micky's side. One-on-one was a different proposition to two-on-one.

"A kiss and I go?" she sought to clarify.

"I'm a man of my word," Micky said, making a cub scout sign.

"Leave her alone, Micky," I said again, this time a little more seriously and slowly.

Purely to extricate herself, she leant forward at that moment and pecked Micky dryly and briefly on the cheek before recoiling back.

He hadn't been prepared for that swiftness of execution. I'd seen him pull the trick off before, seizing the girl as she leaned in, and finding her lips before laughing hysterically to himself.

He shot an angry look my way, and I ceased rubbing the bit of grit, but retained it in a pinch. I gave him a small warning look, just a dip of my chin and a challenging downturn of my mouth.

"I didn't say where I wanted you to kiss me," he said to Elle.

She tried again to turn him and clear a path for herself, but he stayed west side of her, the sun shadowing him from behind, and lighting her up so that the concern on her face was impossible to mask.

Oh, and still I was rapt by her - even then in that moment, I was so taken by Elle that I failed to really grasp the gravity of the situation unfolding.

"This is where I want you to kiss me," I heard Micky tell her, and I looked at him to see that his dick was erect and poking out the front of his jeans.

"Leave me alone, you filthy little sod," Elle said, turning away, and still trying to sound calm.

The grit fell from my fingers, and I got to my feet in a fluid motion.

"I said leave her alone!" I snapped at Micky.

"Fuck you!" he screamed at me, viciously, spit spewing from his mouth. "You've been different since she arrived. You and Debbie and everybody. You've all become fucking wankers because of this prick-teasing bitch!"

Elle stood, rooted to the spot. She could have run in that moment, but she didn't. The sudden escalation in violent energy stalled her.

"Leave her!" I said again, and went to posit myself between them.

Micky punched me, but I drew my leg back and he only succeeded in landing a glancing blow on my chin. I went towards him, but his penis comically swaying out the fly of his jeans distracted me.

I actually laughed. It was ridiculous. All of it. It was just a laugh that had got out of hand. I turned to Elle, and was about to tell her to go, when I felt a sharp jab in my flank.

My hand went to it instinctively, and emerged with blood coating my fingers. It dawned on me that Micky had slashed me with his penknife. Still I wasn't concerned. Still I felt like laughing. It wasn't life threatening or anything.

But in a blink, Micky was going to Elle, the knife point at neck height.

I punched him in the back of his skull as hard as I've ever punched anything. It made a sick sound on impact.

Still he was going at Elle, squeezing her back towards the bank of the old railway, not far from the precipice. She was a foot away from falling - one step.

Feet first, I lunged at him, side on, my heels connecting solidly with the outside of his lower leg, and he went down.

I didn't once consider the matches. He carried them loose, tucked down his sock so that they wouldn't rattle in the box and alert his parents to their presence. They hated smoking.

The sulphur spat to life. Micky gave a scream, and as he instinctively rolled away from the flame, so he slipped over the edge, and fell down through the branches before thudding down on the ground below.

A boulder broke his back on landing, but he was still alive when the parched long grass caught the flame and washed over him.

I tried to get down to him, but I couldn't get there quickly enough.

The official cause of death was the fire, but he'd have been paralysed had he survived. By virtue of his paralysis, he would have felt no pain until the flames reached his neck and head.

Someone found Elle an hour later, wandering around the Humpty Dumpty Field in shock. But I was at the hospital by then, having stitches and treatment for the burns on my hands and the smoke I inhaled.

Squatting down, I pick up a single grain of grit. And with Bean leading me back to number three, I rub it between my thumb and finger until we reach our destination, at which point I release my grip and let it fall on the rockery.

16.

Have you ever gone three minutes without uttering a sound? It's not too difficult.

Try three hours. It'll get to you.

Now try it for three months.

That's how long I remained in complete silence. Elective Mutism was the professional opinion.

Busying myself with Dad's worldly goods, I reflect on the fact that I cried over the signalman's anguish, but seven years on, and I didn't shed a tear over Micky. Over thirty years after that, and I'm incapable of crying over my own father.

Does life inoculate us against pain? Does repeated exposure to it render us immune? Is it a survival mechanism, no different to having to learn about water and fire, and the dangers associated with them? As a child I dabbed my finger on the glowing element of a car's cigarette lighter, and suffered the pain and endured the blister. But I never touched it again.

Avoidance isn't always possible, but detachment is. As an adult, I trick myself into believing that men have to be men. We are, it is commonly believed, the strong ones; the breadwinners and providers. And as such, we can't afford to break down, or the whole of everything would come crashing down with us. So we carry our stiff-upper-lips and bear the load.

It's all bullshit. But it's a lie that I'm happy to attach myself to, and through it I achieve my indifference and am able to carry on.

It doesn't mean that it isn't there, buried away.

Bean lies resting in his day-bed after our walk. He usually maintains a watchful eye on me, moving around the house to where I am if I'm absent for any amount of time.

His eyes are closed now, the black lashes linear slits in his sandy brown coat as they form the triangle of darkness made by his nose and lips, up to the tips of his ears. He looks happy, those shiny moist lips set in a slight crescent, his breaths coming soft and even.

With his legs curled inside the foam wall of his bed and the curve of his body, he resembles a prawn; cooked and ready for peeling.

A flinch passes through him, and after a lull, his front paws begin to move rhythmically but jerkily. Is he listening to jazz? Ah, he's running in his sleep, perhaps dreaming of a rabbit or squirrel, him in hot pursuit.

An involuntary soft whine comes from him, and a shudder. In his dream is it a bark? Did he just land on his prey?

Or is he running towards Dad, and was that a happy yap of joy and excitement on reunion? Was the shudder the bliss he felt as my Dad's expansive hand found his fur and ran down from nose to tail?

Or is it a nightmare he's enduring, and is he, in fact, the one being chased? Is he running happily towards, or away in terror? I hope he's enjoying a happy memory, and not that night he spent with my Dad sitting still in a chair, as he muzzled him and felt the warmth seep from him over the hours as he smelt the death.

"Bean," I call gently, as I shuffle over to him from my packing of old VHS videos for the charity box, and lay a hand softly on his hind quarter, barely touching.

His eyes snap open, and I see the alarm and fear for a second, before he regains his senses and his chestnut eyes soften in relieved recognition. I rub his ear with my thumb, and he brings his head round and finds the side of my hand with his tongue.

"It's okay," I whisper to him as I continue massaging his ear before stroking the smooth fur between his eyes and up to his forehead. "It's all going to be okay."

He can't speak. He would if he could, I'm sure of that. But he does speak in his own way, as I've come to understand him in just a few days. I know the standing staring look and wag of his tail means he wants to go out. If he sits and stares and shuffles his feet under him he wants food. And if he puts his feet up on my thigh and tilts his head to one side, he wants attention.

You simply have to read the signs; speech is unnecessary and less efficient. Speech is more open to misinterpretation or misunderstanding. Words can be skewed by the hearer to meet an agenda.

Even before Micky died, and I didn't utter a word for three months, I was always more comfortable expressing myself in writing than I was in speech. The letter writing that Elle and I embarked on would have happened anyway, I think, because it suited both of us. Elle liked it because there was a permanence to it. Unlike spoken words, they couldn't be denied later. If you were going to say it, mean it, and stand by it.

But she didn't, did she? Ultimately she didn't mean it or stand by any of it.

A rattle on the porch snaps us both back to the here and now, Bean rising and growling a warning, a ridge of fur raised on his shoulders.

Elle? No, it's a man. Immleigh? No, wrong shape through the moulded glass.

"Oh, hello Mr Glenn."

"Good afternoon. I hope I'm not disturbing, and that this is a good time? I said to myself, I said, chances are he'll have had his luncheon, and not yet be preparing his evening meal, and seeing how the weather's fine, and his car is on the driveway, now may well be an opportune moment. Am I correct?"

"Yes. Come in, please."

"Getting sorted, I see," he observes, as he steps inside and removes his tweed cap to reveal a few strands of over-swept grey hair.

"No sense in delaying. And it gives me something to do."

"Agreed, agreed. A man of action, eh? I like that, I do. We have to keep busy, Digger, that's my motto in life. We stagnate, else, I say, and that's a slippery slope. I applied it to my work, and I apply it now in my retirement."

We take seats at the small dining table at the front of the living room, closest to the hallway and kitchen.

"Well, if I may speak freely, and not beat around the bush, as it were, as I see no sense in making small talk when there's business to be attended to?"

"I wish you would."

"Good! Well, the fact of the matter is, the point of this visit, is that I saw your note in the envelope that you delivered last early evening, and I've been thinking about it ever since. So much so, in fact, that I have to confess to you that it kept me awake for part of last night, and I have always been a sound sleeper, regular in my sleeping habits."

"I'm sorry if..."

"No, no, Digger! No apology necessary. My restless mind is my concern, and you played no knowing part in upsetting my routine. I am not here to complain, I say."

"Oh, good." I hope the tone of surprise in my voice isn't too obvious.

"It's this here dog business that brings me hither, and disturbs me in the way I have described."

"I always pick it up in a bag," I protest.

"What? No, no, you misunderstand."

"Do I?"

"Yes. I wish, if it were agreeable to you, to adopt the beast!"

"I'm not sure I understand."

"I wish to have Bean come live with me."

I'm struck dumb. This is a man who has complained for close to fifty years about every dog Dad ever had. He complained about every bark, snarl, crap, piss, shed hair, cocked leg, yellowed lamppost base, disturbed tuft of grass and attempt to show him affection.

"Why?" is all I can say.

"Ah, yes, a very astute question. And the truth of it is," he begins, settling one wrinkled old hand on top of the other as it rests on the curved handle of his wooden walking stick, "I say the truth is," as he again pauses to clear his throat and drop his eyes down so that they're bent on his hands, "I say, I'm lonely, Digger."

And suddenly I see his frailty and fear and it shocks me.

He adds, "I'm so desperately lonely without her, you see," and his voice falters at the end and barely makes it all the way there.

"What was her name?" I ask.

"Mrs Glenn?"

"Yes."

"You never knew her name?" he asks me, raising his worn-out eyes up to me, a sign of moisture lurking in the corners.

"No. She was always just Mrs Glenn, and you have always been Mr Glenn."

"Glenda," he informs me.

"Glenda Glenn?"

"Yes."

And I laugh. He laughs too. I've never heard him laugh before.

"And my name is Reg," he informs me.

"It's good to finally meet you, Reg," I say, and offer him my hand.

He takes it, and I can feel the tremors reverberate through him, but his shake is warm and sincere; firm but not imposing. It feels gentlemanly, but difficult to achieve given the arthritis that swells his knuckles. I know that it pains him to deliver it, but that is how he has always shaken hands, and so the pain must be endured.

"You obviously miss her terribly," I state, rather obviously.

"I can't begin to tell you."

It's him now being taciturn, and me leading the way.

"How long were you and Glenda married?"

"We weren't. That's the best of it. That's the big secret."

"Really?"

"It's the truth. Her father refused to give his blessing, and she promised him that she would never marry without it."

"So you lived together?" I ask.

"In sin?"

"I wasn't going to say that."

"No, but plenty did. I say, plenty did. It was different back then."

"When was this?"

"1949. We were sixteen when we met. I'll save you the mathematics of it - I'm eighty-four years of age."

"So you were together for - what…?"

"Sixty-seven years," he says before I can calculate it. And I bet he could tell me the months, weeks, days and hours.

"Wow," is the only word that comes to my mind.

"It's never enough, I can tell you that."

"You loved her," I state, because there's no need to ask.

"Every day. But not enough, I say, not enough."

"What do you mean?"

He leans back in the chair, the heavy folds on his face showing his full age and the extent of his loss all of a sudden. I never before noticed how thin and frail his wrists are as they protrude from the sleeves of his shirt and jacket. He clears his throat. "You think that there will be time enough later on. And there isn't. One day your life is ahead of you, and the next it's all behind you. I say, I worked countless irretrievable hours when I didn't need to. What was the money for, I ask you, at time-and-a-half? If I could sit and work it all out, it'd reckon up to half a lifetime that I squandered when I could have been with my Glenda. So, I say, you tell me, Digger - what did I love the most - my lower-management responsibilities at the works, or Glenda? I didn't even take retirement when it was offered to me at fifty-eight. Nor again at sixty-two. And I worked past my sixty-fifth. I was sixty-seven when they finally got shot of me."

"Why did you stay on?"

"Because I allowed it to define me, Digger. Your father was the same. I needed the routine and the motivation. Or so I thought."

"And you didn't?"

"No. I say, it was all rhubarb! But I was afraid of upsetting the status-quo. I'd always worked, and Glenda had always been at home. And we were happy. We loved one another - I say, loved! That's the truth of it. And I worried that if I was with her all the time, she'd see through me. She'd see that I wasn't what she thought I was. She'd fall out of love with me. So I kept it all the same for as long as I could. As I say, work defined me, lad, to such an extent that it was all I saw and valued in myself."

"And you want a dog for companionship?"

"I do. I'd enjoy walking him, I think. And I'd like the company about the house. There's nothing worse than waking up to an empty house, Digger; especially when you've known something different for so many years."

"You never had children."

"No, that's a fact. Seems there was something amiss regarding that. Whether it was Glenda or myself, we never knew. But it wasn't meant to be. Besides, I was happy with my lot."

"And Mrs Glenn?"

"I believe that she was happy. But I'd catch her all the time, watching you lot running and larking about in the street when you were so-high. And, I say, I'd see a happiness in her as she watched you through the net curtains. After all, that was why we moved here."

"I don't understand."

"It's not difficult, lad! We were nearly forty when we came to live here. We were part of the generation before - the fuddy-duddies, didn't you used to call us?"

I smile shyly.

He smiles back at me, thin-lipped, a knowing little twinkle in his eyes. "She loved watching you all play. So did I. We'd spend hours just sitting together in front of the window watching and smiling at you. You were better than television, I can say that! And she'd open the little window at the top so she could hear your chatterings. She'd do that in all weathers, and I'd worry about her catching a chill. But, I say, she'd wrap a blanket round her, and say, 'but it's like music to me, Reg, hearing the children - just like music to me!' Relax, before you go thinking too much - there was nothing improper in it! But Glenda got such pleasure from watching you all. Such pleasure."

"I always thought you were monitoring us, looking for us to do something wrong," I say honestly.

"You thought she was a nosey old bag?"

"No, not that..."

"Ha! She'd worry, though, Glenda. I say, she was a bit of a fretful woman when it came to children. I suppose it came from not having any of our own, that over-protectiveness. 'Tell them, Reg, please,' she'd say to me, 'tell them to be careful of the thorns on the roses.' So I'd have to come out and tell you to stay away from the roses. Or, 'tell them, Reg love, will you, make sure they don't go getting in that dog muck over by the lamppost.' I say, she did fret about you all. Especially you."

"Me?"

"Yes, I say! You were her favourite. She never had much time for that Micky up the road, though I probably shouldn't say that. She always thought he was a bit - now, what was the word she'd use? - a bit of a sly one. That was it. But you? She kept a close watch on you."

"I never knew."

"No, well. There's plenty we don't know in this world, and that's not a bad thing, by my reckoning. Always something to learn, I say, and put me in the ground when there isn't, if you'll pardon my insensitivity at this time, what with your father and all."

"I hope I was good when she watched."

"Not always, but that's how it is, I say. She'd watch you sneaking in to that lass at number nine, I can tell you that."

"She knew about me and Elle?"

"Elle and I!" he scolds me, and for the first time I know that he's correcting me because he wants the best for me. "Oh, yes, and she was rooting for you two. She said that you reminded her of us when we were about your age. She said, I say, that if we'd have had a son, he might have been a bit like you. The fair hair, and the openness of your face, and the way you'd walk and run. She saw something in you. And she liked your quietness and kind nature; the way you could sit and occupy yourself, perfectly content in your own company. That was what she said. And she saw herself in that lass next door, I believe, though she never said that outright."

"You mean Elle, not Debbie, right?" I ask.

"Yes! Aren't you listening, lad? Smart and polite. She had a dignity about her; a grace, you might call it. Once you got through the daft clothes and hair! And she was tall and slim like my Glenda. Oh, yes, she was rooting for you two even before you were sneaking round there! 'Just let him grow up a bit,' she'd say to me, 'and they'll be together, you mark my words. Made for one another.' She could see it all, could Glenda Glenn, and just by watching."

"She was wrong, though, wasn't she?"

"I never knew her to be wrong. Ever! Not when it came to affairs of the heart. If it didn't work out, that will have been because of something daft one of you did. 'Ditch him,' she'd say to the window, when she saw her with that Perry in his car, 'he's the wrong one for you, pet! That Digger's the one for you.' Or, 'watch yourself with her, Digger, that Debbie will be the ruin of you if you let her be. You hold on for that one at number nine!' It was like a soap opera watching you young ones. As I say, it was better than anything on the television!"

"I've always loved her," I find myself telling him. "I've loved her from the moment I first saw her, and I love her now as I sit here."

"Then tell her!"

"I can't."

"Then you aren't the man my Glenda said you were."

"She ended it with me."

"So what, I say? So bloody what! She made a mistake. Have you never made a mistake in your life? Is that why you ran away, is it?"

"I didn't run away."

"Then what do you call it? Running away is what we called it! What are you now, nearly fifty?"

"Forty-eight."

"And this Elle?"

"Just fifty."

"Then don't waste any more time, I say! It's running out, Digger. And it'll be gone before you know it. Trust me on that." He wags a knowing hooked finger at me, before switching his attention to the dog. "So, this is the beast! Bean, you say? I say, come on Bean, what do you reckon on coming to live with me, eh, keep one another company?"

"He's a good dog," I report.

"One question, if I may; why did your father call him Bean - because he's full of beans?"

I lick my lower lip before saying, "something like that. Like I say, he's a good dog."

"I know. I've watched him with your father enough. But I recognise the mournfulness in those eyes of his. I see it in the mirror every day. My Glenda always said that there's only one true love for each of us in the world, and the trick is to recognise it and hang on to it, and I reckon Bean here had his with your father. And I had mine with my Glenda. Still, we can both help plug a gap for each other, I say. What do you say, Bean? Eh, I say, what do you say?"

17.

The Riverside restaurant, est. 2012, is as high-end an eatery as there's ever been around Millby. It sits on the east bank of the river Tred, just after it merges with the river Jem, and is set up with large windows all along one side so that diners might gaze out at the sunset over the river.

But there is no sun to set on this Wednesday evening. I sit at the bar, leaving the lack of view to couples who stare at their phones rather than their partners.

If I was here with Elle...

Millby has improved; restaurants like this prove the point. A Chinese takeaway is no longer a novelty.

It's been a long day. I packed and labelled all the boxes I purchased. I'll need more. Fifty years in one place equates to a lot of stuff.

I felt a need to get away for an evening; away from Dad's house, Oaklea, Elle's house, Debbie, the old railway, Micky, Immleigh, the Humpty Dumpty Field et al.

So what did I do by way of escape? I came to where I know Elle was just eleven days ago, on Saturday September 30th; her birthday. Her fiftieth birthday.

I wonder where she sat? What did she order? Has this cutlery been in her mouth?

If I understood Tony Swann correctly, she wasn't with anyone except Pat and Pat, and it was her fiftieth. If she had a partner, wouldn't he have been present? Ah, but what's the difference? With someone, not with someone - she still chose not to be with me. That said, Swanny and Mr Glenn's words remain with me. Was it a mistake? Has she regretted it for all of this time, but was too proud or timid to attempt reconciliation? She was never timid; that was part of the attraction. Too proud, then.

For the first time, I wonder if I acted hastily by leaving that day.

I order a vegetarian dish, this being the first decent meal I've had in several days. My body tells me that I could use the nutrients. Thus, a veggie pasta dish follows my soupe du jour.

I've survived. I'm half way through this week, just as I'm half way through my meal. Come Sunday, I shall pack my case, load my car, and head back to my life. And, to some degree, the adage concerning 'out of sight, out of mind' does play out true.

There are always reminders, those chance encounters that come out of nowhere and feel like a punch in the guts. A song on the radio, for example, or the hearing of a word or expression. Driving up from London on Sunday, I heard 'Eleanor Rigby', the Ray Charles version, but it was sufficiently evocative. Last year, during a visit to Dorset, I encountered a humpy field like ours, and was rendered immobile before I willed myself to step on it and cross it.

If I can survive the next three days, particularly Dad's funeral on Friday, then a lot of my concerns will go away.

My concerns? They are many fold. I try to list them out in my mind as I play absently with my noodles.

Dad's funeral itself, of course, and my getting through that in one piece is paramount.

It's a relief to know that Bean will go to Mr Glenn - I still call him that - Reg on Sunday before I leave. That way he can prepare the home, and get a few things in. It's a satisfactory solution, even if I do have some worries about Reg's age. But he seems well and active enough, and Bean isn't a demanding dog. He may turn out to be just what he needs. And I've given Reg my number and told him to call me should there be any issues.

In addition, Mum and Debbie being present at the funeral, and, as is their wont, making it all about them plays on my mind. It would be nice if Dad could be the centre of attention for this one day at the very least. Though that may be advice I would do well to heed for myself.

Immleigh is still sniffing around, but when I leave on Sunday, I hope to leave him behind. After all, he hasn't been in contact for twenty-plus years. Not since they warned him about harassment. It must have held his career back, those warnings. Great; another reason for him to resent and pursue me.

The Will being read on Saturday morning worries me. If it goes the way I think, it's going to involve some explaining and managing. I have a dreadful feeling that it will drive a wedge between Paul and I.

And, of course, last but not least, there's seeing Elle. I dread that as much as anything else I have to face. Yet, the thought of not seeing her bothers me just as much. I feel that I can't win. In a way, I hope that I see her, and she is nothing like she was. I secretly hope that she will have altered to such an extent that I won't even recognise her, and we shall have to be reintroduced.

Glancing down, I smile at the approximation of the outline of her face formed by the pasta on the white plate.

But the orange tomato sauce conjures up Debbie, so I destroy it with my fork.

Sitting with just my thoughts, I begin to relax. There's something appealing about the pace of life here. I've enjoyed my walks with Bean, and the fresh air and greenness of the landscape. I haven't smoked any more than I would have at home, and I feel healthier, my mind free to roam and wander. Yes, there's a danger in that, as it inevitably takes me backwards. But there is something to be said about giving the brain opportunity to exercise.

Despite all my concerns about what I have to face, I feel, in some ways, more at ease here. Would I have ever had impetus to leave had it not been for the last letter?

Life is certainly less stressful. How long did it take me to get here? Barely time enough to listen to three songs in the car. So, ten to fifteen minutes. That same journey in London would take half an hour at least, plus another fifteen minutes parking. And everything is less expensive, I note, as my bill is handed to me.

Why did I never come here with Dad? Paul, Jen and the girls could have met us. I'd have paid. Why did I never do that?

I didn't suggest it, and Dad never wanted to go anywhere, always using the dog as his excuse for non-attendance. Instead, we'd sit at the house and drink a couple of cans of beer, the television always on; always a distraction.

To some extent, he gave up on life after Mum left. I recall going to the pub with him on my eighteenth, but Mum came back for it, and Elle was there. It didn't go well between those two. It should have been just he and I. And Paul, perhaps.

All of the projects - the driveway, the patio out the back of number three, the rockery and the porch, the decorating and the new dining table - they were all done prior to Mum leaving. Nothing was embarked on after she left. I never thought of that before. She was his motivation, and without her present, he didn't think himself worth the effort.

However, he did touch up my room and repaint my bed.

A sadness accompanies that thought. It's time to depart.

My journey back to Dad's old house is soundtracked by 'Where Are You?' by Cat Stevens. I play it on repeat. It's winding down as I pull on to the driveway, so I sit and let it finish. It would be rude not to do so.

Other people aren't so considerate, it seems, as a rotund man approaches the driver's door.

Opening it, I call out, "can I help you?"

"Ah, would you be Douglas?"

"I am, but everybody calls me Digger."

"Ah, Digger, yes. Ah, did you not get told I was coming?"

Does he begin every sentence with 'ah'?

"No."

"Ah, a miscommunication I think. I'm Ralph Brierley, the, ah, funeral director. My condolences at this, ah, sad time."

"My brother, Paul, and his wife are dealing with that," I say, taking his chubby cold hand in mine as I alight from the car.

"Ah, indeed, Paul and Jennifer. However, I wished to gather some information about your father for the, ah, eulogy, and have spoken with some of the neighbours here. Could we have a chat, if that's, ah, convenient?"

"Of course," I say, and gesture for him to follow me to the house.

We stand in the kitchen, him filling the doorframe, a drink, ah, declined. Bean sniffs his suit trousers, but discovers nothing of interest so lies down and observes.

"Will you be delivering the eulogy?" I ask.

"Paul and Jennifer have, ah, requested that I do."

"Good. So, how can I help?"

"I wish to get a sense of your father, from those who were, ah, closest to him. I appreciate that this, ah, might be difficult at this time, but what do you most fondly, ah, recall of him, for example?"

My mind is a complete and utter blank as a mild panic overtakes me. I hadn't given this any thought; my memories are fragments. He wasn't the kind of dad that... But he was a good dad. He was...

"He loved his dog," I blurt clumsily.

"Ah, yes, that has been mentioned. I'm more interested in, ah, your relationship with him."

"He was my Dad."

"Ah, yes, I meant more..."

I wish I'd had time to think about this. "He built a rockery. And a porch."

"Perhaps consider it from a more, ah, personal perspective, might I suggest?"

"He rarely shouted."

"Good, so he was a gentle man, would you say, a gentle and loving father?"

"I suppose so, yes."

Was he? Yes, he was.

"Excellent. And, ah, can you recall any examples of that?"

"Ah..."

I'm doing the 'ah' thing now, it must be infectious.

"He kept my letters," I say, for reasons I can't begin to fathom.

"Letters? Ah, were they letters you sent to him?"

"What? Er, no, they were letters to me from someone. But he kept them."

"Ah, I see," he says, but in a way that implies he doesn't see it at all. Still, he pauses to make a note. "They are very, ah, dear to you, the letters?"

"They were. They are, I mean."

"And he kept them for you because, ah, he knew that they were precious to you?"

"I think so. I don't know."

What am I talking about?

"Perhaps one of them could be read out, if you think that would be, ah, applicable," he suggests.

"They're very personal."

"Good! That's exactly what I need, something, ah, personal."

"To me, I mean. They were nothing to do with Dad, really."

"Ah, I see."

"And he kept my school reports. And my Subbuteo and tapes."

"Ah, right. Very good! So, he was a man who never forgot the important things in life, would you say?"

"I would. I would say that."

"And these letters…"

I wish I hadn't mentioned the bloody letters.

"…they were very, ah, personal, you said?"

"To me, yes. Yes they were."

"And he kept them, ah, safe for you?"

"He did."

"So, ah, he was a man you could rely on - a man you could trust?"

"Yes!"

"A man who was, ah, always there for you when you needed somebody?"

"Well, he worked a lot, so…"

"Ah! So, a responsible man; a man who took his responsibilities seriously?"

"I suppose so, yes."

He makes more notes.

"Well, you've been, ah, very helpful. Again, I'm sorry for your loss."

"Thank you."

~~~~~

January 9th 1987 "...My Love, what a perfect day today was. A bonus day! I love the snow because it cancelled everything and allowed me to be with you. And I love it because it meant nobody else was around as we took our walk. Oh, Digger, why can't every day be like that? Why can't we live in a world where there is nothing to be done except what we choose to do? And where there is nobody to see except one another? You would have kept walking and never turned back, but aren't you glad that I suggested we did? I honestly had no idea that P&P would be out all afternoon! I hope that I didn't wear you out too much, but I felt so randy! Making love in the snow was incredible, but taking our time and repeating the performance in my room was even better. God, you turn me on! Prior to meeting you, I never thought of sex as being that vital in a relationship. I honestly believed that there were more important things. And there are, I know - or things just as important, such as communication and respect - but I now know that sex with you is so life-affirming and vital to me. I could barely stand after the third time, my legs like jelly. And I have never experienced sensations like I did at the end! I had to wash the bedding after that! Oh, my perfect Lover, you enchant me and have created something new in me that I never knew existed. I glow even now, hours later, and I still crave more! Why can't you be here by my side all night and every night? It is all we both desire, and so why should it not be? Know that I am yours for all time, every cell of me! Do with me everything and anything you want, as *long as it is done in the name of our Love! Sleep time now. I am tired. I am satisfied. I am in Love with you. Lx."*

Extinguishing the light, I lie in the single bed that remains from my past, only the mattress and bedding having been replaced. I feel the sticker residue on the pillars of the headboard. Dad must have picked them off at some point when they went yellow and began to separate.

It feels as though he semi-glossed over them rather than go to the trouble of sanding them smooth. I don't blame him. How many times did I stay here across three decades? Thirty? It's about right; one night a year on average.

Perhaps he didn't even remove the stickers. If I were to pick at them and flick the lamp back on, would I be terrified by Kevin Keegan's perm?

Sleep won't come tonight. The food was a bit rich, perhaps. And my struggle to describe Dad bothers me, but my relationship with him is private. I know what I feel about him, and don't have a need to share that with all and sundry. Still, I should have had more to say.

I was asleep one night close to forty years ago in this very bed. Was it 1980 when we had the heavy snowfall? I remember the school being closed for a few days as the oil heating stopped working, or ran out of fuel and they couldn't get it delivered.

A gentle shake awoke me, and at first I resisted and clung to the warmth and comfort.

It persisted, though, so I came to and opened my eyes to see my Mum kneeling by the side of my bed, her face set and sad. Not quite sad; more dreamlike, as though she were sleepwalking and not really conscious.

"Come with me," she whispered, "and put your socks and slippers on."

I did as I was instructed, and slunk down the stairs in her wake, sensing and not needing to be told that I should move quietly.

Dad had built the porch by then, and Mum led me to it by my hand. It was late, I knew, but not as late as it felt. The stillness made it seem like the early hours.

She silently levered down the handle and opened the inner door so that we could step inside, where there was just enough room for us to sink down on our haunches, our feet tucked under us and our legs crossed, and all the while Mum held my hand in hers. I can recall the warmth and softness of it.

Outside large flakes of snow padded down relentlessly, and not a sound did anything make.

The world was as still as I've ever seen it. All life had ceased to move, as it seemed to have instinctively gone into hibernation. Everywhere I looked, the carpet of white was untrod and pristine. It sat on every surface, thick and thin, on which it could gain a footing; and once established, it steadily accumulated as it adhered to itself.

It evened everything out, that snow, and softened the edges of all I could see; of all that I knew. Cars morphed into smooth mounds, and trippy kerbs disappeared. Sharp tree twigs became feathery fingers, and fragile windows appeared as cotton wool.

The world looked unbreakable and incapable of causing harm in that moment.

"Lovely, isn't it?" my Mum sighed.

"It is," I agreed.

And then she asked, "if I ever went away, would you want to come with me?"

"We won't get far in this!"

"No," she chuckled, "we won't. But what about another day?"

"Where are we going - the seaside?"

"I don't know. Would you like to go to the seaside?"

I nodded at that. We hardly ever saw the sea. "Dad said he'd take me fishing on a boat the next time we go."

"But what if your Dad wasn't with us?"

"Because he has to work?"

"He always has to work," she sighed, and hugged her knees to her chest as she uncrossed her legs. It made her smaller.

I began to comprehend, then. "I wouldn't want to go away from here. What about school? And Micky? And Ringo!" I said, as he came to the front door and sniffed around its base. "And Dad and Paul! We're not going away, are we Mum?"

"No, we're not going anywhere. I was just dreaming of being out in the snow," she said, and put her arm around my shoulders to draw me to her. I felt her lips on the top of my head, and then a wetness fell on me.

Mum held me to her so that I couldn't see her face above me, and I wondered if the porch was leaking. But then I understood that the wet drops were warm.

"Will you make me a promise?" she asked me breathily, giving the moment a sense of importance.

I nodded that I would, as I tried to work out how quickly the snow was accumulating and how much there might be come the morning if it carried on at the same rate. I imagined how big a snowman Paul, Micky and I might build.

In the same hushed voice, she said, "promise me that, if you ever feel unhappy, you'll change your life."

And I said that I would, as she hugged me tightly.

A warmth sweeps my face, and I open my eyes to see two beads of light as the air in my bedroom shifts.

I reach out my hand and it connects with the coarse fur of Bean. He wants attention and the comfort found in human contact.

"Don't we all," I say to him in the dark, and a patted hand brings him hopping up on my bed where he curls up behind my knees.

18.

After four days, Bean knows that I open the back door for him on rising, and while he sniffs around out there, I boil the kettle. I drink two cups of tea and have some toast while he eats his breakfast, and I give him the final piece of crust as a reward.

Thereafter, we head out through the porch door and go for a walk, him leading the way.

For all I know, it's exactly what Dad did, and perhaps Bean taught me his way, rather than the other way round. After all, I require the routine as much as he does.

He trots obediently by my side, switching to my left or right depending on where something stands that his nose might investigate. His legs take about three sets of short steps to my one, until he veers away to check a scent.

Knowing the length of his retractible lead to the inch, he nearly always breaks off and jogs back to me before it can pull on his neck. Yet, I notice, he isn't looking at me. Does he count my steps and know the limits? Has he calculated the timing from my pace? We are in harmony. Only very seldom does that leash pull in my hand, and force me to turn and wait for him, and it's usually because he's relieving himself.

We both perceive a car alongside us, but pay it no immediate heed.

I know it's Immleigh before I turn my head.

"Morning!" I call chirpily.

"I've been watching you."

"So I noticed."

"And I noticed."

"What did you imagine you noticed?" I tease him.

"I noticed where it is that you don't go."

"What does that mean?"

"It means that you aren't as smart as you reckon yourself."

"Is that right?"

"I knew you being back here would bear fruit. You've been everywhere walking that dog."

"It's public land," I point out.

"Oh, it is that. Yet you never once set foot on the eastern side of the reservoir."

I try not to betray myself, and keep my features calm. A slight smile of indulgence is all I show him.

He continues. "So I called in a favour. Guess what I discovered?"

"That my Dad owns that land."

"That's right. Well, he did, at least. But you never go there."

"I go where the dog leads me."

"Of course you do. Take care, won't you?"

Wanker. You know nothing. But I'm happy to let you carry on thinking that you do.

We walk on, along the ring-road that encircles the old part of Oaklea estate; the original part before they built the newer, bigger, shinier houses where Debbie lives for now.

She'll solve her problems. The likes of Debbie always do. Some new host will appear for her to parasitically attach herself to, and she'll drain him dry and everybody will move on. Repeat till death. Survival; that's the name of the game.

There are enough men out there for whom sex is a big enough pull, as it blinds them to the true agenda. And, deep down, Debbie always knew that about herself. Dad would tell me the details of her life, recounting it like an episode from a crappy predictable drama. 'She's married again. Only known the bloke for three weeks. I wonder how long this one will last?'

She always married them quickly, because she knew that she'd be found out. So, better to nail them down during the early stages, when all relationships are at their finest and most passionate. Play on that thrill of the chase and get the paperwork signed.

It's another decent October day, the sky pale blue and a long way away. I wonder what it will do tomorrow for the funeral? I should check the forecast, but what's the point? It'll be what it'll be, and there's nothing I can do to change it.

I'm not sure there's anything that I can do about anything. It all has to play out and run its course. But Immleigh is correct. I do purposefully avoid that land of my father's. And it's also true that Bean never takes me there. In fairness, there isn't much to see, the council having left it unmaintained as it isn't their responsibility. As a result, the grass is high and the shrubbery dense and vicious. Ticks abound as the foxes and badgers use its corybantic neglect as cover and shelter.

Rather, he steers me towards the Humpty Dumpty Field once more, and we cross it, rising up and sinking down its amiable rounded ridges. And I'm okay with my life being like this field, and comprising of gentle ups and downs. Only when they become steep and jagged do things become complicated and jarring.

Bean clumsily navigates the harsh descent to the Lane, and shakes himself a little anxiously when safely reaching the road surface. I jump down beside him, and we walk along to where it abruptly ceases at Curtly Brook.

Much like the old railway, this Lane epitomises my memories of Oaklea, in that both appear to be heading somewhere, only to suddenly end without warning. Yes, I know that both came into being for a reason, but the sense of being trapped is what emanates from them now. And being trapped is all well and good when you desire whatever it is you're trapped within. But as soon as that desire wanes, or is removed altogether, so it feels akin to incarceration.

I had the option, just as Paul did, to go with Mum in 1985, when she and Dad calmly and soberly announced to us that they were 'splitting up for a bit.'

Mum was going to Jemford Bridge, where she was originally from, and had a job lined up. She'd live with her sister initially, until she and Dad decided what the future held. Jemford Bridge wasn't that far away, about thirty miles to the north, and serviced by a main road and a train line. It was the end of the county, not the end of the world.

And none of it was the end of the world. I'd turned sixteen that year, and Paul was coming up on eighteen. I'd finished secondary school a few months before, and had somehow emerged with nine O-Levels despite my lack of effort.

It earned me the option to stay on at school, and get my As, but I decided on Millby college in the end, because of the greater freedom it would afford me. With hindsight, the stricter regime of the school would have been a better fit for me, but hey-ho.

I was with Elle by that summer when decisions were being made. I didn't care about anything else.

There was a confidence in me that came from being with her; a sense that everything would be fine. Even in those fledgling weeks of our relationship, I was changed by her, and possessed a self-belief like never before. Not that I'd ever been a shrinking violet, but there had always been a shred of self-doubt. Particularly then, in the aftermath of Micky's death.

I was sat electively mutely on the grass at the side of our house, my cassette player with me. Dad had picked me up some new batteries because I kept burning through them.

My world, of course, wasn't silent. It was I who was silent, and therefore the people around me who suffered it. And I kind of knew I was, but I also had doubts as to whether I really was. Perhaps it was simply that I operated on a different level and my words couldn't be heard or deciphered?

I can't explain it, even now; not any of it. I suppose I didn't want to talk about Micky dying, and what we'd all been through. Then there were the police asking questions, Immleigh on his first case as a detective out of uniform and keen to make an impression. Micky's parents wanted answers, and the therapists talking, talking, talking, asking their endless questions. I shut down. I verbally cut myself off and waited for it all to go away.

Through my cassette player and radio, I immersed myself in music, so that the sense of hearing was always occupied and otherwise engaged. If I couldn't hear, I didn't need to answer anything. Thus, I wouldn't have to speak.

Mum and Dad worried about me, but I was, in every other way, normal. I ate my meals, went to school - albeit with less of an inclination to raise my hand - washed and shaved, and went about my business.

I was always quite quiet, I think; a person of few words. Elle once said that I gave her the impression of someone with a million thoughts going on in his brain all the time, but only a tiny fraction of them would ever be released. She was right. I like holding on to my own ideas and developing them. Paul and Micky would blurt; no sooner had a thought come to them, then it was out in the public domain.

So, to go from quiet to silent wasn't, perhaps, so much of a behavioral shift in me as it might have been in others. And I was fifteen. As a result, my mind was full of dreams and hormonally driven fantasies, all of which evolved because of, and revolved around, Elle.

Yes, I was sad about my friend dying, but Micky and I had drifted apart by then anyway. I'm not even sure why I was on the old railway with him that day. I think we encountered one another in the street, and decided to slope off for a smoke.

As I sat listening to music in my muted world, that was a large part of my depression; that I didn't care enough about his death. I didn't miss him, and a part of me was relieved that he was no longer around.

"What are you listening to?" Elle asked, startling me that day as I sat on the grass, my shoulder-blades against the fence.

It was the first time I'd encountered her in the couple of months since Micky had died. He-Pat would talk to me, and ask his Counsellor questions, but I had a sense that Elle was kept away from me because of her direct involvement and presence at the scene. And, I reasoned, she probably had some things to overcome, as well. But I'd missed seeing her.

"Sorry," she said, remembering that I didn't speak.

By way of answering, I handed her the tape inlay with the tracks written on it.

She sank down next to me, adopting a similar position and read the listing.

"The Cure, Talk Talk 'Today', Echo & The Bunnymen, Icicle Works, Joy Division 'Love Will Tear Us Apart'…" she mumbled aloud. "I love 'Closer'. 'Decades' is so stunningly beautiful."

So are you.

They were all songs about love on the tape, something I'd compiled to conjure up Elle. I'd written 'Music for L' on the spine, I suddenly recalled with dread, and hoped she wouldn't notice it and guess what it denoted.

I felt an approval as she scanned my music, and 'Love Is A Wonderful Colour' began to play.

On side two of the recording were songs I'd taken from my parents' records; Andy Williams' 'Music To Watch Girls By', The Kinks, Donovan, The Monkees 'I'm A Believer', Beach Boys 'God Only Knows', Zombies 'Time Of The Season', each chosen because of a line or a sentiment that I associated with the girl reading them.

And then she turned the inlay card over and read the spine. 'Music For L', and a heart alongside it.

"Is it for your girlfriend?" she asked, again forgetting that I couldn't reply.

I felt myself blush hot, and I smiled shyly and closed my eyes, a tautness in my cheeks and the tendons at the sides of my neck tightening. I couldn't look at her.

'Eleanor Rigby' was the final track, but I'd run out of room, so I'd written it on the reverse side.

I heard the scrape as she turned the card further, and I knew that she must have seen it.

"Oh," was the only sound she made as the penny dropped.

And I hoped above everything else that she wouldn't think that I was like Micky.

~~~~~

Bean and I stop and turn back when we reach the main road linking Millby with the town of Oakburn thirty miles to the northwest, the cars and trucks blasting by and spewing out fumes.

Elle went away that day without a word, and I silenced my cassette player and continued to sit in agony, my throat tight to an extent that swallowing was uncomfortable.

Two excruciating days dragged by, most of which I spent shamefully locked away in my bedroom, not wanting to encounter anyone in the world. Least of all Elle.

A knock on my door was followed by a narrow opening, in which a slice of Mum's face appeared.

"Someone's here to see you!" she happily informed me.

The door opened wider, and Elle stepped forward from behind Mum.

Mum said, to my abject horror, "well, I'll leave you kids to play."

Elle smiled and handed me a cassette.

'Music For D' was written on the spine in slanted writing, but there was no heart present.

Beaming my thanks at her, and breathing a stifled sigh of relief, I popped her tape on, and sat on my bed.

She sank down on the floor, her neck supported by the edge of the mattress, and New Order's 'Temptation' built steadily from the speakers.

Her back was essentially to me, as I kicked my legs back up and reclined, my cheek leaning on my open palm.

And so a routine was established. She'd come and see me with a new cassette every Saturday afternoon, and I began rating the tracks by writing down a score out of ten, so that she could get a feel for what I did and didn't like. After a couple of weeks, I began indicating my score by holding up my fingers. But I only did that so that I could look at her.

And after four weeks, or so, one day, and in a way that I wasn't even aware of until after it had happened, I said, "I'm sorry."

She shot round and looked at me, her eyes wide with surprise. "What for?" was all she said in reply. It was a smart response, to simply answer the question rather than make a big deal out of me speaking.

"Everything. For ignoring you. Would you like a drink?"

"Er, yes. Please."

"Tea?"

"Yes."

"Milk and sugar?"

"Yes, that'd be nice."

"How many?"

"I'm not bothered. I'll have it how you have it." That should have been a clue to me, a red flag, as she forsook her own preference and aligned herself with mine. She was compromising herself even then.

It was November, and too cold to sit outside, so my bedroom became a haven for us; me on the bed, Elle always on the floor leaning against it. Sometimes, when we were discussing something, she'd turn and face me, perhaps to see if I was being flippant or teasing her. And that image of her is my favourite and the most enduring. It was as though her face hadn't quite had time to settle to the fixidity that we all adopt when facing the world. And her eyes were searching, as she turned from the brighter light coming through the window to the comparative shade of where my bed was situated. It gave her a slight look of vulnerability as her pupils adjusted. The natural look lasted less than a second, I suppose, but it never failed to excite me, and it is the facial outline that I've spent thirty years attempting to replicate.

Her hair had grown out somewhat by then, but remained bottle-blonde, and asymmetrically cut, so that her shining fringe would sweep from right to left as I looked at her, before it disappeared behind her ear. It didn't look like hair, but more like a silken sheet not composed of strands. Only close up, and when the light passed through it did I see the individual hairs.

Oh, and her ears, so perfectly mother-of-pearl in the shell. So many times, as I lay behind her, did I long to reach out a hand and touch her ear and hair, but I was so afraid of driving her away. Had Micky not done what he'd done, I'm sure I would have risked the rejection, but I couldn't bring myself to behave even slightly as he had. It had to come from her, I decided.

And if it never came, I would be okay, just as long as she continued being with me. To smell her and be that close to her was enough. For then, at least. After she'd leave, I'd sit where she had and sink my face into the bedding she'd made contact with, in the fabric of which she lingered.

I'd lie awake for hours at night because I could smell her in my room.

I ached, but I welcomed the pain that came from it, and I came to relish and preserve that feeling I had when I was with her, and try to maintain it when I wasn't, because the cramps of longing in her presence were preferable to the sheer agony of her absence.

Looks, I freely admit, first attracted me to Elle. But as time passed in that non-contact way in my bedroom, or on walks around Oaklea on permitting days, so it grew from the physical immature love that I always retained, and grew into a deeper love that went beyond the epidermis and into her innermost being.

Will anybody understand my thoughts? We can only truly appreciate and grasp what we have direct knowledge of. How many people have shared this experience? Who can really understand? After all, it can never be identical for two people.

My own Mum has never truly known love. My Dad loved her, I know. But she didn't love him to anything like the same depth. She left in pursuit of that love, but never found it. And it's made her what she is.

Mum's one of the lucky ones, I believe. At least she changed her life and went looking. Better to do that and fail, than to stay still and end up bitter and twisted and full of regret. She's not angry. She tried and failed to find someone to love, and so now that love is primarily directed towards herself.

How best to put it? The most important person in Mum's world is Mum. The most important entities in Dad's world were Paul, myself and Bean. I'm unsure where Dad was on the list.

But Mum has been loved. By Dad and others. But it wasn't enough. She wanted a reciprocal love; an equal harmonious love. She wanted Love.

Which is the opposite to me. I loved, but was not loved back, it transpired. Yes, I feel anger, but I suppress it and dissolve it through my thoughts before it can come to the fore physically.

As a result of it all, I lack self-worth. I know that. I hide it well, but I know it about myself.

Debbie mentioned her life being fake. Well, so is mine, and it always has been, I now understand.

A relationship founded on pity was always doomed to fail. He-Pat probably had the notion that Elle visiting me would be therapeutically beneficial to us both. And, yes, a deep affection, I believe, undoubtedly grew out of that. But Elle got somewhat forced into something initially, that grew as a consequence of exposure. She may have even loved me, but not in the way I desired.

I'm sympathetic with her side of things. How could she not indulge me, given the catalyst? She was too decent a human to break me again after she'd been the main person involved in my reconstruction. So she waited a reasonable amount of time, those two and a half years, two of which we were involved, and then cast me off when she could be more certain of my ability to cope.

I was too in love and immature to see it from her perspective. She did love me, I believe that. But it was pitiful love.

At the time, though, with Elle so close to me, I was largely oblivious to that and everything else. At school there was a wariness of me. Thanks to Immleigh and Micky's parents, there was an element of doubt surrounding the circumstances of the accident. Only Elle's honest account of that day saved me from more probing interrogation. Well, that and my condition. But Immleigh believed my mutism to be a fabrication; my version of the right to remain silent. And policemen, I learned, hate silence. Silence is the enemy of justice, it is believed by some.

That perceived change in me, from a quiet but popular lad to distant loner, wasn't anything psychological. It was purely circumstantial. My only real friend since memories began was dead. And I had Elle in my life, but I shared that with nobody.

Debbie seemed immature amidst the staples of my life, whereas just a few months earlier, she'd been the more knowing instigator and controller. Less than six months before, she'd been able to somewhat pull my strings like a puppet-master, but now I felt as though they'd been cut.

I was sixteen in the March, and Mum pushed me to have a little party at home. I'd learn that she was preparing to leave, and I think the party was a final opportunity to enjoy a childish moment before she departed and I grew too old.

But I already was too old in my head.

I agreed for her sake, because I sensed a change was coming for her. Was it a mid-life crisis that finally gave her the impetus to go? I'm not sure. I don't think, to this day, that she is either. She just felt a need to redefine and pursue her own happiness. And she waited until we were old enough for it not to matter so much. The fact that she didn't find her happiness is irrelevant. At least she won't die wondering. Which is why she's so afraid of death; because she still harbours hope.

It was unfortunate that the day of my birthday was also the day Micky's mum and dad happened to be moving out. They, too, were going their separate ways, the strain of it all having ruptured them in equal opposite measure to Elle and I coming together.

Debbie, Donnie and Davie came, as did a couple of people from school, and a few mates from the estate, but it was a small gathering as such things generally go. Mr and Mrs Glenn called in, as did Pat and Pat. Elle arrived with Perry, much to my chagrin.

Mum, Dad and Paul got me a new stereo system, an integrated stack, with a built-in turntable on top.

Perry gave me something for which I forsook the Wanker prefix for a few months on consumption of. He presented me with a pile of his old albums. They're worth a pretty penny now, and I still have them all. There were Vertigo swirls and green Brains and private label folk LPs - about twenty records in all. He had duplicates from when he worked in a record shop somewhere at some time.

Seven or eight months earlier, and I'd have sneered at them, but no more. I didn't know a track on them. I'd heard of none of the artists. So I approached them with my mind and ears open, without any Micky prejudgement. And, in most instances, I loved what I heard. Indeed, I've been attempting to fill in the gaps ever since.

All that said, he was still sitting on our sofa with Elle when I opened them, one knee crossed over the other so that his flares touched her leg, his arm along the back of the settee so that it disappeared behind her. Wanker.

I don't recall what Elle was wearing that day, but she looked stunning. Even my Mum dryly remarked to me during the evening, "she is a strikingly attractive girl, that Eleanor. But a bit serious and aloof. And she's too old for you, Digger. Watch yourself there. Anyway, are you having a good day, my love?"

Piss off.

Debbie had somewhat embraced the fashion of the moment. It was just as the much revered Madonna was transitioning from spiral permed cuteness, to something more darkly serious. Depeche Mode had got the balance right, and were singing about kinky sex and god having a sick sense of humour. Dead Or Alive were spinning her head like a record. But, at the end of the day, David Cassidy still had the last kiss.

Everybody had left bar some of the neighbours, and while the adults, including Perry, sipped at their Liebfraumilchs, us younger ones swigged from cans of lager and listened to my new records on my new system.

Mainly to appease the adults, I stuck to Perry's oldies, and fell completely for Folkal Point's take on 'Scarborough Fair'. It is to this day my favourite interpretation of that song. And there are a lot of versions to choose from.

But I held back on the Sisters Of Mercy LP that Elle gave me. I'd play that when I was alone, through the headphones that Mr and Mrs Glenn had got me, "so we shan't have to hear all that modern rubbish! I say, give me music where you can hear the words. That's what I say!"

To which Mrs Glenn had smiled sympathetically at me, and warned, "don't play it too loud through those phonio things, Digger, or you'll damage your ears."

"Damage your brain, more like, listening to that rubbish!" Mr Glenn summed up.

Being a Sunday, Pat and Pat departed at the same time as the Glenns; work on the morrow. About half an hour later, Perry went to leave, asking Elle if she required walking home. She didn't. She'd just listen to the other side of the current album, and then think about going.

Colin shot off next door to put the boys to bed, but came back and joined Dee, Mum and Dad at the dining table. Debbie idled sulkily in a chair biting the skin around the nail on her thumb, and Paul sat slumped in an armchair reading something or other to do with UFOs.

I stretched out on the now vacant sofa, and Elle slipped across and took up her familiar position in front of me, just as she would in my bedroom.

She turned and presented that view of herself to me, the one I so adored.

"Happy birthday," she said softly, and smiled with her feline eyes.

"We haven't played Elle's record!" Debbie exclaimed, rising abruptly.

"It's Digger's record, not mine," Elle pointed out.

"Yeah, I know that," Debbie replied, and shot a look that told of Elle's stupidity.

"Then it's up to him if he wants to play it," Elle said, a little nervously.

"I'll put it on for you, Digger darling!" Debbie sang as she opened the gatefold cover.

And as the 'First And Last And Always' LP was drawn out, so a note with slanted handwriting fell to the floor. 'Digger x' graced the envelope.

Elle leaned forward and grabbed it before Debbie could react.

"Is that a love letter?" Debbie asked quietly.

"It's just a letter," Elle answered.

Clumsily the record was cued up, and the needle descended, missing the run-in. The title track came through the speakers, the wrong side having been played first.

Elle turned to me again, and handed me my letter. As I took it, I was sure that she deliberately found my fingers with hers.

Paul read on in his chair. The chatter continued from the dining table. Debbie pulled a face at the music, and mumbled something about the strange voice, and was it on the wrong speed?

At that moment I reached my hand forward and delicately touched the back of Elle's neck.

She didn't flinch or pull away. In fact, she shuffled slightly closer to me, and tipped her head to one side so that I might find her neck more ably and move up to her ear. I traced it with the tip of my middle finger.

I knew then. My life made sense to me.

Looking up, I saw that Debbie knew it too, and such a look of hatred, undiluted detestation, twisted her entire face. I thought she might start crying. I thought that she might actually vomit.

Elle didn't see. She had her eyes closed when she half turned her face so that she might gently kiss my hand.

And later, when I walked Elle home, all the way to three doors up, our arms around one another and our hips rising and falling with un-clashing symmetry as though we were made to measured order - that was when I saw Micky's mum leaving number thirteen, her gaunt white face and hooded eyes staring at me out of the side window of the car.

A look of hatred was projected at me, its poisoned barbs peppering me.

How dare I be happy? Barely six months had passed. And with her, of all people!

My self-satisfied elated grin dissolved, and a shudder swept through me that Elle picked up through her arm.

She saw and she felt my anguish.

For one day I'd succeeded in forgetting about everything, but there it was laid bare before me again.

I didn't have opportunity to think another thought. Her lips were on mine and opening me up. My senses began registering one by one; the beer on her breath, the warmth of her lips on my mouth; the softness of her tongue as it entered me; the taste of her saliva. And my eyelids swept down, removing the image I'd just seen as it was stricken from me. For then, at least, and for all the time that I was with Elle.

It was more than just a kiss; it was more like a kiss of life.

19.

The porch rattles. Bean growls a warning, and I rise to answer it. It's a familiar friendly face that I welcome.

"All right, pal? I'm sorry to call unannounced," Johnny Peters says.

"No problem, Johnny. It's good to see you. How are things?" We were at school together, and he's an Oaklea man.

The handshake is warm and sincere.

"Not bad at all. I was sorry to hear about your dad. He was always good to me when I was a kid, and always had time for me later."

"Thank you."

"The funeral's tomorrow, isn't it?"

"It is. At Millby Crem at eleven. Come by and have a drink at the Mill at midday, Johnny. Please. You'd be very welcome."

"Ah, work, Digger. If I can, I shall, you have my word. But I'll be honest, it probably isn't going to happen."

I bend and pick up the post. Bills to be paid, which Paul said to leave until the finances had been sorted by the solicitor.

"Come in," I say.

"I can't stay, but I wanted to catch up with you." I see the silver regalia on the shoulders of the black uniform beneath his coat, and it dawns on me that this may be more than a friendly call. The coat is unnecessary on this warm autumnal day, so he wore it to hide his police uniform. And he came in his own car; no sirens, blue light or orange stripe to draw attention.

"What's up?" I ask.

"Nothing. I wanted to call anyway. But I need to ask; has Immleigh been bothering you?"

"Ah, not really. He follows me sometimes, and I've seen him watching me. He's harmless enough."

"Would you say that he's harassing you?"

"No, not quite that."

"You're sure?"

"Yes. Don't worry about it, Johnny."

"Have you spoken with him?"

"A couple of times. He called here, and he pulled over in his car."

"And what did he say to you?"

"The usual."

He nods his understanding. "He's eaten up, Digger. He's a private citizen now, so I can't rein him in in any official capacity. But there are laws in place to deal with this kind of thing."

"Honestly, I don't think it'll be necessary. He's saying the same things he was saying thirty years ago. I can kind of understand it. His niece went missing on the same day that I left town, and given my history with him…" I cut myself off, not wanting to go through the Micky situation again. I don't need to; Johnny was around at the time.

"It was just a coincidence, wasn't it, Digger? You seeing her at the station in Millby, and again in Tredmouth?"

"Absolutely. I give you my word. I boarded the train and travelled alone that day."

His dark hair is worn away at the sides of his forehead where a hat has been donned for years; the constant friction exhausting the new supply from the follicles. The remainder looks like a number two buzz cut. He's still handsome, though, and in good shape. He always had the type of build that would stand the test of time.

"And where did you stay in Tredmouth?"

"Nowhere. I told him that. I walked the streets for hours, snatched an hour's sleep in the waiting room, and boarded the first train to London in the morning."

"Where you stayed with your uncle, correct?"

"For several weeks while I found my feet. He gave a statement at the time."

"Okay, sorry to ask," Johnny says, shrugging at me.

"It's fine. Hey, so Dad said that you'd risen through the ranks. Congratulations."

"Thanks. Somehow I've ended up as Chief Constable of Brakeshire," he chuckles.

"Like I said; congratulations," I repeat, and offer him my hand.

The shy self-effacing dimple-inducing smile he had as a child is still present. He was always one of those kids - the first to be selected for the team, whatever the sport might be. And he was smart. Perhaps not academically, but he was smart when it came to people. And I never met anyone with a bad word to say about him. Had I considered it at the time, I'd have pegged him for a career in the police force. Whatever path he'd have taken, he'd have been a success.

"Sorry to intrude, Dig, especially given the timing. I'll be thinking of you tomorrow. And I'll always smile when I think of your dad."

"Much appreciated, Johnny. I'll see you."

"See you. And get in touch if Immleigh bothers you, okay? Promise me, Dig?"

"I promise."

"Don't go doing anything stupid."

"I won't."

He nods a final time, and wheels away, his highly buffed black shoes cracking like a cap-gun off the paving slabs.

Johnny Peters knows me. As captain of the school football team he'd pick me from the touchline early on. He always said that it wasn't because I was a better player than some of the others, but he knew that he could rely on me. He'd play at centre-back, and put me alongside him. 'Dig in!' was the apt instruction as he took the ball forward. And I always would. He was a good leader even back then - the kind of bloke you'd want next to you in the trenches; the one you'd go the extra mile for.

He was by my side when the two lads said something about my role in Micky's death; some comment that mentioned Elle and compared her to Myra Hindley.

Those cracks of his shoes remind me of the sound of a skull being driven in to the brick wall of the changing rooms.

Johnny stopped me that day, but the police were still called. Immleigh came sniffing and asking his questions, and this was long before his niece went missing. He had it in for me even then.

I discovered that a reputation was very easily established, but so hard to shake.

~~~~~

I'm waiting; killing time. Wasting time should be added to the list of commandments. Thou shalt not waste time.

A script for a radio play has sat unmolested in my case since arrival. Work holds no interest for me here. Consoling myself with the fact that it is just one week of my life, and that by this time on Sunday I will be back home, I find energy enough to tackle Dad's bedroom. Bean accompanies me.

Dad's clothes hang in the wardrobe and lie in drawers. I'm compelled to check the pockets, and squeeze his socks for anything neglectfully left behind or stashed for safekeeping. There is nothing. I lift his mattress, but no gold sovereigns or secrets lie under there, but I still feel guilty for looking.

His clothing gets folded in half and laid into black bin bags, each with red pulls pinching the tops closed. If I can get this done in time, I'll run them down to the Heart Foundation shop in Lower Millby.

Removing his clothes feels so final. It's the first time it's really sunk in that he won't ever be requiring them again. A thought occurs to me, so I call Paul and ask if Dad will be needing a suit? He won't. There's no viewing, and it's too late now, anyway; he'll be cremated in whatever he arrived at the undertaker's in.

All of Dad's garments are a bit shabby. There is no colour in his attire. I take a silk tie, charcoal to almost black, and decide to wear it tomorrow for the funeral. I'll keep it afterwards. It'll be nice to wear something of Dad's on the day; something old, new, borrowed and black. The oils from his hands will still be on the fabric where he tied the knot. perhaps on the day of Mrs Glenda Glenn's funeral.

Except that she never officially was a Glenn. Nor was she ever a Mrs. She was simply Glenda, but not to Mr Glenn. To him she was everything.

Bean leaps away, startled by the rustle of the bags as I begin to lug them down the stairs. He watches me through the balusters as I toil, the third trip up and down leaving me short of breath. I am older.

Am I old? It doesn't seem that long ago that I could have run up and down here all day long without pause. All of those thousands of days - ten thousand and more, comprising hundreds of weeks. I dread to think of the hours, but can't help myself. I work it roughly, rounding the numbers up or down, whichever is closer. That can't be right, can it? Fifteen million minutes in thirty years can't be correct?

It is, I find on checking. And that works out to about twenty-five million in my life. How many can I even recall accurately? When you condense it down, my entire life, all of its notable moments can be captured in perhaps four hours. Two hundred and forty of twenty-five million defines me. I think that's about 0.001%. Is that one hundred-thousandth?

Moreover, is that normal? Are those proportions the same for everybody? I have no idea.

I play with the figures some more as I stand outside the back door and smoke a cigarette, Bean territorially checking the perimeter of the garden.

Elle and I spent roughly four hours a day together as a couple for two years. That is about one half of a percent, or a two-hundredth of my life. It is, I realise, insane that I've spent so much of the remaining 99.5 percent of my life thinking about her, and allowing her to shape my decisions.

Yet she has. Even at the most intimate of moments with others, she would populate it. Debbie described her as 'an alien species that escapes and infiltrates the world', and perhaps she's correct.

When having sex with women, I've checked to see if they clung to me on withdrawal in the same way that Elle would. And I know that sounds strange and was the wrong thing to be thinking of in that moment, but I couldn't help myself. That minute or two that I observed Elle in similar circumstances left such an impression that I've carried it with me for fifteen million minutes since.

The answer is that it never did in the same way. Nobody fitted me as snugly as Elle did. Nobody was ever quite right after her.

Dad's life may have contained a higher proportion of minute memories than mine, because he did marry Mum, and he did have Paul and I to help create them. But really, when you boil it down, how many of his forty million minutes truly mattered and were recalled at the very end? Even if he tragically lay there for hours before he expired, how many did he make count?

~~~~~

September 2nd 1986 "...My wonderful Lover. You complete me. It is as though I've never been whole before, and just having you close, as close as it is possible for two people to be, fills me with something more than just the physical. You enter me in every sense, and I feel elation beyond anything I've ever known before. I could happily die in that moment, and know that there would be no better time to go. If that memory and sensation could stay with me for all time after death, I'd take it, just so that I could preserve it. But no! How could I be without the physical you? I hope we die together, Digger my Love, eighty years from now, having never been apart for a single day or night. Will we still have sex when we're nearly a hundred? Perhaps we could both die of heart attacks at that exact moment? But that's all too morbid! I prefer to think of my life with you, and the millions of minutes we have ahead of us - will you savour every single one, just as I shall? I feel braver because I'm with you. And I know that you say the same about me, that I give you strength and confidence, but I fear nothing when I think of us. It feels so perfectly right. You feel so perfectly right for me! Tonight, when you withdrew from me, it felt a little as I imagine death might feel. That was why I reached out to you, just to be sure that you were still there and that I was still alive and capable of feeling all that I am incapable of describing accurately! Do you really want to marry me, my Love, or was that just something said in the afterglow of intimacy? If you were serious, then I submit in writing that I absolutely will - nothing would make me happier. I just know, Digger - I know that we are right for one another, so where is the sense in waiting? My feelings shall never change. All of my love is yours.   *Lx."*

20.

Everybody is staring at me. Some people look at me a little concernedly. I nod some greetings to familiar faces, both the vague and better known, but don't smile. And I look for her.

She isn't present.

I think the people stare because I have Bean with me, a black piece of fabric from the lining of one of Dad's suits cut to a triangle and tied around his neck.

Either that, or I'm naked and this is all a dream.

I couldn't leave him behind. He looked so sad as I dressed...

"What the bloody hell are you doing?" Paul hisses in my ear as he steers me away from the fractured gatherings of people.

"What do you mean?" I tease.

"You can't bring the dog!"

"Why not? It's not like they serve hot food, is it?" I ask, turning my head to the chimney stack rising high from the rear roof of the low building.

"You'll have to take him back to Dad's."

"No!" I say, a tetchiness allowed to colour the word. "Dad would have wanted him here," I add dismissively.

He deserves to be here, and I need him here.

Paul knows better than to argue. "Keep him under bloody control!"

Seeing how my brother distanced me from the doors, I light a cigarette. I'll give up after I get home.

"I think it's no smoking," a voice says, and I turn to see Debbie's father addressing me.

"All right, Colin?" I say, and switch the lead to my left hand, the ciggie between my fingers as I greet him with the traditional handshake.

"All right? I was going to come round in the week, but our Don and our Deb said they'd seen you. I thought you'd have probably had enough of our lot after that!" He laughs at his own little joke. He always did that, laughed at himself. It's nerves, I think.

"Ah, Paul's had me busy at the house, Colin," I say, as I continue smoking, "and I've had the dog to tend to. Is all the family here?"

"Should be. Dee's there look, being talked at by Mr Glenn, and Don and his wife are by the wall. Dave was picking Debs up, but she'll cut it fine. That way she gets the grand entrance and maximum attention!" He chuckles again, and I smile along and squeeze some air out my nostrils to keep it company. There's nothing sadder than a solo laugh.

"Who else do I know, Colin?"

"Having trouble remembering? Well, it has been a while, lad. I'm assuming you know your sister-in-law! Heh-heh. Hey, you know who that is on the left of your Paul? That's Perry!"

He looks... He looks like I'd hoped he'd look. Gone are the smart Yuppie clothes he left here in, and back are the flares and a black velvet jacket with silk lapels. He has a black scarf knotted jauntily around his neck. It looks a bit like Bean's neck scarf. His hair is long, straggly and grey, with enough grease in it to fry chips. A cragginess completes him, as his little eyes peer through a pair of silver rimmed round Lennonesque glasses.

He spots me looking at him, and flutters a hand and a crooked white-toothed smile.

I can't stop myself scanning the car park to see if his Perrywanker blue MG Midget is there. It isn't, sadly.

But I do see Immleigh sat in his car watching me. He can't even let it go today, of all days.

He-Pat and She-Pat walk up the slope. Alone. They hold hands, and it makes me smile to see them like that. She's an inch taller than him, more with her slight heels, and she looks classy in her black suit and blouse. He looks proud to have her by his side. Love still burns between Pat and Pat.

And I think of Mr Glenn, Reg. The last time he was here may have been for his Glenda, the poor old sod. It must be breaking his heart all over again, the being back.

"All right, Pats!" Colin calls out, and laughs.

"Hello Colin," they reply, "Digger."

"All right?" I say.

"I should go and rescue Dee!" Colin announces, "hey, I heard Reg say he was having Bean. Is that right?"

"That's the plan," I confirm. "I reckon they might be good for each other. Everybody needs somebody."

"Oh, aye, it'll suit Reg Glenn," Colin says as he readies himself to depart, "having something that can't answer back! Heh-heh-heh!"

"How are you holding up, Digger?" She-Pat asks kindly.

"I'm fine, thanks."

Where is she? Where's Elle?

It's awkward, the lack of anything to say. I can't say what I want to ask. "Weather feels like it'll hold off," is my safe option, my eyes following a car that pulls in, a silver Toyota.

Is this her?

A man emerges first from the passenger door of the car followed by a man and woman from the rear; Tony Swann and a couple I don't know. The car must be a cab, as it drives away.

Immleigh watches on.

"They're saying rain at about one, I think," He-Pat says, "but we'll be done by then, and in the pub."

"I could use a pint," I truthfully admit, even though it's the ante meridian.

"There are some nice beers at the Mill," Swanny booms, greeting everybody enthusiastically.

"I was telling Digger that the other day," Don chips in as he joins us, and lights a smoke when he sees that I'm smoking.

Suddenly hands are in mine, and women are putting their motherly arms around me as I'm re-introduced to people I once knew, and introduced to those that I never have known.

And it's okay. All of it is fine, the fractured assemblage coming together as any degree of separation is addressed through someone knowing someone who knows someone. That was always how Oaklea worked, and Millby more generally. You could never get away with anything, because somebody always knew somebody.

The talk is vibrant and friendly, and it pleases me, just as I know that it would have pleased Dad. This is a day for him, I decide, and turn away from the car park. To buggery with everything else until I'm alone again.

A summons comes from Jen, and Don and I look for a bin for our cigarette butts. There isn't one. All that ash, and no ashtray. I tug a crap-bag of Bean's from my pocket and we deposit our extinguished trash in there. I'll get rid of it later.

As we enter the crematorium, a man looks at Bean, but I must cut a figure of a man who it's best not to question on this day.

I'm ordered by Jen to sit on the front pew, "with me and the rest of the family."

Bean sits at my feet on the far right of the bench.

Mum appears, breathing heavily as though she's been running. The greetings are swift, the time arriving, a body to be disposed of.

Music plays. Pachelbel's 'Canon', but the slower version from more modern times. Every wedding and funeral tends to use it. And it is beautiful. But did Dad even know it? He did, I remember. He liked the Christmas version with the choir adding words.

Mum sits behind me, relegated to the second tier, and I feel her hand on the side of my face; cold, like the dead. She's alone; no funeral-face Jim by her side.

I turn, smile, and can't help looking over the room.

Where is she?

"You brought the dog?" Mum whispers.

"I know," I reply, in case she thought it had occurred by accident, or stealth on his part.

"Oh, good grief! Well, I suppose he did love his dogs more than he ever loved me!"

Let it go, let it all go.

A kerfuffle at the rear shifts my focus, Debbie arriving with Davie, her timing ensuring that all heads swivel to see her. Her eyes meet mine as she scans the room, and rest there for a millisecond before continuing. I think she's looking for Elle, and a little smile tells of her satisfaction at not seeing her. She sits alongside her family on the opposite wing.

The weeble figure of Ralph Brierley fills the stage, as he addresses most of his comments to the family on the first row, but taking in the rest of the room where applicable. Bean gets a mention, and the gathering titters or tuts in unison.

A list of who he leaves behind; two sons, Paul and Douglas; Jennifer, his daughter-in-law being like the daughter he never had, and two beautiful granddaughters, Charlotte and Hannah.

All of the buzz words are reeled off - we should have had a bingo card. Caring, thoughtful, trust, honest, responsible, gentle, hard-working, conscientious, a good neighbour, reliable, loving, 'a man who knew what was, ah, important in life.'

House!

Letters are mentioned, and my head snaps up. It's a letter by Paul. Not that one, I quickly realise.

It's a biblical passage, but Humpty Dumpty seems to look at me as he reads it.

"If I give away all I have,
and if I deliver my body to be burned,
but have not love,
I gain nothing.
Love is patient and kind;
love is not jealous or boastful;
it is not arrogant or rude.
Love does not insist on its own way;
it is not irritable or resentful;
it does not rejoice at wrong, but rejoices in the right.
Love bears all things,
believes all things,
hopes all things,
endures all things.

Love never ends;
as for prophecies, they will pass away;
as for tongues, they will cease;
as for knowledge, it will pass away.
For our knowledge is imperfect
and our prophecy is imperfect;
but when the perfect comes,
the imperfect will pass away.
When I was a child,
I spoke like a child,
I thought like a child,
I reasoned like a child;
when I became a man,
I gave up childish ways.
For now we see in a mirror dimly,
but then face to face.
Now I know in part; then I shall understand fully,
even as I have been fully understood.
So faith,
hope,
love
abide, these three;
but the greatest of these
is love."

Some modern track I've never heard before is played through the speakers at low volume. I'm grateful for that because it's bloody awful. Ah, that explains it; it was selected by his granddaughters.

Paul offers the explanation, and prattles on awkwardly about someone I don't really know, the black necktie choking him, the collar of his shirt a size too small and making his neck bulgy and red. The top button will be unpicked before we get to the pub, I'll wager. A loving grandfather. A good neighbour. A man who was respected and liked by all he met. His summer projects and ex-wife. His two sons, his work, as he provided and never complained. A man of integrity. A hard-working man of honour.

I hear Mum tut behind me, and imagine her shaking her head.

Too soon the pine box is propelled on rollers towards a black pair of curtains.

Did any bastard check that he was dead?

I find Bean's neck with what nails I have on the fingers of my right hand, and he pushes against me. I grip the dense fur that lies there beneath his black sash, and I hold everything in check.

I have an urge to toss Dad a final smoke now that he has a light handy.

It makes me smile, that thought, and I have to clamp my lips to stop it manifesting as a laugh. Is it nerves, like Colin, that makes me want to laugh? Is it based on only being able to show one emotion at any time, and so I laugh rather than cry?

Bittersweet is a fallacy.

Bean presses more firmly against my leg; enough to make me believe that if I were to remove it he would topple over. I use the flat of my hand to smooth the whiskery sides of his face, as we hold each other up.

Oh, Dad, I'm sorry! I'm sorry that I didn't spend more time with you. I'm sorry that I never asked the questions that needed asking, and that I never heard your answers. I'm sorry, Dad. But I couldn't.

The coffin is gone, the curtains sweeping closed - no panto screw-up, I'm delighted to report. There's a noise, an eerie sound of fire intensifying, I think, and I want to be outside so that I can see him go up in smoke - that last conversion of what he was to what he now is; dust. The result of that conversion is dust and what else?

Smoke. As it spews from a chimney, and is carried, I hope, to the north where it can sink down as it cools, and settle in the shallow ravines on the Humpty Dumpty Field, so that he shall never have to cross it again.

Bye, Dad. I love you.

21.

'Let It Be' escorted us out.

All the while I looked for her, but she wasn't there. I was offered lifts, but declined, citing the dog as my reason for so doing. We both needed the air and exercise. We both needed to be alone together.

"I owe you one," I say to him, as he pauses to investigate a tuft of grass at the base of a road sign.

He glances askance at me with those shining eyes of his, and pops his purple tongue out by way of reply. It looks like a smile of gratitude. It looks like he's been eating a pack of Chewits.

It's another half a mile to the pub, but I feel no need to hurry now as I let Bean dictate the pace. I'm happy to linger and let him sniff. It's his walk, after all, not mine. All of them were his, and would never have taken place were he not present.

What do I feel? Relief, I think. There's a sense of relief stemming from the funeral being over, and from it going off hitch-free. There's a relief from being a step closer to departure. Just a couple of hours in the pub and the Will reading and aftermath to get through.

Even Immleigh had gone when I emerged. I saw him standing at the back of the hall when Debbie sought the limelight, but he wasn't present when I turned to leave.

So that Bean might feel grass beneath his paws, I cut a corner across a modest triangular expanse of open land towards Mill Lane and the Old Mill public house. The pub appeared in the late-nineties, and it is the ruinous mill in close proximity that carries the age.

I can't enter with the dog, but I knew that when I decided to bring him. I'd reconnoitered the establishment when I dropped Dad's clothes off, and ascertained that they had an outdoor seating area, replete with propane heaters and a roof overhead. It breaks up the crowd that way, and allows me to not get lost in it. I've always preferred small gatherings to large ones. To be honest, I prefer one-on-ones to small gatherings, but this is a day when that won't be possible.

"What are you having, Dig?" Davie and Donnie ask before I can get through the gate.

"A pint of what you have looks good," I say, greeting Davie like the old friend he is. "But I'll get this one. Look," I continue, "here's two hundred, cash. I need to stay with the dog, but could I ask you to stick that behind the bar and make sure everyone gets a drink? Do you think it'll be enough?"

"Sod that!" Don smilingly states. "We'll hold the dog. You get in there and say hello. People want to see you, Dig."

"Thanks lads. I didn't like to ask," I lie.

'This side of the pub is closed for a private function', I read on a blackboard. A tide of bodies part to allow me passage, and I smile grimly and exchange words with people as I head to the bar.

A chat with the landlord sets everything up, and he announces that everyone can claim a free drink at the bar 'on the family'. He'll let me know when they run out of money.

Paul grabs me, his tie yanked down and collar gaping, a pint in his hand, another shoved in mine. "Thanks for that," he says, and nods towards the bar, "we can't really afford it, with the kids and everything."

"It's fine. I wanted to do it," I tell him, which is true.

"How was my speech?" he asks me quietly, his mouth close to my ear.

"It was great," I report to him. With Dad gone, I suppose he needs my approval now.

"I spent hours on it. Jen helped a lot."

"She's been brilliant," I tell him, because it's what he needs to hear.

"Thanks for what you did in the house. It'll make things easier."

A word catches my ear; more a letter than a word. "L," is called over the crowd.

I'm on my tiptoes, taller than most present, and looking for her.

"L," it comes again, and I see the caller is Swanny, and he's waving at someone. I spin and search for her.

A woman appears, a path clearing for her. It can't be!

An enormous woman looms into view. Yes, she's tall, but she's almost as wide as she is high. And with a red face that erupts to reveal yellow teeth...

I search for her amidst the folds. What colour are her eyes behind the thick tinted lenses? And why is her hair vaguely purple?

"All right, Lindsey?" Paul says to her as she passes us, "I don't think you've met my brother, Digger? This is Lindsey - Swanny's wife."

"All right, love!" she booms, because she is one of those warm open-hearted people who don't do reserved.

I'm seized and pulled to her, my pint slopping a tongue of fluid that slaps the floor playfully, and I'm buried in the folds of her ample bosom. "Sorry about your dad, love."

"Thanks," I mumble.

"Leave her alone, Digger!" Swanny says, "the woman needs a bloody drink! Pint of lager, Linds?"

"Please, please. Spitting feathers, I am!"

And after I've blustered out a few civil words, Paul does the most astute thing I believe he's ever done.

Bringing his mouth close to my ear again, I hear him breathe out, "relax, Pat told me that she'll be here soon. She's been on a teacher training course in York, and her train was delayed. And she's still gorgeous. You wanker."

We both laugh, and it feels good. It's a long time since we laughed together.

And so I move through the fair, pulled here and there by the energy of the day. Brief words and actions blur by as I make my way back to Bean and the fresh air. I hear 'sorry' and 'loss' a score of times, and smile at anecdotes and memories.

She'll be here soon.

Bean lies by the side of a table, a bowl of water placed for him by some person more thoughtful than me.

It is a happy wake, full of sound and friendly chatter. It went that way naturally, as these things tend to do, I imagine. Some may be maudlin and morose, people sat around tables in small groups, muttering sentiments about the deceased, a wail of grief pervading through the scene every now and then. But this is one of the happy ones - a celebration of a man. My Dad.

Bean wags his tail at me, and rises to his feet. I sit by him, Davie shuffling along to accommodate me, another pint placed in front of me by Donnie before I'm half way through the last one.

Debbie appears and smiles her smile at me - 'all tits and teeth' as Dad would have termed it. Her orange skin has been suitably tempered down for the day with a trowel full of foundation, her eyes made up darkly so that the bright blue irises look like patches of blue in an otherwise stormy sky.

"Sorry about the other day, Digger," she says sincerely when she gets the chance, the conversation having moved away from us momentarily. "I'm just going through a bad time, that's all," she adds, and rests her hand on mine.

Her black hat and little black dress suit her; a neat and tidy curvaceous bundle held up by black suede boots with high heels, black fishnet covered legs connecting the parts.

"It's fine," I tell her, and smile placidly. I remove my hand from hers in order to grasp my drink, the other occupied holding the dog's leash.

She'll be here soon, and I don't want her seeing that.

Music seeps out through the pub door, live and acoustic, a man and a guitar. Jen's brother, performing for free as long as we provide his drinks. I've seen him drink. It would have been cheaper to get the Rolling Stones.

You can't always get what you want.

Debbie is gone; to the bar for another drink. A gin that will be her ruin. Bob and Diane are here with the twins, Mark and Kerry-Anne. They sit for a while and we exchange pleasantries, all of them bedecked in sombre blacks and dark greys that I imagine aren't much of a deviation from their regular clothing.

Kerry-Anne finds my leg with hers and I feel it gently rub up and down me, her face a picture of purity as she sits across from me, the contact hidden by the wooden table. She does it in a way that it could be interpreted as being in innocence, and she believes that she's touching the table frame. But a little sly glance up at me betrays her, along with a smile that could either be sympathy or lust.

I'm not interested. Too young. Too silly. Too dishonest. Get someone your own age and have a happy life. Break a fucking rule or two, and stop acting a part for mummy and daddy.

I turn away from her and chat with Bob, my back to the pathway leading in as I face the pub. I make introductions as required; Perry to Bob and Diane and their little children. He already knows them, but he takes them off my hands.

Bean is turning away from me, his lead unfurling slightly. My thumb on the lock, half depressed, stops his progress. He stands still, his tail wagging and shifting the air.

Rain begins to pad down, large lazy dollops of moisture that splotch on the light brown pathway and begin to darken it to the colour of Millby mud. The roof keeps us dry, the wind calm and not moving the rain in on us.

Turning a semicircle on the bench to see what Bean is attracted by, I know that it's Elle solely by the way she moves.

Her head is masked by the black umbrella she carries, tipped forward to protect her from the rain. She wears black - trousers and a jacket, both nicely cut to extend her height and nipped in at the waist. Sensible black shoes find purchase on the damp pavers, and a small line of light grey shows at her cuffs, matched by the triangle at her neck.

My stomach feels as though it's falling through me, and my face, in the space of ten seconds, goes from a dreadful cold paleness I can see on my nose and cheeks, to a red flush of intense heat. Is that what Dad felt at the last?

My ears burn as though two people are arguing over my character.

Left for love, right for spite.

I draw a fortifying breath and will myself to settle. The cool air lessens my glow, and I fix my eyes on her, waiting until she has no option but to lower the umbrella. I set my face to the slightest of calm smiles, just my lips showing it, but it tugs ever so slightly at the outside edges of my eyes.

Bean appears to her first, and she sinks down, her knees stretching the material of her suit, her thighs slim even in a squat.

"Hello Bean boy!" she purrs as she fusses him, not caring about the hairs on her black clothes, and I remember the voice. I remember all the things it said to me as it whispered in the dark.

As her umbrella is tipped to one side, she raises her head and my pulse pounds as my eyes mist over and all I can see of her is an outline that matches every outline I've ever sketched of her.

I blink rapidly and reset my vision. And for the first time in thirty years, I look on Love.

She is an older version of what she was. But I would have recognised her. All the while, as I looked, and wondered if I'd missed her, I now know that I didn't. She is as she was. I simply never saw her again.

"Hello," is all I say.

"Hello." She blinks but doesn't remove her eyes from mine. A little ripple of something - emotion? - darts from the corner of her mouth and along her pronounced cheek bone. She must feel it, and brings a hand up to smooth it away. It's as though she's wiping a tear that isn't there.

"I'm glad you could come," I tell her.

That's an understatement.

"Sorry. Sorry for not being here before now. And I'm sorry about your dad, Digger; so very sorry." It feels like she's apologising for more than she states, so I smile a little broader, and nod that it's all fine. Everything is fine. It always was when she was with me.

Her hair is bay with blonde highlights and cut to the shape of her neck...

"All right, Elle!"

"Come on in out the damp."

"Can I get you a drink?"

"What was wrong with the trains?"

Our connection is broken.

"Hello!" Elle calls generally.

She collapses her brolly, shakes it, and leans it against the table. "Will you look after that for me, please, you beautiful boy?"

She's talking to the dog.

Her hand finds my shoulder as she passes, our first physical contact since Monday May the twenty-fifth, 1987 - a Bank Holiday. It was almost midnight when Pat and Pat told me that I had to go, that Elle had an early start the next day.

"We'll talk," she says, "let's talk later."

And she's gone from me again.

My eyes follow her up the path; such elegance. Such dignity.

He-Pat watches me from the doorway, a pint in his hand resting on his folded arms. He nods and turns away. Debbie stares through the front window, her top teeth chewing her bottom lip anxiously.

Turning back, Kerry-Anne moodily avoids looking at me, her lips set in a pout, her arms folded over her chest, one hand playing rhythmically with the heart hanging from the gold chain around her neck.

I bring Bean's face to mine and put my hands where Elle's were, my face where hers went, and another pint is placed before me, sent out by someone inside.

Jen's brother strums away earnestly, and has a stab at carving out 'Wonderwall'. Stab and carve being the correct words, as he butchers it.

My hand drops to my side, slips inside my jacket, and finds the scar through my shirt where Micky slashed me with a penknife.

Each time I look the scene changes. Don and Davie stand to free up the bench seats as they smoke and drink, laughing with Paul and Swanny, as Mum appears by my side, Jen opposite.

"Where are the girls?" I ask.

"At school."

"Of course. I keep forgetting it's a Friday."

I would have liked to have seen them. I put some money in a card for them, which I hand to Jen. I couldn't think what else to do. She slips it in her bag and smiles at me.

She's steady. I've always liked Jen. Even the money thing; it's only because she wants the best for her children, and, to be honest, I'd have a problem with her if that wasn't the case.

"I'm sorry I haven't seen you all week, Digger, but there was a lot to do," she says, and I nod that I understand.

Elle said that we'd talk later.

Mum takes over as Jen's brother rewards himself with a barely-earned break, a CD more than adequately replacing him.

"Are you all right?" Mum says to me.

"I am. Are you?"

"I still can't believe it."

"Where's Jim? I thought he was driving you up?"

"Ugh, don't even ask me. He wanted us to get a hotel for the night - a double room! I don't want that! Not with him, anyway! I mean, I like him, and I know that he likes me, but I only like him as a friend. That's all. Why do they all want me, these men? I don't understand it. I don't know what they see in me, do you?"

"It's not my place to say."

Stephen Stills' 'Love The One You're With' reaches my ears in the lull.

I hate this song with a passion. Not the tune, but the sentiment. If I can't be with Elle, I know that I will never love. That was true before today, but is reinforced by seeing her again. I will be alone for the rest of my life, I now understand for the first time.

"Don't you want a relationship, Mum?"

She sighs and takes my hand in hers. "I do. But not like before; not for the sake of it."

"Was Dad for the sake of it?"

"Not at first. But I stayed for you and Paul. I should have gone sooner, Digger. Sorry to say that."

"It's okay. I get it. Do you remember when you told me to change my life if I was ever unhappy?"

"No. When did I say that? Phhh! You can't expect to be happy all the time, Digger."

"No, I don't suppose I can."

"Besides, I love my life! I love my house and being by the sea. I love my friends and I have my health. Oh no, I wouldn't change a thing in my life! I was just saying to Dee about my new carpet, I love my new carpet..."

Love the one you're with. Especially when you're on your own.

~~~~~

Time marches on. One or two people head out, hands shaken along with heads. Healing hugs are administered. It all tells me that I am not alone.

But I am.

The rain has stopped, the shower having freshened everything and wiped the slate clean. The money ran out at the bar some time ago, but it isn't stopping anyone. I slip Paul one of the pints accumulating that I don't have the stomach for. It feels like a good time to walk Bean around the pub garden.

Wanker Perry is at my side unannounced, as Bean leads us to a hedge he deems worthy of further investigation. A likely place for squirrels to lurk, and birds to hide.

"All right, Dig man?"

"All right, Perry?"

"It's going well, I think."

"It is," I confirm.

"Nice to see a few old faces."

"Yours included," I say, and smile at his thin old face.

"I won the lottery," he suddenly states.

As I look at him with his shabby suit and unkemptness, it strikes me that he could probably use a few quid.

"Literally or metaphorically?" I need to ask, wondering if he's found religion or something.

"Oh, I see! No, literally."

"How much?"

"Just under three million pounds."

"What will you do with it?" I ask, the enormity of the sum not really sinking in.

"Hey? Oh, no, no. I won it twenty years ago. But I ticked the box about no publicity. Funny, really," he says.

"Is it?"

"Yes. I never needed the money, so I don't even know why I bought a ticket. I come from a rich family, see, so I've never needed to work unless I chose to. That's how come I could buy number eleven when I was in my early-twenties. But money's like that; it attracts itself, like eggshell. There's them that have it, and them that don't. Your Paul is always looking for it, and that's why he never finds it. Even if he did, the burden of having it would probably send him mad." He pauses from speaking while I light a cigarette, refusing one for himself, but I don't understand why he waits for me to do that. "Nobody knows," he softy tells me, and taps the side of his nose.

Is he across the Humpty Dumpty Field with the fairies?

"Why are you telling me?" I ask.

"Because I told your dad."

"Why?"

"Because I knew he was a man who could keep a secret. And I believe that you're the same. We all need someone to share things with, Dig. When it comes to a public face, you play everything here," he says, and draws his hands to his chest.

I smile. He's right. I always thought he was a bit stupid, but he's quite sharp.

"And he told me about the land," Perry continues in a knowing tone.

Now he has my full attention. Dad always maintained that he told nobody but me about that.

"It's a burden, Dig man. And it'll change everything for you when people find out. That's why I kept my inheritance a secret when I moved to Oaklea. It was a fresh start for me, and I wanted to be accepted on my own terms; for what I am, rather than what I have. Does that make sense?"

"Yes. Yes it does. But I can't keep mine a secret, can I, because of the Will?"

"No you can't. But be aware, Digger. Watch out for the worms that will come crawling out of the woodwork."

"I will. Thanks."

I'll be out of here. Nobody need know anything where I live. Besides, the land is worth nothing unless it's sold.

"I know you will. You're like your father. That closed nature of yours, though," he says, and waits to see if I nibble on the bait.

"What about it?" I ask nonchalantly.

"There's a downside to it."

"I'm not sure that there is."

"Oh, there is. Love is like money, you see," he says to me.

"In what way?" I ask, humouring him.

"It attracts itself. Ever noticed that it's always easier to get a woman when you've got a woman?"

"Erm, not really, no."

"You and Elle. If ever I saw a couple perfect for one another, it was you two. What happened, Digger?"

"You'd have to ask her."

"And she said that I'd have to ask you," he reports.

"Did she?"

"Yes."

"Just now?"

"No. The last time I saw her. At Mrs Glenn's funeral. She was there alone, and I couldn't fathom why. And now I see you here alone, as well."

"It's complicated."

He laughs. "Things are only complicated when you don't have all the information."

"I have all the data. And it's… It doesn't help," I tell him, the merest unintended hint of annoyance in my voice.

"Hmmm," he muses, "something's not right here. Something is amiss. And I wonder if it's because of that closed nature of yours. Do you love her?"

I feel my lips draw in, the single word affirmative response suppressed before I can utter it. "I did."

"Present tense: Do you love her?"

I find his eyes through the little round lenses and nod, before I return my focus to Bean and my smoke.

"I wanted her for myself. I wanted her more than any woman I've ever met," Perry tells me, "but I didn't stand a chance as soon as she really saw you. I would have given her everything. Every-fucking-thing, Digger!" he snaps as he takes a step closer to me.

I wonder if he's going to have a swing, but no. His hand finds my arm, and grips it tightly in passionate pleading, "but I may as well have been invisible from the moment she fell for you. All my money, all through the years, I would happily give away in exchange for her love! And you had it. But, as your dad said to me once - 'one of them fucked it up, and the other couldn't ever forgive. That's as much as I know.' But you remember, Digger; I won the lottery despite being rich."

With that, he wheels away, and I stand with Bean and finish the last few drags of my smoke. What did that mean?

A purpose takes hold of me, and I march back to the pub, Bean having to trot to keep up. Paul takes the lead, not that he had much say in the matter, and I'm inside, resenting every delay as Mr Glenn has a quick chat about his preparedness for the dog, and Mum and Dee give me cuddles as Debbie pouts, and Colin chuckles at something I can't focus on. Something not funny.

She's with Pat, Pat, the Swanns, and a woman called Fran who works in the newsagent.

There are men called Trevor and Gareth to meet, who Dad knew from work, and I must play my part and shake hands, exchange a few words but refuse a drink.

Finally, I reach her side, and she's prepared. She watched me slowly advance through the merry throng, her face cool, her glass empty. I saw no dread at the impending encounter. She said that we should talk later.

Now is later. Is it too late?

And I watched her the whole while, answering questions without fully turning to people, her eyes watching my progress as she smiled away the attentions of all around her.

She knew that I was coming to her.

"Can I get you a drink, Elle?"

She looks at her glass, but she already knows that it's empty. "Yes please, I think I'm ready for another."

"I'll get them," He-Pat says, "what would you like, Digger?"

"No, Pat, thank you. My shout. Pint?"

He nods, and I list the drinks in my head - three Best bitters, one lager, two pinots, one gin and tonic, no ice.

Three bitters, one lager, two pinots, one gin and tonic, no ice.

"I'll give you a hand," Elle says, and I instantly forget the order.

"Hi! Two Best bitters, a gin..."

"Three Best bitters, one lager, two large pinot grigios, and a G and T, no ice, please," Elle corrects from beside me.

"Thank you. How are you, Elle?"

"I'm pretty good, thanks. Forgetting this week, what about you?"

"I'm fine. Can't complain. You're teaching, I heard?"

"I am. Infants."

"That suits you, I think."

"Because it matches my intellect?" she says, and holds her face steady.

"No," I reply, wondering if she's annoyed but sensing that she isn't, "because you always had such patience."

"Not always."

"No, not always." An image of us falling into bed in desperate urgent need flashes across my mind. Is that what she means? It momentarily arouses me, and her eyes are fixed on mine when I regain focus.

"You do something with music, is that right?" she asks.

"Yeah. Nothing exciting, but I choose music for films and television shows, as well as radio and adverts. That kind of thing."

"Anything I might have watched?"

"Give me a list of everything you've ever watched, and I'll let you know," I beat out, partly because I'm nervous.

Her smile broadens. "It suits you. I always told you to do something with your interest in music."

"You did."

The drinks are assembled. "What do I owe you?" I ask.

"On the gentleman over there," I'm informed, and glance over to see Perry watching us.

I mouth the words 'thank you' over to him, and he gently bows his acceptance, a little flourish of his hand showing his long-hidden class for a moment.

Elle and I ferry the drinks over and remain side-by-side.

I want to take her hand, but daren't. That was all it took, on that day of my sixteenth birthday party. I reached out and touched her, and the rest came naturally. All it needs is a spark.

I've been hugged by all the women here, my hand taken by all the men present, yet the one that really matters…

"There's a sight for sore eyes! I say, a sight to warm the soul!" Mr Glenn bursts in, "seeing you two stood there side-by-side. Well, it takes me back, that does, I can say that! That's where you two belong, that is. My Glenda knew, and she knew a thing or two when it came to matters of the heart! Concerns of that nature, I suppose I might say!"

Awkward laughter emanates from the gathered. Elle and I move a self-conscious inch apart as eyes wash over us.

"Mind if I jump in? Now, Reg, what's this I hear about a partial parking ban on the old street?" Perry says as he squeezes in alongside me, forcing me back towards Elle.

And as Reg Glenn explains his reasoning, and fends off resistance, so Elle and I pick up where we left off at the bar.

"How was this course you were on? York, was it?" I ask her.

"That's right. It went well. I was presenting to a newly qualified group of primary school teachers."

"Presenting what?"

"I was trying to prepare them for their first day in a classroom."

"How many people were there?" I ask.

"About a hundred and twenty."

"I couldn't do that. Were you up on a stage?"

"Yes. You get used to it, I suppose. I just kind of block it out. Besides, they can't be any worse than a classroom full of seven year-olds."

I laugh. "No, I suppose not."

"You must have to present your music ideas?"

"I do, but it's usually around a table, and to no more than three or four people at the most. I still get nervous."

"You always were more a one-on-one kind of person. We both were."

Only when you were the one. Since then, I've been more one-on-none.

"You never married?" I ask her, making my comment sound general.

"No. Nor did you, I heard."

"No. After I left here, I never found love."

"When it comes to relationships, love is lies. It has to be," she comments and shrugs.

"Why? I don't disagree, but why does it have to be?" I push.

Don't push too hard.

"Because of the imbalance."

"Because it's always unequal, you mean?" I ask her, and think of Auden's poem.

"Yes."

"I think I agree with that."

"We always did agree," she smiles.

"Not always. But if love's balance is always unequal, is it better to be the more loving or less loving?"

"Auden?" she asks me, even though she knows the answer.

I smile by way of reply.

"It depends," she cagily says.

"On?"

"On whether you're together or not. If you're with the one you love, and you really love them, I think that you overlook that imbalance. In which case, I'd want to be the more loving one."

"And if you're not with them?" I ask and wonder if she knows that I'm talking about us.

"Then the more loving one will always suffer the greater hurt."

"So, better to love a little less?"

She contemplates the question. "No. I'd still take it the other way round."

"That's insane. Why, Elle?"

She thinks about it, looking off through the window as she ruminates. She's so beautiful. "I'm a primary school teacher. And I've honestly loved a dozen or more of the children I've taught. But they cannot love me in the same way, and nor should they. They have their parents, siblings and friends; they have their lives and the lives that lie ahead of them. Whereas they are my life. They will go forth and forget about me in time, but I never forget them. And yes, I know that they will leave - I know it when I meet them, but it doesn't stop me loving them. I know that I will ultimately meet with abandonment and rejection, but I fall for them every time, even so."

"They're children. It's different, I think - a different kind of love, perhaps."

"Perhaps. But the point is, who gets the most from it? Mine is the greater love, and mine is the greater reward. Part of love is knowing when to let go, I suppose."

"I did love you," I tell her, and feel my cheeks glow at the admission.

She turns her face fully on me, and I want to reach up and trace the outline that I've replicated so often and know so intimately. "I know you did. But you were too young."

"So you let me go?"

A dark shape looms in from my right, and the bubble bursts around us as Mum forces her arm through mine.

"Ugh, what a day! It feels so strange, me being here with all these people from when I was with your father, and him not here with me. Mind you, he never was really with me, I suppose. I always felt alone anyway, so..." she lets it drift away somewhere.

"Oh! Eleanor?" she begins again, "I didn't recognise you in a suit and with your hair all normal! I was just saying to Dee - I've been having such a laugh with Dee. She's known me for nearly fifty years, you know? Fifty years! I can't believe that, I don't look old enough, do I? Anyway, we were laughing and remembering all the things these kids used to get up to when they were small. You won't know, because you didn't arrive till later, and you were always so grown-up in a way. Apart from the hair and clothes, of course. But I suppose that was the fashion then. I always thought this one here would be with Debbie," she says, indicating that she means me via a tug on my arm.

"Mum, it's not really the..." I try to stem the hemorrhaging.

"She was like my own daughter, Debbie was! And she's kept her figure like I have, don't you think, Eleanor? It's hard when you have shape, like Debbie and I do!"

Swanny steps in to save me. "Come on, Dig lad. We've finally got Paul drunk enough that he's buying a round!"

22.

Bean and I prepare to head off around four o'clock. He needs his dinner. That's my excuse.

The crowd has thinned out, and those remaining seem to be in it for the long haul.

I express my gratitude, shake hands and accept hugs once more.

Elle shakes my hand. Formal. Dismal. That is all we now are. I force myself to smile at her, and wonder if it will be the final time I will ever look on her face.

I arrange to meet Paul at the solicitor's at ten tomorrow.

"Thanks for coming, everyone. Good to see you. Bye," I call generally, and know that there are many people here who I will never meet again.

I turn my back and trudge wearily towards home. It's about a mile and a half, or thirty minutes at a steady pace.

A car slows alongside me, and I know that it'll be Immleigh, so don't bother to turn my head.

Not today. Just not today.

"I fancy the walk. Do you mind?" Elle asks me as she alights and steps by my side.

"No. I don't mind in the slightest."

The taxi drives on with Pat, Pat and Mr Glenn inside.

"So, Bean is going to live with Reg, is that right?"

"That's the plan."

"I'm glad that I'll still get to see him. I hate it when people go away for ever."

"I had to, Elle," I say resignedly.

"Oh, no, I didn't mean you. It's okay. It was a long time ago. But I'm glad that we can be friends now. We can, can't we?"

I think about it. "I don't know, Elle. That's the truth. On Sunday, I'll go away from here. And what is there to come back for? Paul is in Drescombe and has his family, Mum's a hundred miles away living her lovely life by the lovely sea, and Dad is dead."

"What about Bean? He'll miss you. You could come back to see him, at least."

"I've spent a few days with him, that's all. He'll forget all about me in a week when he's with Mr Glenn."

"He won't," she says softly but with assuredness. "I watched him today, through the window. And every time you went away and left him, he looked for you. He tried to follow you, and had to be restrained. When you went to use the toilet, he whined for you as he lay forlornly on the ground. He didn't want to know anybody while you were absent. And as soon as he heard you or saw you or smelt you, his tail started moving and his eyes brightened in anticipation at being back by your side. All the while, when you were present, even when someone else was holding the lead, he went to be by you. And you don't notice, Digger. You see everything to do with everybody else, but are blind when it comes to yourself."

She falls silent, and we walk along for a minute, our footsteps perfectly in sync. When I look round at her I see a single tear scoot silently down her cheek.

"Elle, don't. Please don't."

Her voice remains perfectly calm, despite the tear. "I can't help it. I know Bean because I've been there. I recognise myself in that dog. But it's more than that. Debbie never took her eyes off you all the time I was there. Or, if she did, it was to scowl at me. Mr Glenn actually admires you! Those two Smith sons, Donnie and Davie, they stayed with you like minders - like pillars at the side of a gate, where you are their opening; their way in and out. That young girl at number five was sneaking furtive looks at you all afternoon. Swanny sought you out every fifteen minutes to make sure that you had a drink and were okay. Perry did the same from a distance. It's always been that way. Your dad saw it: 'Digger's coming back on Saturday for my birthday - Digger's coming home!' Imagine how hard that is for Paul? You get all the attention, but you're blind to it. Your mum craves it, yet it never comes her way. It's something enigmatic. Like an energy force. But you? You're oblivious to it all! And Bean sees it. Just as I did."

"Did," I point out.

"Do! I still feel it. There, you broke me. I admit it. Happy now? I still love you. I always bloody well have! And it's ruined my life!"

"You said that your life was pretty good. You clearly love your work."

"It fills a void! That's all!" she blasts out, angry at herself, I think, for letting things get to her.

"So you fucked up, Elle, is that what you're telling me?" I say, my frustration rising, as I turn to face her, Bean standing stock-still by my side.

She nods, her cheeks wet with tears. "You were too young, and I drove you away."

"Age is irrelevant! I would have died for you!" I scream at her.

"I died a bit when you left," she replies, attempting to soften everything down with her tone. She doesn't want to argue.

"Then why did you never get in touch? You could have contacted me through Dad," I growl angrily, because when all other emotions are exhausted, anger is the one that remains.

"How could I?"

"What? It was all on you, Elle! It had to come from you!"

"I let you go because I love you!"

"That makes no sense! Why did you dump me, Elle - why?" I plead.

"I never dumped you. What are you talking about?"

"The letter! The last fucking letter!"

"What? I didn't dump you in that letter!" she says making no sense.

"You did, you..."

"I told you that I was pregnant!"

I'm moving before the lead hits the ground. I can't stop her crumpling, but I can be there to sink down with her as we make contact with the damp earth.

In time with her sobs, I keep repeating, "I didn't know...I didn't know...I never knew..."

She's curled up, her knees raised, her back and shoulders rounded to form a ball, her head down and forearms wrapped over it - an instinctive position of protection and impenetrability, all of her vital organs shielded by her skeleton and muscles.

She rocks shudderingly with the violence of her emotions, and I try to absorb them and hold her steady - hold her together - hold myself together.

"I never knew, Elle!"

"I got back... You were gone... I miscarried... "

"Oh, no, no, no, no, no!"

"Why, Digger? Why did you leave me? What did I do wrong?"

23.

We read them together.

January 22nd 1986 "...Digger my Love - my Lover! Here I lie, unable to sleep once more, my mind full of the past, present and future, all of which you seem to permeate. I wonder sometimes if it was all meant to be, that it all happened for a reason. When I think of you, I begin to understand. It becomes clear to me that my mum had to die and my dad and his family had to reject me so that I might be sent here to P&P. How else would we have ever found each other? How cruel it seems that Love comes from death in that way..."

November 28th 1985 "...I'm sad, my Love, because I didn't see you today. I ate dinner, but it didn't fill me. I drank tea, but it didn't quench me. I watched television with P&P, but it didn't entertain me. I bathed this evening before I came to bed, because you weren't on me and there was nothing of you to wash away - I had nothing to lose. I listened to music in my room, but I heard none of it. Even one day without you is almost unbearable! But I will bear it, because I know that I will see you tomorrow! Oh, but in the future, let us never go a day without each other, Digger! Always come to me, or let me come to you, even if it's only for a minute. I sound pathetic, I know. I've never been this person before, and I always detested the girlie-girls who wrote a boy's name on their books and encircled it with a heart. That was never me, and I vowed that it never would be. Yet here I lie, unable to embrace anything because my Love for you is so strong that nothing else can get through to me! But I am embracing something - I hold in my free hand the shirt you gave me because I was cold, and it retains your scent on it that I breathe in greedy lungfuls, and absorb into me through my lungs and blood so that it can penetrate me and flow to every cell of me! I will sleep in this collarless shirt and have it against my body all night, and I will tuck it between my legs and grip it there as I sleep. Today that is as close to you as I can get. In some ways it frightens me, that you are my whole world - you are my life. Oh, don't think of me like DD and her ilk! You know that you hold my happiness in the palm of your hand. You can hold it for all the time we have, or you can sling it away, and I am powerless in that regard, and wholly dependent on you to always want me - to always make me happy. Hold me for ever, my Love. Or, at the very least, for as long as you desire to. Lx."

October 1st 1986 "...Digger Darling Sweetheart! Does the age difference bother you, I wonder? Or is it a feather in the cap to be with someone who is older than you? Thank you for my day today - I feel so Loved! I am nineteen, my Love, and therefore, seeing as it is past midnight, I am in my twentieth year. This is my final twelvemonth as a teenager! We talk about marriage, and I want nothing more. Yes, we are young, and P&P say that we don't yet know what we want, but I do know, Digger. I am certain. So, yes, I will marry you. I betroth myself to you! But... You are still only a tender seventeen, and I have to be the responsible one. Responsible? God! I beg you to come inside me, and I'm talking about taking responsibility! I hold you in place, with my legs wrapped around you so that you are as deep inside me as it is possible to be! Am I bad? Ah, but it is only eighteen months between us. What is that in real terms? H-P is three years older than S-P, and why should it make any difference because he is the male? It doesn't matter. Nothing matters as long as I'm with you. Time passes so rapidly, after all. This, as I said, is my twentieth year, and if I live to a hundred, I am almost twenty percent done. A fifth, my Love! So, as I review my life as another year is ticked off, I am deeply in Love and deeply happy. But I am impatient, as you are, because every day we spend together is so very precious. But they will slip by and one day exhaust the supply. It is tragically inevitable. I see people all the time, wasting their days as, I believe, they wait for something to happen. We shan't wait long. Life is short, and I am certain of my course! I will marry you when you are nineteen, and I am sure that you are certain of yours. Life may be short, but it can feel long if you choose wrongly. I owe you the time to be certain, my Love - I couldn't claim to Love you completely if I didn't. It is eighteen months to wait, and I ask you to indulge me on this. Will you wait for me until you are the age that I am now? And come tomorrow, and for always, I will wear the beautiful ring you gave me. I accept, my Love. I will take that gold ring with its diamonds, and you and I shall have a little private ceremony and become engaged! Shall we tell people? I want to, but you must decide. Only then shall I know which hand to wear it on in public. And I hope your Gran will love me from wherever she is, and have certainty that I deserve the heirloom and the title of your fiancee. Lx. PS - I'm wearing it now in bed on my left hand and I feel so good - so proud! Thank you, my Sweetheart! I Love you."

"I kept all of yours," Elle softly tells me.

"My Dad kept these for me," I honestly inform her.

"You didn't know?"

"Not until this week. They were boxed up as you see them."

"Do you think that he read them?"

"No. I thought about that. He was too decent, Dad. He'd have glanced at them, realised what they were, and packed them away."

"I wonder why he kept them, though?"

I consider her point and put myself in his slippers. "He wouldn't have seen it as his place to destroy them. He kept mentioning the boxes of stuff in my old bedroom, but I never bothered to look."

"Why not?"

"I didn't want to revisit the past, Elle. It was too painful."

"Micky and everything?"

"That. But, no; not really. It was you more than anything else."

She sits on the floor just as she once did, and I sit on the edge of the bed alongside her. Bean naps by the door, his eyes closed after a long and active day.

Elle continues flicking through the envelopes.

"Here's what I don't understand," she begins.

"Go on."

"Well, most of these envelopes don't have stamps on them, because I'd hand them to you in the morning when I saw you."

"Okay."

"But that week when you didn't get the letter, I was away on that college course. So it would have had a stamp on it, and would have been delivered by the postman."

"Perhaps he delivered our mail to Debbie next door. Remember how that used to happen fairly regularly?"

"It still does. So... She intercepted it, steamed it open, copied my writing..."

"She always had a gift for forging writing," I inform her, "Micky and I would have to pay her to write notes to the shop so they'd sell us cigarettes when we were kids. She could do his Dad's writing perfectly."

"Okay, that makes sense. And so she wrote a letter breaking up with you in my writing, and reused the envelope my true letter came in?"

"It's perfectly possible."

"This looks like the one," she says flatly, and as though she doesn't want to handle it, hands me an envelope held between her thumb and index finger. She pauses half way.

"That isn't my writing, Digger. That isn't even my writing on the envelope. And look, the postmark looks like biro. It's stamped, but it never went through the system."

"Is that important?" I ask.

"Probably not. But I always got the feeling..."

"What?"

"I always got the feeling that she never knew about my pregnancy. Yet she would have done had she read my letter to you."

"She's sly, Elle."

"There's something more to this," she muses.

"There's only one way to find out."

Elle turns to me, her face asking 'what?'

"Go and ask her," is my simple reply.

"Not till the morning, Digger. We'll get her when she's sober and less likely to react badly. Besides, she's probably still at the Old Mill."

I don't open the letter. Not yet. I have an urge to march down to the pub.

Elle breaks the brief silence. "I should go and tell P&P where I am. They might be worried."

"Worried about you being with me?"

"Hmmm, yes. It was very hard, Digger, after you left. They were so kind to me, so supportive."

"You should go."

"Come with me. We owe them an explanation," she urges, and takes my hand.

"I'm not sure that we have one yet."

"Oh, I think we're on the right track."

"Your letters to me, Elle?" I say, and remain seated.

She stands over me, our hands still joined. "Yes?"

"Did you mean them; all the things you wrote?"

"Oh! My Love! I meant every word, and far more for which I didn't, and still don't, possess the words!"

"It was real, wasn't it, Elle? You and I - it was real?"

She nods and smiles at me with her eyes. "Don't be angry, Digger. Don't be too angry with Debbie," she adds, the smiling eyes replaced by concerned ones.

"All of the wasted years," I bemoan.

"Then waste no more. Not one day - not one."

~~~~~

He-Pat accompanies me when I nip out for a smoke, leaving She-Pat and Elle side-by-side and deep in discussion, as explanations are best put over and questions answered.

"I won't lie," Pat begins, "I always liked you, Digger. Just as I always liked your father. And don't kid yourself that Pat and I didn't know what was going on between Elle and yourself back then. You didn't invent it, and we knew. But we could see that there was nothing we could do to discourage the pair of you, and that if we tried, we'd lose you both. Do you mind if I have one of those?" he asks, and I hand him my cigarettes and lighter.

"I've never seen you smoke," I observe.

"Ah, just the odd cigar. One of these I have about once every couple of years, usually when something bad happens," he tells me after sparking up.

"And this is bad, Elle and I?"

"I hope not, Dig. I really do. Look," he restarts, "it wasn't that we wanted to keep you apart, but we were worried about the depth of it all - worried that you'd both get hurt. We thought that you were both too young.

"I'll be honest with you. I have doubts even as we stand here. Perhaps you did get Elle's letter to you, and you did know that she was pregnant. You got cold feet and ran. I could kind of understand that. As I said, you were very young. So, thirty years pass, your life doesn't pan out the way you dreamed of, and so you come crawling back. It does happen."

"I promise you, Pat, I never knew until this afternoon."

"Okay. Then you need to understand how bad Elle was after you left. I suppose you had to see her to really know. She was very deeply traumatised, and I'm qualified to judge. At the worst of it she weighed ninety-two pounds, and I honestly believe that she wanted to die. Prior to that, she miscarried, and I think she purged that baby out of her. We tried to tell her that it was contradictory, what she was doing - that she was claiming to love you, and if that were true, would she not want your baby in her life? But she said that it meant nothing without you. She only left her room to go to the toilet, and rarely washed. This went on for six months. She dropped out of college, and was told by the GP that if she didn't eat or exercise, she would die. And when he told her that, she smiled.

"She would read your letters to her over and over again, looking for some clue as to why you left and what she did wrong. And ultimately she blamed herself for falling pregnant and pressurising you - entrapping you, I suppose is how she thought of it.

"She begged us to never tell anyone, as she didn't want you to be judged. She believed that you'd been through enough. And we gave her our word and kept it.

"I don't think she ever fully recovered, and it was a year before she picked up her life to some degree. It was probably five years before some normalcy was reached. Even then, a song on the radio or a mention of your name would set her back.

"I worked in grief and loss counselling for forty years, Digger, and I never witnessed such pain. Yes, it ran deeper with Elle because of her mother, father and step-father, and she was more sensitive to abandonment as a result, but I have never dealt with any case this bad that didn't end up in suicide or a mental health facility.

"Every time I left the house, I half expected to come home and find her dead. It was horrific, to be honest with you, living with that kind of time bomb, but unable to see the clock counting down.

"We thought about moving away, but Elle was adamant that she wanted to be here. She was thirty before she went out with a man again, but no relationship got beyond a couple of dates.

"She left here to work in Jemford Bridge when she was thirty-three, but transferred back before she was forty. Teaching saved her, I think. Being around children allowed her to skirt much of the adult world. The children were where she focused her love. And she has so much love in her, Digger. But I don't think I need to tell you that.

"Here's where I am on this. None of what I've just told you even comes close to making you understand how bad things really were. I didn't know that someone who weighed so little, and who rarely ate or drank could keep crying relentlessly as she did. Surely one ran out of tears at some stage?

"If you hurt her, Digger, I will kill you or I will die trying. I'm sorry, and I have no wish to provoke you or threaten you. I'm simply stating a fact. I used to think that it would be better for Elle if you were dead - that way she could have had some sense of closure, and not blame herself. I'm old, around the same age as your father, and I love two things in this world; Pat and Elle. And I will do anything to protect them.

"Do more than just love her, Digger. Love her enough to make up for all the years she's lost. Love her enough to replace all of those hundred-thousand tears she wept over you. And love her enough so that she can love herself again.

"So, are we okay, you and I?" he concludes.

"We are," I tell him. "I hear and begin to understand every word you say, and I'm sorry for my role in it and everything suffered by all involved. One thing, though..."

"Go on."

"You wouldn't have to kill me, Pat, because I'd do it myself."

He nods his understanding, and accepts the hand I offer him.

~~~~~

"Stay with me tonight, Elle. Please?"

"It's probably not a good idea..."

"It is. It's the best idea I've had in three decades. You said not to waste any more time. So, I begin right now; I will not waste this night. Come with me. Nothing will happen. But I need you to be with me. You being by my side is enough."

"But you leave here on Sunday, Digger? What then?"

"I won't go. I'll stay."

"Where will you stay?"

"A hotel... Dad's house for now. With you, here, at P&P's! I'll rent a place. It doesn't matter where. Who with is all I care about. You could come with me to London!"

"I have my children; my job. What about your work?"

"I can work from anywhere. I work from home most of the time anyway. Oh, Elle, I don't know the answers yet. But I have to be with you."

"Tomorrow. I will come to you in the morning, and we'll go to see Debbie. Then we'll talk and decide what the future holds."

"I have to meet Paul at the solicitor's at ten," I remember. I'm losing track of the days. It's still Friday, I have to remind myself; it's still the day that I said goodbye to Dad.

"Then I'll be round at eight. We need her sober."

"Come round at seven. I won't sleep anyway."

"Seven," she confirms.

We stand in the golden glow from the streetlights.

"I don't know what to do," I tell her.

"What do you want to do?"

"I want to kiss you goodnight."

"It's like you're sixteen again! Kiss me, then!"

And so I do. It feels like the first time on this very street, just a few yards along. She must have anticipated this, as I taste the mint of toothpaste in her mouth. Did she brush her teeth when I was outside with Pat? Do I taste of cigarettes and stale beer?

I open my eyes, and hers are closed. We stop, but don't break away, and I feel her cheek lightly brush mine, minimally making contact like a static charge, her ear touching my face that I kiss lightly and whisper, "I Love you, Elle."

We keep moving around each other with gossamer light touches, like dandelion spores playing with one another in a warm breeze just strong enough to lift them from the ground; like strands of a spider's web that threaten to break apart, but always maintain a connection at the last. We are butterflies dancing around each other, and our faces are their wings.

"And I Love you," she whispers as her hand rests on my chest, over my heart, and checks that it beats and that I am real and here.

"Come with me," I implore.

"Tomorrow," she promises and backs away.

Just our outstretched hands connect us, and then our fingers, until the connection is broken.

Before she can reach the door, I spin around, and call to her. "I shall marry you, Eleanor! I always said that I would. And I shall."

And as I turn back, the curtains at number seven shift in the window, and I hear a man's voice say through the open pane, "she always knew, did my Glenda. I say, she was always right when it came to matters of that nature! Matters of the heart, as I should say!"

"Night, Mr Glenn," I call happily.

"Night, Digger!"

On the other side of the street adjacent, I see Immleigh watching from his car, and a feeling of utter dread shoots through me.

24.

We drink tea as Elle reads the letter written by a false hand.

May 28th 1987. "...Dear Digger. You know that I love you. Please don't ever doubt that. But the truth is that I love you as a sister loves a brother. I didn't know, because I never had anything to compare it with. Until now. I met someone who I want to be with more than I want to be with you. Its that simple. And I know that you will meet someone who you will want to be with more than me one day soon. We've had some really good times together, and I mean it when I thank you for them. I will try to never forget those times, or you. 'All good things must come to an end' is a line in some song or other, and it has been good. But I believe that something better lies in store for me and for you. Please don't be sad or angry. If you love me at all, wish for my happiness and don't make things difficult when I get back from my trip. I don't think I could bear it if you were angry with me! I see no sense in drawing this out, so will stop now. A little of my love will always be your's, and I hope we can always be friends. L."

"It's not bad," Elle says appraisingly, "but you should have spotted the apostrophe in yours. There is no apostrophe when it indicates possession. And the lack of an apostrophe on 'its'"

"Yes, Miss," I say, and hang my head in schoolboy shame. She smiles.

"But the handwriting is uncannily good, I must admit."

"She always did have a talent for that. Did you get much sleep, Elle?"

"I sleep better now than I ever used to. The children tire me out, and my trip and a few drinks yesterday helped. But, no, I lay awake for a long while last night after you left."

"And what did you think about as you lay there?"

"Honestly? I thought about getting up and coming to you here."

"Why didn't you? I lay awake and waited for you to come."

"For Pat and Pat. They needed a night to digest all of this. Did Pat tell you much yesterday when you had your chat?"

"He told me enough," I say, and leave it at that.

"You put sugar in my tea," she says.

"I always did."

"That was how you had it."

"And you don't now?" I ask.

"Not generally."

"I'll make you another," I offer, advancing towards the kettle that still has a little of my Dad's water in it.

"I like it like this," she says, and wraps her fingers round the warm cup, threading them through the handle.

There are no rings on her fingers.

"Do you still have that ring I gave you?"

She smiles. She is the same as she ever was. I smile back at her, because I never could help myself doing that.

Elle fishes for the gold chain around her neck, and tugs it free of the taupe cashmere jumper that adorns her slim form. The ring alone hangs from it.

"Do you want it back?" she asks teasingly.

"No. That's yours, with no apostrophe."

"Thank you."

"Have you always carried it?"

"Every day of my life since the day you gave it to me."

"Initially on your finger, though," I point out.

She nods, and I see a tiny shadow dull her eyes.

"I chose a name," she says, and I can barely hear her.

"A name?" I ask for clarification.

"A name for the baby."

It's my turn to feel the shadow enter me.

"What name did you choose, Elle?"

"Tilly."

"Tilly," I repeat, and feel the word on my tongue. "A girl?"

She nods. "Till."

"To dig," I realise.

"To dig," she echoes.

I hold out my hand and she takes it.

"Let's find out the truth together, Elle," I propose, as I go to her and wrap my arms around her.

~~~~~

Debbie looks ill. She was in bed when we arrived, repeated knocking rousing her eventually.

"What time do you call this?" she asks.

"Half past eight in the morning," I tell her as we follow her through to the white kitchen.

"And what do you want at this time of day?"

"We want to know about this," I say, and place the letter in front of her.

She struggles to focus as she blows air from inflated orange cheeks. Her face looks like a mini space-hopper.

"Did you write this, Debbie?" Elle asks pleasantly.

I see the temptation to lie occur to her, but she shrugs it off. "Yeah. It was just a laugh. So what?"

"Hilarious," I snap, "do you know..."

Elle cuts me off. "What's done is done, Debbie. But what did you do with the letter I sent to Digger that day?"

"What letter? What are you talking about?"

"Try to remember, Debbie, please. Did you switch the letters?" Elle says. I can imagine it's how she speaks with the children she teaches.

"No. I didn't switch anything. I'd seen your letters in Digger's room, and I practiced copying your writing. Then, when you went away for that week, I posted that through the letterbox. It was just a laugh, that's all. And, yes, I was hoping he might believe it and come and see me till you got back. That was all it was. I didn't expect him to piss off for thirty years."

"Promise me, Debbie. You didn't take the letter?" Elle persists.

"I promise," she sneers petulantly.

"Why did you do it, Debbie?" I snap.

"I told you why."

"To split us up?"

She shrugs at me. "Did you get your precious land, did you?"

"You know about that?" I ask, surprised.

"It was in one of the stupid letters I read. You don't think it's funny that she's back with you just as your Dad dies? You always were a bit thick, Digger, when it came to stuff like that."

"I don't care about any of that," Elle states dismissively.

"No, well, whatever. She's no better than me, Digger," Debbie continues, "despite her always thinking that she was."

"You're pathetic," I say, and turn to leave.

"Am I? Pathetic, am I?" she calls after us. "At least I'm not being made a mug of! Thanks a lot, you fucking bitch! I'm set to lose everything, and she gets it all like always. Have a nice fucking life, because I won't!"

~~~~~

"I believe her," Elle says as I drive back to Dad's house.

"Me too. Besides, she didn't have time. The letter was with the rest of the mail. She wouldn't have had opportunity."

"That was the Friday?"

"Yes."

"And I posted my letter on the Thursday morning, first class."

"Perhaps your real letter didn't arrive until the Saturday," I speculate.

"It was sent from the middle of nowhere, so it may have taken longer. And you were gone by then. You left that very day, right, on the Friday?"

"Correct."

"The letter isn't in the boxes your dad kept because I checked last night."

"So who took it, Elle? And why? And why wasn't it sent to me, or shown to me when I came back to visit? Why have I never seen it?"

"I don't know. Perhaps it simply went missing in the post. It does happen."

"Perhaps," I mirror, parking up on the driveway Dad built.

"Or perhaps it was never mailed. I gave it to somebody to post for me."

"Did you trust them?"

"I was promised that it went. But the whole point of the course was that we were meant to be cut off."

We remain sitting in the car.

"Let's assume that it did get sent. Dad would have got it to me," I say with certainty, "or, at the very least, he'd have let me know that it was here waiting for me."

"It would have been inside the porch, and the porch was locked," Elle continues the process.

"Yes. So, Debbie might have added her letter to the post, or she posted hers first, and the other mail joined it. But I don't see how she could have got to your actual letter unless someone let her in."

"Paul?"

"I can't see how. He was at work that day. I was the only one at home."

"Then it must have come on the Saturday."

"It must have. But that still doesn't explain what happened to it."

"What happened that day, Digger? We need to relive that day."

"I didn't go to college. The Monday was the Spring Bank Holiday. That was the last time I saw you prior to yesterday," I say sadly, and turn in the driver's seat towards her.

She rests her hand on mine as I continue. "I had this idea about coming to you for a couple of nights. The plan must have been quite advanced, because I'd checked the train times. It probably explains why I was up so early, to be honest."

"I wish you had come to me."

"I know that I was thinking about it. I had some extra cash because Paul had got me a couple of days work at his place that week. I figured with you being away, I might as well do that and kill the time. I know that I missed you, Elle. It was the longest we'd been apart since we'd been together, those six days. I got through four of them, and couldn't wait until Sunday, so I thought about going to you.

"Let me think? Eddie was a puppy. Do you remember that Ringo had died in the night at Easter?"

"Yes, I do," she replies, and squeezes my hand, "and your dad came home with Eddie on the May Day weekend."

"That's right. And with Paul and Dad working, I had to let him out in the mornings. He was just old enough to go for walks by then, but not far. Did I take him out the front and leave the porch door open? I can't remember. That was when Debbie could have switched..."

"I don't believe that she did. She seemed genuine."

"She's a good liar, Elle. She always was. And she'd stop at nothing to get what she wanted."

"And what did she want? Was it you or the land she really desired?"

"The land and the money, probably. Even this week, she was very amorous with me, and she told me about her financial situation."

"No wonder she scowled at me all afternoon. Okay, so perhaps she had opportunity. Had the post been when you took the dog?"

"Erm, no. Definitely not. Had it been, and had I read your letter - the fake one, I mean - I wouldn't have taken the dog. I'm sure of that."

"So you walked the dog, came back, and was the post there then?"

"Yes! Yes it was. I picked it up as I entered. I remember, I remember! The porch door lock has always stuck where Dad misaligned it. I got back, and had to wrestle it open. I was struggling with the puppy, and scooped the mail up as I came in. I didn't see the letter at first."

"Could the dog have got the letter and chewed it up?"

"I don't think so. I don't know, Elle. Maybe. But there would have been residual evidence."

"Go on. What happened next?"

"The next thing I remember is reading the fake letter, and my world fell apart. I lay in my room for... I don't know how long. Hours, anyway. I re-read the letter a couple of times, and tried to decipher it, to see if there was some hidden message that I was missing. I went over and over the last night that I saw you, looking for any clue as to why.

"There was a rattle on the porch at some point. I got up, peered out of the window, and saw Mr Glenn. I couldn't face him, so ignored everything and laid back on my bed.

"I heard Dad come home from work. He had someone with him, and they were arguing. He didn't know that I was in the house."

"Who was he arguing with?"

"A woman. I didn't know who she was. She sounded upset, and Dad was getting angry with her. I couldn't deal with it all, so I lay with my arms wrapped over my ears and... It's the only time in my life that I've wanted to die. In that moment, I didn't care about life. I wished for it to end so that I could stop feeling anything."

"I'm sorry, Digger. I'm so sorry."

"You have nothing to be sorry for. You went through worse than I did."

"Who was this woman?"

"I honestly don't know. I heard the back door open and slam, and more shouting from the garden - mostly coming from my Dad. He wasn't a shouter; he was never an angry man, Elle. You knew him. Mum once said that she wished he'd have got angry sometimes, because it would have shown that he cared. I never heard him like that before or after.

"The next thing I know, I could hear him doing something in the back garden, and I heard the side gate open and blow shut. A minute later and the car boot slams, and all the while I'm trying to block it all out and understand why everything is happening. Why was my whole world disintegrating around me?"

"What happened then?"

"Nothing. Silence. An unbearable silence. Wind pummelling my bedroom window is all I recall hearing. I opened my eyes and uncovered my ears, and because of the angle, all I could see through the glass was a livid black sky. A storm was coming.

"And I knew that I had to go. I simply couldn't face seeing you and not be with you. I grabbed my bag, added clothing until it was full, pulled on my black trench coat, that old cap I used to wear, and my boots.

"I didn't stop to look at anything. I didn't acknowledge the puppy. I don't even recall seeing him, and I left number three and walked down the hill. I did not look along at number nine, and I did not look back. I knew that if I did, I wouldn't go.

"I've never told anybody this, but as I reached the ring road, my head down to keep the wind from my eyes, lightning hit the path in front of me. It was one of the most exhilarating and surreal moments of my life. Amidst all of this chaos, I witnessed this incredible power and beauty. I heard it fizz, Elle, as it hit the tarmac and advanced towards me. It was all over in a second, and it struck no more than twenty feet ahead, disappearing when it was maybe ten feet in advance of me. It passed through me, some of the electricity, and made the hairs on my arms and neck stand up.

"It stopped me in my tracks, wide-eyed and awed, and I could smell it, Elle. I could smell the energy. And I knew that it was trying to prevent me from leaving. But I thought about that saying - lightning not striking twice in the same place - and I walked on to where it had already struck. And as I passed over the point of impact the thunder roared savagely above me, and I marched on and crossed the Humpty Dumpty Field.

"The rain came as I dropped down on the Lane, and I turned west towards Curtly Brook. Had the rain come sooner, I believe that it would have conducted that lightning and perhaps fried me right there and then.

"My plan was to walk to Millby station. From there I'd get a train to Tredmouth, and from there I would go to London and my Uncle Brian.

"But as I headed away from Oaklea, I had this urge to go to the old railway for one final time. I wanted to see where Micky had fallen, Elle. I was angry at you, and I wondered about that day, and how it led to us getting together. So I deviated to the north, skirted the reservoir, and made my way up to the old line.

"I reached the sheer drop, and looked down at where he fell. I saw the spot where you were standing, and I thought about the tramp who spent a couple of summers in the old signal hut before it got burnt down. I blamed the rain and wind for me crying, and vowed that I would never again shed a tear over any living thing.

"I turned to go, and when I looked down at the plot of land my grandfather bought from the railway company, there was my Dad wielding a shovel as he tossed earth into a hole he'd dug out.

"In the hole I could see a black bin bag disappearing beneath the soil and pooling water.

"I think dad looked up and saw me, or saw a dark shape against the black sky and through the steely rods of driving rain, my coat flapping violently in the storm and a black bag slung over my shoulder. Perhaps he thought I was the ghost of the old signalman, or the devil itself watching him that day.

"He never mentioned seeing me. And I never mentioned being there. Only he and I, as far as I knew, were aware of his inherited land. Though, of course, I'd told you. And I discovered yesterday that he told Perry some time later."

"And Debbie knew," Elle adds.

"Apparently. And at ten o-clock today, his Last Will and Testament will be revealed, and everyone will know. And Paul and Jen will want to cash in that land by selling it to the developers that covet it. And they will dig it up for their foundations and roads, and whatever lies in the earth will, at the very least I fear, be the ruin of this family."

"Bloody hell, Digger."

"I know."

"Do you think that this ties in to that girl who went missing?" she asks, joining the dots.

"No. I know that it has nothing to do with that."

"How do you know?"

"Because I know all about that."

Elle withdraws her hand from mine.

25.

"No, no, Elle. It's not what you're thinking. Please, give me a chance to explain," I implore her.

"I think I want to go."

"I retraced my steps along the track, and I headed back across the Humpty Dumpty Field. I recrossed the Lane and went to the station at Millby.

"When I was there, hanging around the platform, I saw a girl. In the gloom, and with her waterproof clothing, for an instant I thought that she was you. She came up to me, and I realised that she wasn't, but she asked me about train times, and getting to Tredmouth. I gave her the information, and we parted. I didn't see her again until we arrived at Tredmouth, and we discussed our onward journey. We were both headed for London, but with it being so late in the day, we'd both get the first train the following morning. We talked for a while over a cup of tea. To be honest, she talked and I half listened. My mind was otherwise occupied.

"That was it. Until, about five years later, I was in a pub and she was working behind the bar and heard my accent. We got chatting about where we were from, and suddenly recalled that we'd met that day on the platform.

"Her name was Michelle. Michelle Blake. Except that it wasn't. Her real name was Trudy Michelle Immleigh."

"The missing girl?"

"Yes. I know where she is, Elle. We've stayed in touch."

"You have to tell someone," she says, resting a hand on my thigh.

"I gave her my word that I wouldn't. That evening in Tredmouth, I promised that I wouldn't tell anyone her story."

"Why did she run away?"

"I can't tell you. I want to, because I don't want any secrets between us. But I promised her that I'd never breathe a word."

"You've been carrying all of this for thirty years?" she says, and slides across the car seat to me.

I encompass her in my arm, kiss the top of her head, and answer, "yes. And Immleigh has never left me alone. He ascertained that I was with her at Millby, and that we were seen together at Tredmouth. I believe that he thinks we came back here, and that she lies buried on my Dad's land. He's been following me all week since I got back."

"And if he digs there, he won't find his niece, but he will find something?"

"Exactly."

Elle thinks about things, her eyes staring unblinkingly off into the distance.

"We need to go digging, Digger."

"We can't."

"We need help. What about Johnny Peters?"

"You're not thinking clearly, Elle."

"I am. No secrets. It's time to dig up the past, my Love, and get it all out in the open."

"Shit. The time. I have to get to the solicitor's. Will you come with me, Elle, please?"

She pulls away from me and fastens her seatbelt by way of answer.

~~~~~

"Yesssss!" I hear Paul hiss as he slaps his knees, Jen grinning by his side.

The house on the corner is his.

"Sorry, Digger," he says to me, "but we need it for the girls education. It takes a hell of a lot of pressure off."

I nod my understanding and smile my genuine warmth of feeling to them both. Will they be so magnanimous?

In addition, all money in my Dad's bank accounts will go to Charlotte and Hannah, split equally, and all contents of the house, barring any personal effects of mine, are to go to Paul.

"You haven't been around, Digger," Paul says as an aside to me by way of easing the guilt he feels.

Ah, but wait, dear brother.

Dad, we discover, borrowed money against the house. Quite a lot of it. And there are expenses to be paid; a funeral for starters, and the solicitor for seconds.

The best guess? Rather than the hundred and seventy-five thousand the house is worth, they should expect to receive something in the region of ninety thousand. Still, a nice chunk of change, but I can hear the air coming out of the balloon.

There's more: The land, and grid references are given, comprising five point eight acres, is left to me. All of it. Solely and in its entirety. Value? Conservatively, given the current buoyancy of the housing market, three quarters of a million.

What land? How much? I can hear the thoughts in the stunned silence.

Elle sits magnificently by my side, her hand not even flinching in mine as the news is delivered.

Yet, despite everything just revealed, I feel so sad.

"We'll make this right," I say to Paul, but he's too stunned to take it all in.

~~~~~

"I'm afraid," I say to Elle.
"Of what, my Digger?"
"Of losing you again. What if this backfires, and they pin something on me. I could go to prison. I can't..."
"Shhhh," she soothes me as we sit in Pat and Pat's place. "I don't believe your dad would hurt a soul. Have faith in him, Digger."
"What time is it?" I ask.
"Just coming up to one-thirty."
"If I ring Johnny and do this, I may be taken away for questioning. They may even charge me for withholding information, or something. I don't know enough. We have to plan for the worst."
"The missing letter doesn't seem so important all of a sudden, does it?" Elle says.
"I'm sorry. It is important to me."
"Oh, I wasn't grumbling. I mean that there are more important things in life, I suppose."
"Crap," I say smiling, "nothing is more important to me than you. It never has been."
"I'm tired," she says stretching.
"Then go to bed."
She licks her lips nervously. "Will you keep me company?"
"Yes. I would like nothing more."
And she takes my hand and pulls me from the chair.
I feel a pang of childish guilt and shame as Pat and Pat watch us head for the stairs. And I suddenly understand

that we are picking up where we left off. It explains why I feel different. I am not forty-eight, I am eighteen. And Elle is nineteen, not fifty.

"We're going up to my room to listen to some music!" she calls out as we ascend, just as she would back then, and we run up hand in hand, giggling away like children.

I glance round to see P and P smiling.

True to her word, she puts some music on as I take in the room.

It's the same bedroom, the same one as mine, Pat and Pat having the master at the rear of the house. All of the houses on this side of the street are replicas of one another.

Her room is a more adult feminine version of what it formerly was. The curtains are floral, the bedding on the three-quarter mattress showing soft swirls in pastel colours. Gone are the posters from the walls, and the room is painted the faintest of yellows; just enough to give it warmth. The last time I was here one wall was painted black. I wonder how many coats it took to cover it?

On the wall above the bed is a painting, but it could be a print, of a woman in a field, the long grass hiding her feet as she sits on a blanket with a basket containing fruit and bread by her side. Her head is turned towards a man who leans on a shovel, his sleeves rolled above his elbows. His adoration for her is plain to see, as he watches her, sweat glistening on his forehead, and the barest of smiles tugging at his lips.

Going to it, and leaning over the bed to see, I read the title; 'The Digger'.

I know this song; 'Death Rattles" by Woods.

"Lovely track," I tell her, because it is.

"It's a CD compilation I made."

"Dad boxed up all those tapes you made for me."

"I made this for you," she says shyly.

"Really?"

She pauses, and answers, "kind of. I actually made it for myself. But it's songs that either reminded me of you, or songs that I know you would have liked."

"Thank you."

"Or songs that I imagined playing when we made love," she adds, catching me off guard.

And I know that it has been the same for her as it has for me. This song is perhaps seven or eight years old, yet it appears on this compilation she made. Over twenty years after she last saw me, she still heard me in songs.

How strange that we're bashful and awkward. Is she nervous for the same reasons that I am; because we don't really know how much we've altered?

It's hard to make that sudden leap across time. Had we grown together, the changes would be gradual and almost unperceived, but here we are about to be laid bare in front of one another, and it's inevitable that a comparison will be drawn against the last viewing.

She must read my mind, as she begins pulling the curtains across the window to lessen the starkness.

I go to her, stop her, and open them back up. I shake my head.

Taking my wallet from my pocket, I slip out a small piece of paper. Unfolding it, I flatten it out on the window sill but cover it with my hand so that she can't see.

Bringing the middle finger of my left hand up, I let its outside edge fall down the left side of her face, barely touching, curving in to her perfect roundly-pointed chin, before it ascends the other side, levelling out as it reaches her prominent cheekbone before following a level straight line up to the curve at the top of her head and arcing over to find the start point.

She doesn't blink during the whole process, and I don't think I do either.

I show her the piece of paper with just the outline of her face drawn on it in pencil, and the date, November 1984.

"You haven't changed a bit," I whisper.

We step away from the window. I stand unresisting as Elle undresses me.

She finds the scar on my flank with her finger, and bends to kiss it.

Does she wonder at the increased broadness of my body and the slight bump on my stomach, and ask herself where the lean young man went?

What does she make of the fullness of my face, the bagginess along my jawline and the bulge of my neck as I look down at her?

Can she see the years around my eyes, the increase in hairs on my chest and belly, and in my ears, and the bushiness of my eyebrows?

If she sees, she ignores.

She cups me in her hand and gently squeezes, and I gasp blissfully.

Holding me in a loose grip, she rises and brings her face to mine.

"Be gentle," she says beautifully.

I nod.

"It's been a long time," she adds.

"I Love you."

"And I Love you."

"Is it equal, this Love?"

"I don't know," she answers, "but it feels pretty equal right now."

And I realise that I'm shaking, a combination of nervousness and anticipation. I am fully erect in her hand; throbbingly so.

How many times have I dreamed of this? Yet, not once did I dare to dream that it might come to be. It was always set in the past in my dreams.

Elle releases me, and I begin to disrobe her, my clumsy fingers tugging the jumper over her head and sending a shock of static through her hair that settles like a just-shaken feather duvet.

I take the gold ring I gave her between my fingers as it hangs from a smooth gold chain, and I lay it carefully back against her skin.

With a pinch of my fingers, her bra releases and falls away. I pause to singly kiss her erect nipples and feel the shudder pass through her just as it did me, as it leaps from one of us to the other and back again on repeat.

Like mine, her skin is peppered with goosebumps, yet neither of us is cold.

Her long skirt concertinas at her feet on release of the button and zip at its rear, and I drink in her slim legs as I sink down. She steps free of the garment, and I lever her shoes from her feet and smile at the black varnish on her toenails - a little nod to her more alternative youth that she keeps hidden.

So carefully so as not to mark her, I slip my fingers beneath the elastic of her underwear, and the small panties roll themselves up as I slide them down her thighs and over her well-formed calves. A tiny click of her ankle sounds as she raises her legs and straightens her feet for removal.

And we are naked together.

At first we stand looking at each other, only our hands making contact.

Elle looks so serious; so stunningly dignified even when stripped bare. She always did.

She leads me to her bed by my hand, folds back the duvet, and lies on top of the sheet-covered mattress. I sink down next to her, and we are so close in this three-quarter size chamber that it almost demands embrace.

We stroke and caress, kiss and nuzzle one another, our feet massaging.

She rolls on to her back, pulling me on top of her.

Not much of an adjustment is required, as we always seemed to fit one another so perfectly, and I feel myself partially enter her, the warmth and moisture coddling me.

I hold and wait, giving her time to adjust and mould to me, and allowing myself time to settle.

Slowly, I begin to pull out and nudge back in, but only half of me. 'Be gentle.'

Elle begins to relax, her eyes closing, her face resting, and I wait until she's ready. I've waited thirty years, after all.

She opens her grey eyes and smiles at me, and I let myself sink into her with all that I have.

A look comes to her - a look that I've never found in another, as the smile broadens and her lips draw in and her head drops to one side slightly so that I can find her ear.

I kiss it, and run my tongue around her lobe, and I whisper into it, "I never once stopped Loving you," as her legs clamp me in place and thirty years of frustration comes pouring out of me.

I don't care what happens, as long as I have this. It isn't the sex; it's the closeness that comes from it. It is the sensations that come from undiluted Love and trust. It is the perfection that can only be found in this dynamic.

"Oh, Elle, where have you been?"

"Right here," she sighs.

I am finally home where I belong.

26.

We read my letters to her as we lie in bed. She felt no need to depart and flush me out of her as Michelle and others always seemed to. Instead, we lie naked together, spooned and close, me reading over her shoulder.

It's a strange feeling to read letters that I wrote so long ago. My writing was better then than now; neater, I mean, because of the practice. I never write now; lists is all.

Is this how it is for famous people who read about their own lives in a biography? This is more autobiographical, I suppose.

The music stopped playing a long time ago, but neither of us has a need for it.

October 3rd 1985 "...Elle, My Love and my life. Okay, so I'm confused. Are we unique, unusual or just like everyone else? To quote The Kinks, 'I'm Not Like Everybody Else'. When I tell people that I Love you, Paul laughs and shakes his head, and Dad says, 'enjoy it while it lasts, son!' Mum tells me that it's simply infatuation, and that I'm too young; that I'll grow out of it. I feel sorry for them all, because none of them have experienced this feeling. But I'm fearful that they have, but they lost it because it did go wrong, and it always does. P&P are the same - they roll their eyes at us always having to be in contact with one another, 'can't you leave each other alone for one minute, ho-ho-ho!' No, frankly, we can't! P&P are happy, Elle, but they don't have what we have. Did they once, and are we witnessing our future through all these people? Will the passion die one day, and will we either opt for friendship or separation? Friendship, I suppose, would be better than nothing. But I don't want to settle for that. Why should I? I want all of you for all time, Elle. Yes, I'm young, as I keep being reminded, but I know that I want you for the rest of my life. Oh god, I Love you, Elle - I think I Love you more than any man ever loved any woman. Some songs seem to capture what we have, but when I listen to other songs by the artist, it falls apart. Did they have a glimpse of this once, but let it slip away from sight? I will never lose sight of it, Elle. Never! I Love you. Dx."

March 11th 1985 "...Thank you for the note, Elle, and for my record (which I adore, and will think of you whenever I play it). I don't know what this is. That's the truth. You kissed me, but was it just a kiss to say Happy Birthday, or was it something more? Or was it simply done because Micky's mum saw me and you wanted to make me feel better - what was it, Elle? I know what I want it to be. I know that I've fallen for you from afar over the past couple of years, and that I am probably in serious danger of loving you since you've been coming to see me. For months, I've been too afraid of driving you away to ever show or say anything to you about how I feel. But when I finally reached out my hand and touched you, I was neither scalded nor scolded, as you seemed to melt towards me. I feel my stomach churn when I write that and recall it. Still now, as I write this to you, my hand is reluctant to tell you too much for fear of driving you away. What will happen, Elle? What do you want? Tell me, and I will act accordingly. Thank you again. Dx."

May 22nd 1985 "...Elle, I am afraid. I had another nightmare last night, in which you had met someone else. You tell me that I'm insecure, and that I have to trust you if I'm ever to truly love you as I claim. And I know that you're right, but the thought of my life without you isn't a *life at all. You have become everything in my world, and the danger is that without you there is no world for me. But I am sixteen, Elle, and you are close to eighteen, and you are beautiful and so smart - there must be others who ask you out? What do you tell them? Are there lads at college who go for a drink with you and Melanie on a Thursday and Friday? No, don't tell me! I want to be older, Elle. I want to share in everything you do. And not so that I can keep an eye on you, or control you - but because I love you with every fibre of my being. It really is that simple. Why do you never tell people that you love me, Elle? Why? Why do we have to hide our love away like this? I am so very proud to be with you. Love me, Elle - just that. Just love me and I shall want for nothing. Love me, and I shall never ask you for anything more. Dx."*

"I did love you, even right at the beginning," Elle tells me, and turns her face to me for a kiss. "But you were so young. I had to protect you and myself. Mostly myself, I suppose. You know better than anyone except Pat and Pat what happened to me as a child, and I was protecting myself from it ever happening again."

"I know. I know that now, and I knew it as soon as you told me. But I didn't have a clue about it then. That letter is dated May 1985. We'd only been together for about two months, and we were still being cagey."

"But you loved me even then, and you were so certain of it."

"I was. I always have been, Elle. I don't know why."

She snuggles back into me.

March 28th 1986 "...I am so very sure of you, my Love. And I am so certain of your Love for me. Nothing can touch me with that protecting me. And when I'm inside you, I feel invincible - I feel like two people! Because, effectively, that's exactly what I become. With you in my life, things that might once. not long ago, have seemed impossible now feel easy. Also, things that might have felt weird or disgusting are now things that I long for! How did it begin that we swap saliva, Elle? Why is it so compelling to me? Yes, we devour other fluids from each other, but I crave your dribble! It satiates me, so warm and fresh and formed from you. That probably explains it. It is you in liquid form, and it isn't a waste product formed of something else. It has your life force contained in it, and is wholly produced by your perfect body. I could live on that alone. It is nectar to me because it tastes of how you smell. Marry me, Elle? Just marry me, and we'll work the rest out later. I must sleep... I don't want to. Sleep feels like a waste of time and life, but if you're not here with me, life and time are wasted anyway. So I may as well sleep, and on waking I can be with you again. This is the cycle of my life! Everything feels like a dream, but it is real, Elle, isn't it? You are real? I won't fall asleep, wake up, and all of this will be a dream that I will begin to forget as soon as I open my eyes? And I'll feel the memories slip away from me and desperately try to hang on to them, but to no avail. That is my worst nightmare, losing what we have. Our future together is all I think about, but the past we've shared is just as important. These letters document it, Elle. Will we always write to one another? I think we will, even when we've been married for twenty years, I will write to you and remind you of how much I Love you. Sleep time, Elle. Be here when I wake up! Be here to wake me up! You know how - that's the best way to wake up, feeling your mouth around me. I Love you. Dx."

March 11th 1987 "My Beautiful Elle, my fiancee, I could burst with all that I feel for you. Don't worry when I'm quiet. It is simply a contentedness that hushes me, and not anything more sinister. You know that you have nothing to fear, and I no longer worry about what is done or what will come. I know that everything will be perfect as long as I'm with you. If you think I'm quiet with you sometimes, you should see me when you're not around! I have no time for anyone, if the truth be told. I know what I want from life, and that is YOU. Nothing more. Just YOU. I don't worry about a job or leaving college. None of it matters. And nor do I worry when I'm told that I'm too young to be settled down. When Mum said that to us, I felt nothing but pity for her. I pity my own mother, because she has never known this! If I have to choose between you and anyone else, I choose you. And yes, that includes my own family. That ring was left to me by my Gran, and there is nowhere I would ever wish to see it than on your finger! It is mine to do with as I choose. So, ignore her, my Love, just as I do. I am now eighteen, and free from all of it! I am a man in the eyes of the world, and I am your man for as long as you want me. You looked more beautiful today in the pub with my family than you have ever looked, and I thought that impossible. Dad's funny, with his little rituals, and having to buy me my first legal pint! I smile when I think of it. But it wouldn't have been right had you not been there. I know Mum wanted it to be family only, but you will be my family for ever. And we shall have a family of our own one day, and she should think about that. I'm sorry, Elle, my Darling, what she said to you was untrue. Had you not been here, I would still have remained here when she left. Don't you worry about a thing, as I will always protect you from harm. If need be, we'll leave here. We'll start again someplace else. As long as you are by my side, I don't care about the where or what or who. You are all that matters. Marry me now and bollocks to everyone! I LOVE you with all that I am and more, the more being what I hope I will be for you in the future. Dx."

May 15th 1986 "...my Love, my Elle. We are isolated and cocooned, and I know there is a danger in that. If anything were to happen to either one of us, there would be nothing for the other to fall back on. I have no friends, because I want no friends. I can't stand the thought of anything diluting you and I. I am perfectly contentedly blissfully happy with that scenario. I feel the need for nothing when I'm with you, and I'm consumed by being with you when I'm not. There is no room for anything else. I wish we could merge and become one. I wish that I could reside inside you and see the world through your eyes, and smell, taste, hear and touch in the way that you do. My desire is to feel everything in the way that you feel it. It is, I've realised, impossible for me to ever be close enough to you. I am IN LOVE with you totally. So fuck the risks. I would sooner have this for a while and nothing in the future, than have never experienced you and your beautiful Love. Dx."

"How do you feel, reading these?" Elle asks me.

"It was a bit strange at first, but I'm okay with it now. How did you feel reading yours to me?"

"Similar. But then I saw the beauty in it all. And a kind of innocence, I suppose. We were so sure of it all, Digger, and it got taken away from us."

"Are you angry?" I ask her.

"I should be. But, no, I'm not. You're here, and that's all that I can think about. But I feel cheated. I feel as though something very personal and precious has been stolen from me. And I want it back."

"I know what you mean. I couldn't even be too angry with Debbie today, and I had every right to be. I saw how broken she is, and always has been. I saw a sadness and loneliness in her. She seemed defeated."

"But what would have happened during those missing thirty years, Dig?"

"How do you mean? Would we have remained here, for example? How many children might we have had?"

"That and more. Perhaps I'd have miscarried anyway. But I don't think I would have done. Between Debbie's letter and my missing one to you, it took a life. It claimed an unborn child, but it also took my life from me. And I think it took a large piece of yours. We were denied the life that we should have shared. Neither of us married. Neither one of us has children. We both drifted after that point in time until yesterday. Yes, we worked and succeeded - we are a successful couple, Digger, in the eyes of many. But those thirty years are not the life I should have lived. I've always consoled myself with the thought that we loved each other too much, and that it would have fallen away at some point. It was so intense, it couldn't burn that fiercely for ever. And what would have happened then? Would we have lasted for thirty years, Dig?"

"I can't be sure. But I have a feeling that we would. Of all the people I know, we stood the best chance."

"Why?" she wants to know.

"I don't know. The depth of it, I think. Reading your letters and mine, we were so exclusively together. I was so definitely yours. But why me, Elle? Why, of all the lads you could have had, did you fall for me?"

"Hmmm. I'm not sure I had many options! But there was something about you. The first thing I ever noticed was the cool confident smile you always had. And you were quiet."

"I didn't speak for three months!"

"But even before that, and after, you only said what needed to be said. You'd express yourself in your letters more, but in person, you were so succinct. Ephemeral, almost. And I noticed your walk before anything else, and the way you'd hold yourself more generally. You'd lie on the grass at the side of your house, or be cleaning your dad's car, and your fringe would be swept over and it would shade your eyes from the sun, and you looked like you were made of gold. No, not made of gold, but surrounded by it, as though it were protecting you."

"My walk - what about it?" I fish.

"Yours is less pronounced, but I saw it in Liam Gallagher and it made my heart leap. You have this slight swing to your shoulders, and you always stand up straight. I noticed it again at the wake yesterday when you walked Bean, and when you came into the pub. It's as though you're listening to music that only you can hear all the time. Your feet point slightly outwards, and you were always a bit leggy - there's a sense about you that you own the ground on which you tread."

"Well, if it was those few acres over the way, I now do. But you make me sound so cocky!"

"Oh no, it's not a cocky walk. It's brash, I suppose, and it portrays confidence and strength. And at first, it may come across as that. But then I got to know you, and discovered that you were anything but cocky. I discovered a humility and sincerity that is still present. I described to you what I observed at the Old Mill; Bean and Debbie, the Smith brothers and Kerry-Anne, Paul and Swanny and Mr Glenn.

You don't blank Bean, for example, because you're being cold and distant, you don't see yourself as above such things and superior. You are totally oblivious to it all. I get the sense that you would find such admiration ridiculous and highly embarrassing.

"Look at you, you're blushing now as you hear this about yourself!" she adds, and I feel myself blush more as a result.

"But besides all that," she continues, "I always got the impression that if you were with me, you'd be with me for ever. I felt that from simply looking at you. And you were quite good-looking... Back then!"

I laugh.

"And there was an intelligence about you; it was in that reticence, and when you did speak you didn't waste words. But it was in your letters that I really saw it. And you were kind and gentle with me. That was the biggest attraction, you know? And today - you haven't changed."

"I have. We have. But I think we've changed in a way that still works for us."

"I hope so. What do we do now?" she asks.

"Nothing. Lie here for another fifteen minutes. It's been such a long time, Elle. And I'll call Johnny Peters when I go back to let Bean out and give him his tea."

"His last supper," Elle remarks.

"His last one from me. I'm pretty sure Mr Glenn understands that he has to feed him."

She giggles.

"And what about Paul and the land?" she adds.

"One step at a time, my Love. One step at a time."

Before I decide on anything, I want to know if he played any role in that letter going missing.

"Stay here tonight," Elle pleads.

"What about Bean?" I point out. "Why don't you come and stay with me at number three?"

"I could."

"Will you?"

"Oh, go on then," she says, and rolls round to face me, her hands tickling my ribs as we both laugh.

"Elle?" I ask when she's settled, her face half hidden under the cover and her breaths on my chest.

"Hmmmm?" she sighs contentedly as I stroke her hair.

"What happened that Sunday when you got back?"

She speaks to me from her half masked security.

"I went to you. I thought you'd come and meet me at the station, but Pat said he'd not seen you for a few days. And I thought that was odd, but that perhaps you'd planned some surprise. Pat dropped me at yours on the corner, and he took my bag home. I ran to you like a silly little girl, Digger. I ran up the path to you and rattled the porch door. But nobody came.

"I grinned, thinking that it was all a scheme, and that you were waiting for me here. So I ran home and called your name as I entered. There was no reply. Pat asked me what I was doing.

"I was bursting with it all, Dig. I was carrying your baby, and I was so, so elated. It blinded me to everything else. I couldn't fathom it. Why weren't you there? I'd tried calling the house from the station, but there was no reply. I just wanted to hear your voice, that was all.

"Why weren't you there, Digger?" she says, her voice beginning to fail her, "oh god, why weren't you there for me? Everything would have been cleared up if you'd been there!"

"You know why, Elle. I thought you'd met someone else."

"How could you think that?"

"Because I always thought that you were too good for me. More than I deserved."

"So you believed it so readily because of that?"

"Yes," I answer her, matter-of-factly.

"I was never better than you," she says seriously, raising her head to face me. "Never."

"You are. You always have been. I always felt like the luckiest man who ever lived when I was with you. I feel that now."

"And I was so stupid!" she says. "Why did I write that letter? I assumed that my news about the baby had scared you away. I could understand it in a way, and it explained your leaving. I should have waited and told you on that Sunday face to face. Oh, but you'd still have been gone! I keep forgetting that it wasn't my letter that drove you away."

"But there is a difference, isn't there? Remove your letter, and you would have returned and had no explanation, as your pregnancy would have been unknown to me. And wouldn't you then have wanted to know why? Wouldn't you have asked questions? Wouldn't you have contacted me through Dad?"

"Yes."

"It was a perfect storm, Elle, when you think about it. When did you realise that I was gone?"

"That same night. Pat went to see your dad, and he told him that he hadn't seen you for a few days. On the Monday I learned that you were in London with your uncle, and that you had no plans to return."

"I'm sorry, Elle. I should have stayed here."

Elle never did swear much, so it gets my attention when she says, "where's that fucking letter, Digger? What happened to my letter to you?"

"I don't know. But I promise you that I'm going to try to find out. Hey, I'd better get up and sort Bean out."

"Five more minutes," she suggests, and snuggles back to me as she tenderly picks out another envelope.

April 3rd 1986 "*...my perfect Elle, my Love. You asked me today to share a secret with you - something I've never told anybody before. And I did that by telling you about the land. Nobody knows except Dad and I, and now you. It seems that it's one of those secrets shared between father and one son of their choosing, and I am the chosen one. But the truth is, it wasn't what I wanted to tell you - it wasn't my first thought. That is something that I know won't come as a surprise to you, but it is something I've never dared tell another person. I can tell you because we share it, this big secret of mine. I am tender. That's it! That is my secret. Tenderness is my foible and my weakness. I hide it, and I over-compensate for it. That was why I lashed out at the lads who called you names. I rage because I'm ashamed to let them see that they hurt me. I hurt them to hide my own tenderness. Yet, with you, I can be myself without fear of judgement or exploitation. We both put on a front, a tough and uncaring face for the world at large, but we are both delicate and... Tender! It's the only word that fits! And that's my point; I see so much anger in the world around me, whether it be at college or on the streets or on the television, and I feel excluded from it. I pretend to be a part of it, but truthfully, I deplore it all. You are my haven, my safe place as H-P might term it. You are my soft warm bed and the roof above me. You are my stabilisers and my arm-bands. You are a hand in mine that will always hold me up, and a kiss on a wound that will cure any pain. Thank you, Elle - thank you for being the one person I know in this world who allows me to be* *simply me. Marry me now, so that I can have that for all of my life? I Love you, Elle, and that is no secret. Dx."*

27.

Johnny Peters greets Elle and I warmly. His smile is telling as he notices we walk hand in hand.

"How did the funeral go, Dig?" he asks.

"As well as they can go," I tell him, which is probably true.

"I'm sorry I missed it."

"No problem. Thanks for the wreath."

"My pleasure, my pleasure. Now, what's this all about? You were a bit cagey on the phone."

The three of us walk across to my Dad's land. The sun hangs low over the old railway, casting an ominous shadow.

"Here," I say, and point at a spot on the ground next to a gnarled old ash tree. It's grown lopsided due to its position, as it has forever sought the light that the railway deprives it of on one side. It leans out, stretching and twisting its neck, its branches braced like arms ready to break the fall that must surely one day come according to the laws of physics. One side of it is dense with happy fronds of yellowing green; the other appears dead. "Dig here."

Johnny waves people over from a van.

"Does this have anything to do with Immleigh?" Johnny asks me as a shovel is carefully inserted into the soft luscious earth.

"No," is all I say.

"You know, Digger, in my experience, things such as these are like medical problems: The truth is rarely as bad as the imagined."

"I hope you're right, Johnny. All I want is that, whatever you find, my Dad will come out of it undamaged."

"You'll know as soon as I know anything. And, erm, I may need to get a statement from you."

"Of course."

"Look, on a personal note," he begins, and encompasses Elle and I in his gesture, "no matter what we discover here, or how that turns out, seeing you two together is smashing. I remember when I heard that you were no longer together, and thinking, 'well, if they can't make it work, what chance do the rest of us have?'"

I blush a little. "Thanks, Johnny."

"I'll call you later," he concludes, and Elle and I walk back to Oaklea, an arm encircling the other, my hand resting on the top of her pelvis, her thumb hooked through the belt-loop on my 501's, and our hips moving in unison.

~~~~~

At an average age of forty-nine, and having been in love with one another for thirty-plus years, it seems a little odd to be preparing dinner together for only the second time in our lives.

It's our treat for Pat and Pat.

Bean sits and waits patiently for his best healthy-boy look to be noticed and shown appreciation by way of a morsel. I toss him a carrot, which he seems to like.

How can this be? Thirty-six hours ago I was a different person, and this was beyond anything I was capable of imagining. Here I am in this domestic idyll.

"You need more wine," I tell Elle, and press behind her as I pass even though I don't need to. I give her backside a squeeze because I can.

She leans back into me, trusting me to be there and not let her fall.

"Are you trying to get me drunk?"

"Do I need to?"

"No," she answers, and goes back to grating carrots for the salad.

"Marry me?" I plead with her.

"Not yet. I want you to continue asking for a while!"

She-Pat enters the kitchen. "Look at you two. It's like when you were kids. Can't you leave each other alone for one second?"

I smile and shake my head.

Bean's back looking for more. I know how he feels.

We eat and drink at the same table, the four of us gathered together. H-P regales us with tales of the neighbours, versions of most of which I'd heard from Dad, even though I barely listened.

"You're quiet," Elle softly says to me, and she finds my leg beneath the table.

"I'm happy."

"And worried?"

"A little."

We continue to sit and drink after Elle and I clear the table and wash up together.

"Look at that dog," Elle points out.

I glance down at him, napping at my side, his soft pink freckled tummy exposed and his legs limply and pacifically in the air.

"Do you see what he's doing?" she continues. "He lies like that so that his back leg is in contact with the leg of your chair, Digger. And he does that so that he can nap, but if you move, he'll feel it and know. He'll know the instant you might be about to leave him, and he'll be able to follow you."

Is she right, or is it an accident of how he ended up?

I take her hand, because the mention of leaving has dampened the mood a little.

"I'm going to stay with Digger tonight," Elle informs P and P.

"We thought you might."

He-Pat catches my eye and smiles as we both reach for our glass at the same time. There's a grimness hidden in it; a concern for Elle that I can appreciate. I draw my lips in but broaden my smile at him, and nod my head as unspoken understanding. It seems to further relax him.

My phone rings. "Sorry," I say, seeing Johnny's number come up, "but I should take this."

I don't leave the room as I have no secrets from these people, but I do stand and leave the table. Sure enough, Bean is up and following me over to the gas fireplace.

"Hey, Johnny."

"Hey, Dig. Well, we did find something..."

"Go on," I tell him, and hold the mantle with my free hand. "Hang on. I'm going to put you on speaker phone," I decide. "Okay, go ahead."

"We dug up where you indicated, Digger, and we found the largely intact black bin bag just as you described. Inside, I have to tell you, we found bones."

Silence.

"Digger, are you still there...?"

"Yes, Johnny. Go on, mate."

"They were canine. It was a dog, Digger. And there was a tag with the remains. 'Ringo' is etched on it. Does that mean anything to you?"

"It does, Johnny. It's all starting to make sense. I'm sorry to have wasted your time and resources."

"Don't be. You did the right thing if you suspected something. Thirty years late, but hey-ho."

"Thanks, pal. Talk soon."

"Take care."

Switching the phone off, I turn to Elle and the Ps. "I need to pop next door to see Mr Glenn for a minute. Please excuse me."

Bean follows me to the door.

~~~~~

We share my single bed, entangled and tightly together, but we don't care. We never could be close enough.

Using Dad's bed felt wrong. Besides, we've never once shared a double bed.

"I walked the dog that Friday morning, and got back to what I believed to be your letter. I didn't see it immediately because the dog had got covered in crap down by the lea.

"So I shoved him outside in the back garden and came back in. Then I read the letter, and the rest of that side of things you already know.

"When Mr Glenn came knocking on the porch, it was because Mrs Glenn had seen Eddie digging in the garden. He was digging up Ringo from where Dad had buried him. Dad had this thing about being buried in the earth. He'd say, 'stick me in the ground, and don't bother about a wooden box. I don't see the sense in it if I am to become soil at the end of the day.' He'd wind Paul and I up about being eaten by worms and recycled. 'Just make sure I'm bloody dead first, though!'

"So Mrs Glenn saw this from two doors up, worried about the hygiene of it for us young ones, and sent Reg round to tell us. But nobody answered. So, they called the council. Mr Glenn saw the woman arrive just as Dad got home. There was some arguing, as Dad defended his right to a pet cemetery, etcetera. That was what I heard as I lay on this bed.

"Poor Dad had to exhume Ringo's body, stuff what was left of it in a bin bag, and take it down to his plot of land for reburial."

"How macabre!" Elle says. "And that's what you witnessed from the old railway that day you left?"

"Precisely."

"But this won't stop Immleigh - he still believes that you know about his niece."

"I've been thinking about that. I'm going to phone Michelle tomorrow, and see if I can't get him off my back. I want to clear the slate, Elle. A clean beginning."

"I like that idea."

"Marry me?"

"Hmmmm."

"Is that a yes?"

"Hmmmm. Keep asking."

"Why?"

"Because I like to hear it."

"Oh, I'll keep asking you. Hey, if I clear Immleigh up, the only remaining mystery is what happened to your letter."

"It doesn't really matter, Digger. Not now. All that matters is that you're here with me."

But we both know that it does matter.

We lie and reflect, each with our own thoughts that, I'm willing to bet, are not too far removed from the other's. Soon I hear Elle breathing more evenly and deeply. Her body becomes heavier, nakedly pressing against me, and I like bearing her weight. The young girl who could never sleep for fear of what she might learn when she was awoken sleeps soundly in my arms.

"I Love you," I whisper to her in the dark, and it must penetrate her somnolent mind and embed itself in her brain, because she reaches a leg back with which to clamp me still tighter to her.

~~~~~

I snatch a breath as though I were drowning.
What? I wake up not knowing where I am.
It is a rude awakening.
I hear a sound that shouldn't be.
I was dreaming.
But it slips away from me the more I attempt to recall it. Why? Stay!
I close my eyes and try to revisit it.
A song. A tune. Tinny and basic.
It's my birthday. I am ten.
'...yudy-yudy-yudy-yudy...'
Micky laughing.
Debbie dancing.
The front garden at Number Three On The Corner.
I'm sat in the porch, the rickety thing that Dad built.
'...yudy-yudy-yudy-yudy...'
 Why? Think!
I'm there because the power cable won't reach any further.
Micky being filthy.
Debbie laughing.
I'm playing records in the porch. It's my tenth birthday. 1979.
'...yudy-yudy-yudy-yudy...'
And it fell through!

The seven inch single I'd taken off so that I could play the next one.

It fell through the gap in the boards.

It had boards because it was raised up to the level of the house.

You step up to the porch, and into the house.

It slipped through the gap and stayed there.

'...yudy-yudy-yudy-yudy...'

Lene Lovich. 'Lucky Number'.

I'm alert, untangling myself as carefully as possible from Elle. She murmurs incoherently.

"Stay here," I whisper to her and kiss her cheek.

Dressing as quickly and quietly as possible, I find Bean lying respectfully by the door. He loyally rises and follows me down the stairs.

I'm searching the kitchen. There's a flat-headed screwdriver that looks as though it'll serve a purpose.

The front door opens, a cold draught shrinking my frame, and I'm down on my knees, Bean alongside me.

"Watch out, boy," I warn him as I lever the tip of the implement between two planks.

Not enough leverage. I withdraw it some, and try again. A creak. More down pressure on the handle. A painful moan as a board begins to lift. I switch to the narrow slightly raised end of the plank. I push down again. It lifts up enough so that I can get my fingers around it.

I heave it up with both hands, and prop it there with the screwdriver.

Fumbling with my lighter, I flick a flame. Lying along the hallway with just my head and shoulders in the porch, I peer in to the flickeringly lit chamber. I see something amidst the dust, cobwebs, fluff and debris.

My hand reaches in and retrieves four pieces of paper and an old seven inch single.

I double check. That's all there is.

My foot presses the board back down, and I close the door.

Inside the kitchen, I switch on the light.

Stiff Records, a swipe reveals.

A bill with Dad's name on.

A christmas card, by the looks.

A piece of junk mail.

And a letter written in her slanting hand.

I don't rush now. The sky is beginning to lighten to the east. A new day is dawning.

I clean the envelope as best I can while the kettle boils; a kettle that still contains a drop or two of the water that Dad filled it with.

As it burbles to life, I calculate the odds in my head - an average of five pieces of mail a day, six days a week, for forty years. Sixty thousand items. I found four. A one in fifteen thousand chance that, as it dropped, the edge of the item would fall perfectly vertically and find that seven inch long sixteenth of an inch gap on the right side of the porch where two planks didn't quite line up.

It remains sealed, the letter, despite moisture having bloated and crinkled the paper somewhat. The stamp adheres. The postmark is illegible, but I think it always was.

Bean goes out for his business, and I wait patiently while the tea brews in the pot. A few minutes later, and he's back looking for breakfast. "A bit early, lad."

Pouring the tea out, Elle's without sugar, I hold both in one hand, the letter in my other, and ascend the steps. Bean knows. He remains behind.

She sleeps on. So tired, after all this time wondering.

I open the curtains and wait for the light to enter.

It crawls in, golden and peaceable, soft and glowing, just like her. And it casts rays all over the room that waltz off the mirror and anything reflective. They dance off her face, and her eyes open. The first thing she sees is me, and I watch her mouth give a little gasp of pleasure at that. It's as if she thought, 'thank god, he's still here. It is real.'

"Tea?" I say.

"Hmmm," she sighs, "thank you."

She doesn't question the earliness of the hour. Such things don't matter a damn. If we're tired later, we'll go to bed together. That has never been said, but we both know it.

"I lifted the floorboards in the porch. I found your letter."

"It was never my letter, it was yours. It was always yours," she tells me as she raises herself up on an elbow.

~~~~~

May 27th 1987 "...Oh, my Love, I am worthless without you. I cannot be without you! I look for you everywhere, but don't see you. I listen for you all the time, but am deprived of your voice. I cry at night knowing that I won't see you tomorrow. Then what is the point of there even being a tomorrow that you are not in? I reach for you, but only find emptiness everywhere. I taste nothing if I cannot taste you, and I can appreciate nothing if I'm not sharing it with you. I talk to you, but you can't hear me! Where are you, my Darling? I tried to call, but there was no answer. I walked three miles each way in drizzle to a phone box, just so that I could hear your voice. 'I Love you' is all I need to hear. If I can hear that, I can cope - I can survive this hell! Yet, perversely, amidst all of that, I have wonderful news! I was sick this morning, my Love, and I honestly believed I was lovesick. But I checked my dates, and I'm late for my period. And I know - I just know - that I have your baby growing inside me. I feel it, Digger! It is half you, and that is the half I will always Love the most! I am so overjoyed! Oh, Digger, are you? You've always been right - we should get married right away. It's pathetic to wait. What am I waiting for? I've never been so certain of anything in my life. I had to write this and tell you immediately. It cannot wait until Sunday. I will never keep a secret from you, and that's how it would feel to me if I kept it to myself. And we always tell one another the important stuff in letters! Is this the best letter, my Love? I hope it is. Oh, Digger, why am I even here on this team-building course? Why did P&P think it would be good for me to be away for six dismal lonely days in the middle of fucking nowhere? Why, Digger? I shall never forgive them. My Love, I lie here writing this, away from the group that I am supposed to be teaming with, and I place my hand on my tummy and feel something. It is as close as I can get to you in this moment. Remember when we talked about this being a possibility, my Love, and you smiled at me and told me that it would be perfect. And then you came inside me. Perhaps that was the time! It happened because we wanted it to. And no baby in the history of the world could possibly have been conceived from a more Loving union. I'm crying now, silently so that nobody will hear. I think my hormones are all over the place! My Love for you is more than infinite, Digger - will you please do me the honour of agreeing to marry me? There, I asked you, so you can stop asking me now! All of my Love and body, my mind and energy are yours for ever. Lx. PS - someone is going to the town tomorrow, and I've asked them to post this letter for me! x. PPS - when I get back, on Monday we will buy a pregnancy testing kit, and you can be there when I pee on it! Won't that be sexy? Lx."

28.

"Why? Why was it always you?"

I think about Paul's question. He's bitter and feels rejected by Dad. I understand it. "I don't think it was that, Paul. I think Dad wanted me to have the responsibility. You have enough with Jen and the kids."

"Why didn't he bloody tell me about the land?"

"Because he didn't want pressure to sell it. And you would have, wouldn't you?"

"Bloody right I would! Do you know what a difference that money would have made to my life?"

"Yes, I do. But I don't think he could let it go. I think he buried all of the dogs there - Ringo, Eddie, Heinz. I actually think it was where he would have liked to have been buried, over by the ash tree at the foot of the old railway."

"We'd play there, remember?" Paul recalls as he softens.

"I do."

"And we got the rocks for the rockery from there."

"We did. And Micky died there, Paul."

"Yeah. I know. Sorry."

"Ah, don't be. Look, I have a few ideas. And don't worry, you'll get half of that money. I promise you that. Do you know what I think?" I ask him.

"What?"

"Dad wanted to protect that land. He kept it so that they couldn't build on it. And I believed for a long time that he did that to hide a secret. But it wasn't the case. He did it so that us kids, and our children after us, would have somewhere to play and run and be free."

Paul considers my hypothesis. "He used to go on about it all the time, Digger - 'remember when you and Digger did this, and you and Digger did that. And that daft lad Micky!'"

We chuckle. It's a shared sound that comes from us both.

He continues. "The television was always on, and if I called in he'd say, 'I wonder if Digger did this one? I wonder if he did that one?' But you were never there to hear it, Digger. You were never around. And when you were, we were all afraid to mention it in front of you. How could we ever mention Micky after what happened? You went a bit mental, mate."

"I know. But we had some good times, didn't we?"

"We did. Remember when we built that go-kart?"

"Dad helped us," I chip in, smiling at the memory, "but you designed it."

"And we took it down to the old railway bank. I thought I was dead."

"We should have probably tested the brake!"

"It stopped well enough when it hit the tree."

"It did," I confirm.

Grins unite us across the table, his soft shy eyes meeting mine.

"And then you suddenly left one day, and we didn't know why. We worked out that it had something to do with Elle, but she disappeared for months at the same time. To be honest, I thought you'd buggered off together, and I was happy for you. Then I found out that you were at Uncle Brian's and she wasn't with you. We had that bloody copper bothering us, asking questions about some missing girl, and it was all a worry. Then I saw Elle one day, months later, and she looked ill. She looked like she was bloody dying. What happened, Digger?"

"A lie. A lie happened, Paul. And a fluke. Nothing was as it seemed."

"And now?"

"And now... Look," I tell him, and point towards the door. He turns to watch Elle enter the pub. My word, she's stunning. She, quite literally, takes my breath away.

"Drink?" Paul asks her.

"Just an orange juice, thanks, I'm driving back to Oaklea."

He's back in a minute, the pub quiet on this Sunday afternoon between lunch and dinner. Another pint is set down in front of me. I'm not used to this.

"Where's Jen?" Elle asks.

"Looking after the kids. To be honest with you, she wasn't too keen on seeing my little brother after what transpired yesterday," Paul sheepishly informs us.

"It'll be put right, Paul. That's why I came to Drescombe to see you. I was saying about the land, and Dad preserving it. But what for? I've been walking Bean there every day for a week, and I've not seen a soul. Children don't play out any more. Nobody appreciates green open spaces. Everywhere else that can be has been built up, so why not there? Let them tear that railway down, and let's allow them to reinvent it. And the money will be split fifty-fifty between you and me. What do you think?"

"I should take your hand off," Paul answers, but he's holding back.

"So why don't you?"

"Because I don't want to see it go. The money isn't so vital now. The mortgage is low, and we have equity. It was in the past when we could have used it."

"You sound like Dad. Think of the money. Think of your daughters."

"I am. And I'm actually thinking about not selling Dad's house, and us all moving back there."

"Bloody hell. I wasn't expecting that," I tell him.

"No, well... I was at the Mill on Friday, and despite the fact it was Dad's funeral, I had a great time! I know, I know... I shouldn't say that. I've missed it. Swanny and Dave and Don. I don't have that here. And I'm having to drive almost to Millby every day for work, anyway. And the schools there are no worse than here. Are they, Elle?"

"No, they aren't," she answers.

"What does Jen think of this?" I ask.

"She's warming to it. We discussed it this morning. Especially as we could sell our house in Drescombe and pay off the mortgage at number three. And we'd pocket a bit of change in the deal. And now you're telling me about the land, and splitting that..."

"Ah, I was going to propose that Elle and I buy Dad's house from you," I interject.

"Really? You're moving back?"

"Yes. Sorry," I answer.

A period of silence stems the flow.

"What are you thinking about?" I probe, as Paul leans back and sips his beer meditatively.

"I'm thinking that right there is another reason for me to move back to Oaklea."

"To stop me coming back?"

"No, you daft prick. *Because* you're coming back!"

~~~~~

"Is it really all possible, Digger?" Elle asks me when we're back at Dad's.

"Why not? Paul can have this place, and we'll sell the land. But part of the contract will say that we have a house built to our design on an acre of our choosing. If the developers are half as hungry as Dad and his solicitor led me to believe, they'll agree. And remember, it isn't just that plot. It's the rest of the land that it opens up. Curtly Brook and the Humpty Dumpty Field will always be protected. They can't go across that."

"So there will always be a place where the children can play," she says dreamily.

I grin at her. I'm enthused about life for the first time in decades. I feel like I did before I crossed that field and left here.

"Hey, Bean boy! Time for you to go to your new life. We're all starting again."

"Can't we keep him?" Elle asks.

"I gave my word. And I said I'd have him there for tea time, so I could teach Reg his routines. I think he needs him in his life, Elle."

Bean is staring at me with his shiny eyes. His tail is still, as though he knows something is about to happen.

"I'll carry him round," I say, "will you bring his lead and the rest of the box of his stuff, please?"

And for the first time, I pick him up.

Elle stands motionless and watches.

What does he weigh? About twenty to twenty-five pounds, I guess.

I bring him to me, his front legs stiff against my chest, our faces a few inches apart. He stares into my eyes, as though he's asked me a question and is waiting for an answer.

I smile at him. "You're a good boy. Thanks for keeping me company this week."

Is that the light, or is there moisture in his dark eyes?

His tongue comes out and he licks my nose. And he sinks in to me, his whole body softening in my hands as his legs go limp.

He places his head on my shoulder and settles in to my neck, his front paws embracing me in a soft clinch.

I hear him sigh close to my ear.

And for the first time in thirty years and more, I break down and cry.

~~~~~

"I knew that, lad. I knew when I heard him whine for you last night when you called round, and I knew when I saw him with you at the funeral on Friday. I said to myself, I said, 'you shan't be getting that dog, Reg, because he won't be able to let him go!' I say, I said that to myself I did."

"I'm sorry, Mr Glenn. I'm breaking my word, and I don't like doing it."

"Understandable! I say, it's understandable that! It's a matter of the heart, as my Glenda would have termed it, and she knew all about that! I wonder, though, would you do me a favour by way of recompense, so to put it?"

"Of course. Anything."

"Would you and the young lady accompany me to a place I found, and help me choose a dog for myself? I say, I'm quite sold on it now, the notion of a canine companion. But I want a good one! I say, I want a good one like the beast Bean there!"

"How does tomorrow suit you?" I propose.

"Ah, so you'll still be here tomorrow, shall you?" he asks, and gives me a look that says his Glenda knew a thing or two.

I nod and Elle slips her arm through mine.

"I say, good for you! That's what I say! Now, what kind of dog would you say I should get? Something not too big, I say, but I don't want one of those yappy dogs."

Elle asks him, "do you want an older dog, Mr Glenn, something already house trained?"

"Well, I had a think about that, and I said to myself, I said, get a little one, a young one that can get to know your ways, and you his. Or hers! I say, I'm not sexist! But I must confess, I did think a boy might be better. Yes, a young lad, a pup, I mean to say. I want the energy in my life - the youth, the playfulness. I want to watch him run, I say, and get into a bit of mischief. We never had children of our own, you see..." He breaks off.

"We'll find what you need," Elle tells him, and takes his hand.

"I know I'm old. I'm eighty-four - I say, eighty-four! But I don't feel it. My Glenda always said, she said, 'you have the constitution of a man twenty years younger, Reg,' - twenty years younger! So I'm sixty-four, if you think of it like that. So if a little one lasts me for fifteen years, I reckon that'll about do us both, and he'll keep me young! He'll fill this house, he will - fill it!

"I want the entertainment, you see?" he continues, still holding Elle's hand, "the television's a waste of time - I say, a waste of time that is! Bloody rubbish night after night, if you'll pardon my language. And all the children have gone. It was you lot that entertained us - as my Glenda always said, she said, 'it's better than any soap opera, Reg - better than any soap on the telly!' And she was right, she was - perfectly correct."

"We'll pick you up at nine tomorrow, Reg, if that works for you?" I suggest.

"Zero-nine-hundred hours it is, then!"

We turn to leave.

"She's made up about you two, you know?" he calls after us.

"Who's that, Mr Glenn?" I say, and turn back to face him.
"My Glenda! I say, she's over the moon about you two."
He must read my expression; a little concern.
"You've got a lot to learn, you young ones! I hear her - when you love someone, they never leave you! I say, not ever! Right, zero-nine-hundred hours it is, I say!"

29.

"Again, I'm sorry to take up so much of your time, Johnny."

"Not a problem, Dig. What's up?"

"Immleigh."

"Has he been bothering you?"

"No. It's not that. But I wanted to do this face to face."

Handing him his coffee as we stand in the kitchen, I beckon him to follow me through and sit at the dining table at the front of the living-room. Elle joins us.

And once we're seated, I begin.

"On Friday May 29th 1987, I left here. I'd received a letter that was forged, but I believed it to have come from Elle. It ended our relationship. I moped around the house for a few hours, and heard my Dad arguing with a woman whose voice I didn't recognise. Once things became quiet and I heard Dad leave, I packed a bag and walked away. On a whim, I visited the old railway, and saw Dad burying what I believed to be a body by the Gnarly Ash. I now know, thanks to you, that it was our old dog, Ringo, and that he had to move the body because the new dog, Eddie, was digging him up in the garden. The woman had been called by the Glenns next-door-but-one out of concern, and the call was well intended.

"Given those two events, and that I was reeling, my mind probably wasn't where it should have been at that moment.

"So I wound up at Millby station that late afternoon, and while I was there a young woman approached me, and I shared information about trains to Tredmouth. I didn't know her name or anything else about her, but I later found out that she was Trudy Immleigh.

"I didn't see her again until we arrived at Tredmouth, where she informed me she was heading to London, as was I. But there was no direct train, and no way of getting there until the following morning. Again, we exchanged that basic information, had a chat over a cuppa, and went our separate ways. I knew that she was running away, and I knew what from.

"Skip forward a few years, and I was in a London pub. The barmaid heard my accent, and we got talking. To both our surprise, we realised that we'd met before. She was Trudy Immleigh. Though by then she was using a different name; Michelle Blake. But I knew who she was that day in the pub, because her uncle, Immleigh, had questioned me numerous times about her disappearance after it emerged that we'd been seen conversing at the two stations."

Johnny drinks his coffee and listens.

"Michelle and I had a relationship of sorts." I squeeze Elle's hand in mine. "She was working the bar and training to be a hairdresser."

"But you didn't report her whereabouts?" Johnny says.

"No, I didn't, because she begged me not to, and I gave her my word. She didn't want to be found, Johnny, and she was eighteen and independent when she left here."

"But you could have taken a lot of heat off yourself had you reported where she was," Johnny points out, reasonably.

"But I'd promised her. She ran away because of the abuse, Johnny. Her father was sexually abusing her. Oh, and she went to her uncle, and he did nothing. He refused to believe her - said it couldn't be possible. That's why she ran.

"Trust me, I was with her and saw the psychological damage it did her. I couldn't betray her."

"But you're telling me now," Johnny observes.

"I spoke with her this afternoon. It's been thirty years, John. She thinks it might be about time she let go a bit. Her mum's in a home, and her father's dead. She wants to see her mother while there's still time. And she knows that I've reconnected with Elle, that I'm moving back here, and she wants her uncle off my case. She always knew about you," I say to Elle, "we never had secrets, and she always knew that I couldn't love her in the way she needed. But I do love her, in a similar way to how I love my nieces. I care for her."

"I understand," Elle says, and Johnny nods along.

"It's up to you how you deal with this," I tell him, "you know better than me, pal. Here," I say, handing him a piece of paper with Michelle, or Trudy's address and telephone number on. "She's expecting your call, and I've told her that she can trust you."

"Thanks, Dig."

I nod. "What will happen?"

Johnny blows his cheeks out and releases the breath. "I don't know. I'll get in touch with... What do I call her?"

"Michelle, I guess."

"That's her middle name, isn't it?"

"It is. And Blake was used because she liked the television series, 'Blake's 7'."

He smiles. "Well, I'll see Michelle. I'll take care of this personally, Dig. And we'll do whatever she wants. Her father's dead, you said, so there's nobody to punish there. But there are still things that can be done."

"I don't think she wants to relive it. She's okay, John. She's turned her life around, and she's happy, I think. She just wants to see her mum."

"They're from Yorkshire, aren't they, the family?"

"Correct. She ran from there and came here. Immleigh tried to send her back. Look, I think there's a lot of guilt with Immleigh. He knows. And it was easier for him to blame me for thirty years than to admit to his own involvement."

"He had a duty to report a suspected crime," Johnny says, a little angrily.

"So did I, if you think of it like that."

"It's different, Digger. He was a cop. You had a duty to protect a victim, first and foremost, and it sounds like you did that. You always were a good man to have as a defensive partner, pal," he tells me, rising to leave.

We shake hands, and he retains his grip.

"I'm glad you're back," he tells me.

"Dig in?" I suggest.

"Dig in," he retorts.

30.

We walk along the old railway. Bean runs free off his lead. He won't go far from us.

"I've never been back up here," Elle tells me shakily.

"Since that day with Micky?"

She nods.

"You always preferred the grass beneath your feet," I remind her, and she cuddles closer to me as we stroll on. "It's okay," I reassure her, and we walk to the end and look down on Dad's... On my land.

After a minute or so, she says, "I don't want to live here, Digger. There are too many ghosts."

I know what she means. "Then we shan't."

"You don't mind?"

"No. I'd happily live in a shed with you."

"It's where diggers belong!"

"Come on," I laugh.

As we turn I see a shape disappear into the bushes.

Bean growls. He saw it, too. Or smelt it.

"All right, boy," I lowly say.

"What's wrong with him?" Elle asks.

"Ah, probably the Old Signalman that used to frequent this line," I reply lightly, but I weigh the chain collar of Bean's in my hand as we turn and head back into the evening sun.

"That was a story. A ghost story for impressionable young boys!" she says delightfully.

"Was it?" I venture teasingly. "Are you sure?"

If she feels my tenseness she says nothing as we walk along enfolded in one another.

Bean sniffs where I saw the movement, his nose busy collecting data. He seems satisfied, as I fruitlessly scan the undergrowth. There's nothing to worry about. The light can play tricks up here when it's low to the west and sits above the long straight path.

We drop down, the three of us, me ascending first and finding the foot and hand holds that I can instinctively locate. She's an Elsewhere, I remind myself, as I assist her in her descent. Other terrain constitutes her. It was always part of the attraction.

Stepping out by the reservoir, we follow the weedy gravel path to the damp arched tunnel that once bore the load of the wyvern fire-spitting trains. Our steps ping off the walls and make us sound like an army on the march.

We emerge triumphantly, side by side, and step on to the Humpty Dumpty Field.

A strong urge to cross it compels me. There's enough light left.

We rise and fall together.

"What song would you choose for this moment?" she asks me.

"I was already singing it in my head," I tell her.

"Well?"

"U2. 'Drowning Man'."

"Ah, that was one I taped for you many years ago."

"From the last really good album they ever did."

"In your opinion," she points out.

"In my opinion," I concur.

On reaching the edge, I clamber down the steep bank of the Lane using branches and roots. Bean scampers down with me, back on his lead.

"Trust me," I call to her, my arms open ready to catch her.

She shuffles down as far as she can, another four feet to navigate.

"Take my hand," I urge her, reaching up, as I repeat, "trust me!"

And she lets go.

She floats down like an angel, me taking her light weight and cushioning her into me.

"How will I get back up?" she giggles.

"I'll carry you if I have to. It'll be like carrying you across the threshold. Or we could walk down to Curtly Brook and get back up there where it's more level."

That's what we turn to do.

A scream of a racing engine is our first warning.

I look back over my shoulder and see Immleigh's hat silhouetted behind the windscreen.

We have, perhaps, five seconds before he's on us.

One... We use it to leap together up the bank and I grab a tree branch, Elle's hand still in mine as she twists round pressed against me.

Two... Her hand leaves mine as I climb higher, my feet finding an anchor.

Three... We reconnect, and I pull her up to me, Bean trying to follow as I heave on his lead.

Four... The root comes away and my feet scrabble the bank, dirt cascading down as Bean launches himself at the car.

Five... She grabs my collar and shields me with her body, the driver's side wheels mounting the bank.

Six... The bank is too steep, the car careering away - wind slaps us, the smell of the engine carried on it as Bean disappears under the front bumper, the lead snatched from my hand.

Seven... Bean emerges from the back of the car, lying on his side on the asphalt, his eyes locked on me.

Eight... A police car enters the Lane, screaming just as loudly as Immleigh's.

Nine... Our feet give way, and Elle and I slide to the road surface, our hands locked together.

Ten... A sickening crash shifts the air, metal crumpling, glass breaking...

31.

"Digger, can you get the post?" Elle calls to me.

"I can't. I can't move."

She comes through to the Ps living room where we live for now while our new house is being built a mile or so to the east of Lower Millby. "What's wrong?"

"Nothing."

She smiles down at us. "How did he get up there?"

"He jumped!"

"Oh, Bean! You good boy," she says, and bends to ruffle the fur on his neck. She kisses me by way of celebration.

"He'll be running with Reg's young pup before you know it."

"Do you think he could manage a walk later?" Elle asks.

His ears perk up at the word. "I think he's game."

"We could take your dad's ashes to the Humpty Dumpty Field and set him free. It's such a nice day. We'll call for Paul, Jen and the girls at number three."

I nod. It's time. And it'll give me a chance to ask him to be my best man.

"Will you get the post? Please, Digger. I want you to," she pleads, as she plays with the gold ring on her finger, the one I inherited from my Gran years ago when my Mum got a gold watch.

I know why. So I scoop Bean up in one arm, and carry him with me as I head to the front door to retrieve the mail.

Sure enough, her slanted handwriting graces one of the envelopes.

"Come on, fella, let's go and see what your Mum has to say today!"

~~~~~

I put a compilation CD on. The Byrds. 'You Showed Me' kicks things off. Elle settles on the sofa with me. We kick our feet up, and she tucks herself into me. Bean lies within arm's reach, and I carefully open the envelope and unfold the page.

And I read.

"...My Darling Digger, my Love! You're here, and only now is it starting to really sink in that I have my life back - I have my Love back. How long will our life and Love last? Forty years? That's twenty million minutes, my Darling, and it sounds like such a lot. But we know that it isn't, and that there are no guarantees that we shall have that many. And so I promise you - I give you my word - that I will make the most of every single one. We've been denied so many that we should have shared, and why? Yes, it's simple to blame others, but ultimately we are both guilty of a lack of faith in one another and ourselves. You too readily believed DD's letter, and I too readily believed that you had abandoned me. Sensitivity and self-doubt have been our downfall. So let us not waste any of what remains to us. I shall fill each minute with you, and relish every moment. But it can never be enough..."

The End Of The Line.

Thank you for taking the time to read this book. It is very much appreciated, and we sincerely hope that you enjoyed it.

A **Morning Brake** Publication.
Contact morningbrake@cox.net

By **Andy Bracken**

Other works by the author:

Full Novels:

Novels set in Brakeshire:
- Reflections Of Quercus Treen
- The Book Burner
- Clearing
- Across The Humpty Dumpty Field

Other novels:
- What Ven Knew
- Gaps Between The Tracks
- Beneath The Covers

Writer Dave Thompson's review of "The Book Burner"

***** "The Book Burner" wasn't anything like I expected. In fact, it's unlike any other book I've read, a tight bundle of psychological dramas that wrap and rewrap around one another, but effectively boil down to one man's search for a long ago truth - which he had never even questioned, until the chance rediscovery of an old borrowed book, while clearing the house in preparation for never having to worry about anything again.

Written with dry, but deliberate wit, a sharp eye for the extremes of emotional nuance and a definite talent for twists, it's a journey through a hidden world of family secrets, dramas and tragedies, set against a backdrop of English manners and morality. I would say "recommended to fans of..." but beyond flashes of Gordon Burn and Andrew Crumley - well, again, it's unlike any other book I've read.

Printed in Poland
by Amazon Fulfillment
Poland Sp. z o.o., Wrocław